G000124110

Dying
in Style

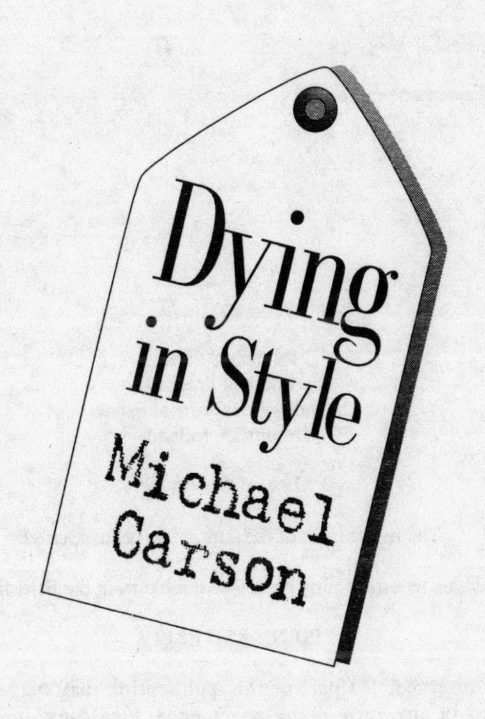

POOLBEG

Published 1998
by Poolbeg Press Ltd
123 Baldoyle Industrial Estate
Dublin 13, Ireland

A catalogue record for this book is available from the British Library.

ISBN 1 85371 817 3

Cover photography by Brigid Tiernan
Cover design by Poolbeg Group Services Ltd
Set by Poolbeg Group Services Ltd in Times 11.5/14
Printed by The Guernsey Press Ltd,
Vale, Guernsey, Channel Islands.

About the Author

Michael Carson is the author of *Serving Suggestions*, a collection of the best of his radio short stories, and seven previous novels including *Sucking Sherbet Lemons* and *The Knight of the Flaming Heart.* He lives near Westport, County Mayo.

For Erika Metzieder

❦ ❦ ❦

Criticism is a disinterested endeavour to learn and propagate the best that is known and thought in the world.

– Matthew Arnold

The opinion of a great body of the reading public is very materially influenced even by the unsupported assertions of those who assume a right to criticise.

– Macaulay

It is impossible to think of a man of any actual force or originality . . . who spent his whole life appraising and describing the work of other men.

– HL Mencken

The trade of critic, in literature, music, and the drama, is the most degraded of all trades.

– Mark Twain

Crime Digest
8 Pepys Mews
London
W2 9YU

Audrey Saunders Ltd
17A Clwyd Passage
London E11 9PS

17 September

Dear Audrey Saunders

It was very kind of you to give my magazine the opportunity of using pre-publication extracts from Arthur Whitworth's new offering, *Dying in Style*.

I have read the work and, to be perfectly frank, I think it exhibits the popping of the poison seed-pod of a terminally-diseased imagination. I have not enjoyed any of Whitworth's output – though one or two of his early novels, *Teacher* in particular, had moments of wit. This one made me feel very queasy indeed.

I do not think I would relish being either one of Arthur Whitworth's neighbours, or any tradesman he frequents. Fail to treat the author well, either with sweet smiles or the best steak in the window, and you risk being painted with livid, rough brushstrokes of vulgar primary colours in one of his novels, prior to being killed off in a most gruesome manner.

The only page I liked of *Dying in Style* was the last. Elsewhere, I kept seeing thinly-disguised people I knew, and friends I love, being done away with because they had dared offend the "fictional" author. But we all know the author is Arthur Whitworth. We all know, do we not, that killing off his enemies would be exactly what Whitworth would like to do if he had the guts. His fiction is merely the crude sublimation of a psychopath with cowardly tendencies.

I have no notion how a novel that takes on the literary and critical establishment will be received. I have the feeling that it is in for a very rocky ride indeed. I am sad to say (for your sake) dear Audrey, that I think the author deserves all he gets. Speaking personally, I would like *Dying in Style* to be totally ignored.

So thank you, but no thank you. If I had my way, Whitworth would be locked up for the duration in a similar prison cell to the one described on the last page of *Dying in Style*, in which the door keeps clanging shut with such ponderous and pompous echoes. I would paint the cell purple, to remind him of his prose. I would also deny the wretch writing-materials. For life.

Of course, this is a totally subjective opinion. I have been wrong before. You still have time prior to publication of Whitworth's book to place extracts elsewhere. Not a task I would relish, but I know you are indefatigable.

All good wishes

James Houston
Editor and Publisher

Dying in Style – *307* –

The warder clanged the cell door shut on the lifer-writer. The convicted man stood, the door behind him, its closing still echoing. What was the sound like? Thunder? A dull, doomy clapper striking a bell? Which note? He tried to whistle the sound that signalled his imprisonment. It faded. Had it faded? Or was it still reverberating around every item in his cell – table, chair, sink, latrine, metal mirror, iron bed – repeating, always repeating, the news of his incarceration?

He listened, trying to discern through the buzzing silence the last zips of sound. It was there. Yes, and it would echo on down the years. Five or six times a day for all his days the door would clang shut, oxygenate the dying twang, the reverberating bagatelle balls of sound, reminding the prisoner that this was home.

He threaded his fingers, forced the fat basket back, hearing each crack one by one like clicked-shut – clicked-open – doors. He sat down on the chair, pulled off the top of his Bic; opened the cheap, hair-flecked paper of the prison-issue notebook. He started to write, facing the tiny barred window of his cell.

Two hours passed. He had written and corrected six pages of the notebook. He stood up and moved his chair to the other side of the table so that his back was turned on the window and the light. He sat again, snuggling his bottom against the metal seat. That felt right.

He continued writing, feeling as if he was in another place entirely. A smile, the first since his arrest all those months ago, bloomed on his lips, spread through every cell of his hunched body until it had soaked through even as far as the writer's free soul.

The End

❧ ❧ ❧

"What did you think of *Dying in Style*? Good read, was it?" Giles Gibbons, owner of Cutting Edge Publications, asked Jim Smart.

Jim Smart eyed a photograph on his desk. The eyes flashed back, inscrutable; the turned-up nose seemed to look down on him, sneering at his puniness: concave chest, short legs, mouse-face . . . and the rest. "Haven't read it," the chief bookbuyer for the W Crisp Books and Media Group replied flatly. "Two of the three readers gave it the thumbs up, though."

"What did the third say?"

Still gazing at the photograph, Jim Smart sighed. "The third's Mandy, and she's not available for comment."

Mandy was Jim Smart's new wife.

"Again? I'm sorry, Jim. I really am," Giles Gibbons said, looking at his wrinkles in the silver hip-flask that lay flat and empty on his desk. His jowls hung down, but he was used to that. What was new were the deep lines in his forehead. Hard to clear, they were. Harder by the day to tense them smooth. It gave him a headache. Still, headache or not, it had to be done.

"Don't know what gets into her," Jim Smart said, though, truth to tell, he had a shrewd, lewd idea. "Should have known something was in the wind from the way she gave your *Tropica Erotica* series such glowing reviews. Thought they were really depraved myself."

"They were, weren't they?"

"Mandy gobbled them up. Thought they were fantastic."

"She was right about them," Giles said. "Sold like hot cakes. Trouble is, what do you do after you've gone as far as you can go?"

"Ask Mandy," Jim said.

"Where is it this time?"

"Sri Lanka. The Jaffna Peninsula."

"Lord!"

"Mandy likes a bit of danger with her tropical adventures. These days."

Giles looked at his watch and the pile of review copies of *Dying in Style* as Jim went on about Mandy. Was the cover right? Covers could make or break a book. Monochrome photo of an impeccably dressed and coiffed woman in the act of swooning down dead. A crimson book was falling from her elegant hand. Too subtle? A cliché? Hard to tell. Hard to tell what was what these days.

"Hmm," Giles said, when he judged Jim to be pausing for breath. "Still two out of three isn't bad."

A short silence on Jim's end of the line. "Don't get you . . . "

"Your readers' reports on *Dying in Style*."

"Oh, yes. Sorry. Get distracted. You know, not knowing what gets into her. Tried to do right by Mandy. Warned me she was a handful before we tied the knot, being Page Three from '78 to '87 and everything. I mean, knew what I was taking on. Theoretically."

"Mmm," said Giles, signalling nautically to Melanie, his secretary.

"Look, hope you don't mind me asking you this; stop me if out of order but, and I don't know quite how to put it . . . "

"Mmm?" He mimed drinking coffee.

"I mean," continued Jim, "you don't have any troubles in the marital department and I was sort of wondering . . . well . . . was wondering . . . "

"There's nothing wrong with you, Jim," said Giles who

had considerable trouble in the marital department – his second wife had just left him taking the kids from both marriages while leaving behind writs. But he didn't wear his troubles on his sleeve.

"There must be something wrong. No one loses wives like me."

Giles held four fingers up to Melanie, who could never bring herself to believe how many sugars Giles liked. "Honestly, Jim!" Giles said. "Haven't you worked it out yet? It's not you. It's the women you choose. Why not try Relate? Worked wonders for me. Look, Jim, how many copies of *Dying in Style* do you think you can take?"

"Realistically?"

"Realistically and fraternally, Jim. We've been shifting books together for two decades."

"Fifteen hundred."

Giles cheered up then. "And what about the book-club?"

"Say another thousand."

"OK, Jim, that's great for starters. Re-ordering won't be a problem. We're doing a ten thousand print-run on *Dying in Style*. We firmly believe it's going to be Arthur Whitworth's break-through book."

"Trouble is, I love her," Jim said. "That's the long and the short of it. Pathetic, isn't it?"

"She'll be back with her tail between her legs," Giles said, for something to say. "Keep in touch, Jim! You should take up reading. It might be just the thing."

"No time, Giles. What with one thing and another. It's hell concentrating."

"Next time I hear from you you'll be re-ordering *Dying in Style* by the ton, or my name's not Giles Gibbons!"

❧ ❧ ❧

13 Duckworth Avenue,
Leeds

The 18th of November

Dear Mr Gibbons,

I don't know if you will remember us: we are Arthur Whitworth's aunties from Leeds. We met you at the big party you had on "The Rainbow Warrior" when Arthur's novel, *The Ends of the Earth,* was published.

We have received our copy of *Dying in Style*. A lady called Roberta Coleman from your offices sent it to us. Thank you very much. It was a very good read, like all Arthur's books. Mind you, you'll probably think we're old-fashioned, but we wish you had tried to persuade Arthur to cut out the smut. We have a lot of friends in Leeds we would love to recommend our nephew's books to. Trouble is, we can't because of the aforementioned smut.

Still, that is not the real reason for this letter, Mr Gibbons. We are Arthur's nearest relatives. We brought him up after his dad went to the bad and his mum died. We love him very much, not just when a book comes out – but all the time. It has really caused us a lot of sorrow, the way his writing has changed him, made him visit us or even write to us less and less. The terrible things that were said about his last novel really upset him and we've seen nothing of him since. Can you do two things for us, please? Tell him to get in touch. (Don't tell him we told you!) And please will you try to make sure that the people who say things about the new book in the papers and on the television are *kind*. We know Arthur better than anybody, from the time he was a little boy. He is sensitive and easily hurt. We don't like the way he has hidden himself away in that miserable cottage in Blubberhouses. It reminds us of how he used to go and hide in the attic at our house when he was a boy.

Do take care of Arthur, Mr Gibbons!

Yours truly,

Anne and Win Whitworth

Giles Gibbons laid Anne and Win Whitworth's letter aside, thought, then asked Melanie to summon Roberta Coleman to his office.

"Thought this might amuse you," he said, passing the letter to the publicity manager of Cutting Edge.

Roberta Coleman read the letter, smiles and frowns alternating across her face. Giles watched her admiringly. Cutting Edge might be a tadpole among publishing imprints, but it had the prettiest, freshest, pertest, sweetest publicity manager of any of them. And, more to the point, one who could shift books.

"I'm not sure we can help them," Roberta said, "much as I'd like to."

"Such charming naiveté!" Giles said.

"This isn't the first time Anne and Win Whitworth have mentioned to me that Arthur never goes to see them. They collared me at *The Ends of the Earth* launch. I mentioned it to Arthur at the time."

"What did he say?"

"He said he needed time to write."

Giles looked doubtful. "Think there's more to it than that. Arthur and I once got pissed together. After *Teacher* was launched. In those days he was a bit more communicative. Anyway, from the sound of it he had a lousy childhood. His aunties saved him as far as I could tell but . . . "

"So wouldn't you expect him to be a bit more . . . well . . . attentive?"

"You would," agreed Giles. "But there's more to it than meets the eye. I'll try talking to him. If he deigns to telephone, that is."

"I'll send him a phonecard. As a hint."

"Do that. It would be nice if we could get the reviewers to write nice things that won't hurt Arthur, wouldn't it, Roberta?"

"It would."

"See to it, would you . . . and that's an order!" Giles said.

"Right away!"

"And tell Arthur to cut out the smut next time!"

"Right you are."

Roberta placed the letter back on Giles's desk. Giles looked at it, feeling the loose skin under his chin. Christ, he was losing his looks! Every encounter with a mirror was depressing. Losing wives, losing looks, losing money . . . losing it. "I suppose I'll have to write back. Lord knows what I'll say!"

"I might be able to help there," Roberta said. "We've booked Arthur in for a reading at the Leeds Waterstones. On the 11th of next month. They'll be able to meet the author then."

"Great!" Giles said. "Now, Roberta, back to your duties. I want you down on your knees every night praying that *Dying in Style* gets a few decent reviews."

"Who's the patron saint of good reviews?"

"Don't bother with saints! Straight to the top, Roberta. There's a lot riding on this one."

Sobered, suddenly worried by Giles's tone, Roberta left

the office, leaving Giles Gibbons to his correspondence and his thoughts.

Cutting Edge Publications
2 Mildmay Mews
London E2 7UN

23 November

Dear Anne and Win

Thank you for your letter.

I well remember our meeting aboard "The Rainbow Warrior" that night. It was a wonderful launch for a wonderful book. A pity some silly and insensitive critics did not agree!

About the smut: to be perfectly honest – and I know how our friends in the North appreciate honesty – it is we at Cutting Edge who encourage your Arthur to add a few "smutty" bits. though we prefer to think of them as "tastefully erotic". You see, we have found through careful market research that the reading public like something a bit "juicy" with their thrillers. Think of it as a tasty gravy to help down the black pudding. So you mustn't blame your Arthur for that. We twist his arm until he gets his characters to take their tops off. I honestly wish we did not have to do this. But the realities of publishing demand it.

Neither, I'm afraid, can I do much about the reviews for Arthur's book. We can only hope for the best. Of course, we really think *Dying in Style* is a great read or we wouldn't be publishing it. But whether the chinless wonders who get their hands on the book before the reading public will agree with us is another matter. I know that your Arthur is sensitive about critical reaction to his books, but we do all we can here at Cutting Edge to make sure that he knows we are supporting him.

I'm sorry I can't be of more help with those two matters. However, I do have some good news: I think you may have an opportunity to meet your errant nephew. He is going to do a reading from his new work at Waterstones in Leeds on the 11th of December. So you'll have a chance to make a fuss of him then.

I will be speaking to Arthur before then. He always rings in when a book is published. I will tell him – in the nicest possible way – that his good aunties deserve better treatment. Still, you know what writers are! Their heads are full of plots and characters and things like that. They're not like ordinary folk. Still, rest assured that whatever I can do shall be done.

Yours sincerely

Giles Gibbons
Publisher
Cutting Edge Books

❧ ❧ ❧

Cyril Parkinson, a Pernod and water sitting on his mouse-mat, prepared to write his weekly review for the Sunday paper. He looked at his Apple purring two feet from his eyes. The screen threw back Cyril's thin, aristocratic face. Yes, he mused, the profile in the Saturday *Guardian* was right. He did have a more-than-passing resemblance to a hungry falcon. Cyril turned his attention to the five books he had gobbled up in the last week. They seemed to shudder under his pitiless gaze, expecting the worst.

"Poison . . . " Cyril mused to his Apple, " . . . or tasty and sweet to eat?"

He cuffed the top book on the pile, the first novel by an Australian nonagenarian called Emily Martin from Alice Springs, whose plot he could not recall. The book fell, fell from grace, from contention, taking the others with it.

Dying in Style by Arthur Whitworth stood revealed. "Poison, I reckon," said Cyril, thinking of LP Lomax, his flatmate. "Revenge is sweet!" he shouted, hoping LP Lomax would hear and hearing realise that he was being avenged.

But LP Lomax couldn't hear. He was buried deep in his earphones, reviewing CDs for a Summer Roundup of Classical Releases.

Cyril Parkinson picked up *Dying in Style*, flicked through the pages. Apart from anything else, this book could not be allowed to get away with it. Every word was a challenge, a "bet you don't dare" to the literary establishment. Well, he, Cyril Parkinson, doyen of the hatchet, "The Sultan of Snide" (*The Observer*), "The critic to whose demolition jobs the public turns to first for their Sunday dose of Schadenfreude" (*The Telegraph*), "That tireless crusader against impoverished prose, armed with velvet glove and titanium shillelagh" (*The Irish Times*), dared. He would blaze the trail and encourage the rest to follow him into the breach yelling: "Destroy the dire product of a diseased imagination!" *Dying in Style* indeed!

The critic took a mouthful of his drink, sucked it through his bridge-work, placed the glass back down on the mouse-mat, and started to write:

For some considerable time now sundry reviewers on these pages have been predicting the death of the English novel. If the publication of Arthur Whitworth's latest opus is any indication, the form has already died and been buried in a dingy council cemetery. No Flowers. By Order. Putrefaction truly Brueghelesque beneath a Hirstian illusion of formaldehyde-induced coma has set in. Where is the soul? If there is a soul – which I doubt – Hell is too good for it.

Your hearts, gentle readers, would surely have gone out to your humble reviewer could you have observed him turning, with gloved hand, ay, and many yawns, each turgid page, sighing at the uneven gnat's-pee prose past, the thick tangled forest still to face. The clock ticked inexorably towards his deadline and nothing . . . not one thing . . . caught his eye and whispered, "There! A Spark!"

I will not bore you with the plot of Mr Whitworth's novel. Suffice it to say that a literary agent is murdered. Then a critic. Then a literary editor . . . a publicity manager at a publisher's. Then another critic . . . on and on. Three hundred (three hundred!) pages of red herrings and meandering, baleful, preachy, prose, before we find out that – Yes! – the author of the book pilloried by the lamented critics, done down by the hapless publisher's minions . . . done it.

It is not my custom to reveal the denouement of a novel of this nature. But in the case of Arthur Whitworth's I make an exception without the least qualm. Read it if you must, but remember who tried to warn you! You are in my prayers that you will resist all blandishments. If, perchance, some enemy were to present you with this opus . . . as a gift! . . . send it back, throw it on the fire, put it in a sack loaded with stones and toss it into the nearest cesspit.

Cyril Parkinson read and reread the review. Then he printed out a copy. He took it into LP Lomax's room, stopping off in the kitchen to make himself another drink.

"Ouch!" said LP Lomax – not for the first time – as he handed back the review to Cyril,

❧ ❧ ❧

Five days after Cyril Parkinson's review of *Dying in Style* had appeared in the paper, the author of the pilloried novel rang his literary agent, Audrey Saunders. Speaking from a public phone-box in Blubberhouses, Yorkshire, Arthur Whitworth complained to his agent about the terrible review that had landed on his mat, and her insensitivity in sending it to him. It would block him for months, he said; it wasn't fair, he said; Cyril Parkinson wouldn't know a good read from a goldfish in a plastic bag, he said. Then, before Audrey Saunders had been able to pour oil on troubled egos, the 20-unit phonecard ran out and Arthur Whitworth was cut off.

It was Friday afternoon and Audrey Saunders was ready for the off. Nevertheless, she called in Lavinia and dictated a letter to her unhappy client.

Audrey Saunders Ltd
17A Clwyd Passage
London E11 9PS

3 December

Arthur Whitworth
Who'll Do It Up Cottage
Blubberhouses
Nr Skipton
Yorkshire

Dear Arthur

I feel for you, really I do! I'm so so *so* sorry that horrid Cyril Parkinson's horrid and unjust review was sent on to you. It must have got through the day that temp with the brain (and the physical endowments) of an ox was sent to us to cover the absence of Lavinia.

Don't take it to heart. Cyril Parkinson has his own agenda. He is also an old Oxford chum of LP Lomax whom, if I recall rightly, you punched on the nose at the Hatchards' Author of the Year bash the other month. Everyone's been dying to do it for ages, I have to say.

Trust me, a bad review – and this was bad, one of the worst I've ever seen, which is saying something – is better than no review at all. No publicity is bad publicity. People will purchase your novel just to see if it is as bad as Cyril says. They will, of course, find that it is the best work you've done to date.

How is the new one going? I ache to curl up with it.

Bye for now,

Audrey

PS: I hope your Waterstones reading goes swimmingly next week. Don't be put off by a few metropolitan twirps. Your devoted fans up north will, I am sure, more than make up for it. *Devastated* not to be able to attend. A.

❧ ❧ ❧

The following Tuesday, one of the sales assistants at the Leeds branch of Waterstones spotted the overweight, florid, balding form of Arthur Whitworth – though she did not know it was Arthur – looking furtive in the fiction stacks.

The sales assistant, a young woman called Farah Picknett, was the proud owner of a First in Social Psychology and History of Art. She was working at the

Leeds branch of Waterstones while waiting for a job to turn up that suited her qualifications and her mother's ambition. Surprising herself, she was finding that working in a bookshop suited her down to the ground.

Farah had just finished laying out sixty chairs for the upcoming reading. Her next job was to uncork the wine, arrange the wine-glasses, and then turn her attention to creating an artful display for a hundred copies of *Dying in Style*.

While working at these tasks, Farah thought what a pity it was that there had not been a couple of decent reviews for the book. In these difficult times, when people had to be pushed towards reading, you needed a few good reviews to blow up on the photocopier and plaster around the place.

Farah thought she had once read one of Arthur Whitworth's books. When Dunstan in "Crime" had described the plot of *Teacher*, Farah was convinced she'd read it while at school, and rather enjoyed it. She picked up one of the display copies of *Dying in Style* and began reading the first page:

"Didn't think much of *Dying in Style*, did you?" the critic asked the publicist.

The publicist smirked. "I've never liked a word that man has written. Speed-read *Dying in Style* just to say I'd read it, but it's a tiresome book."

Neither the critic nor the publicist knew, as they discussed the novel during its launch-party, that the author of *Dying in Style* was listening to the conversation.

"Latitia," said the publicist, " – and don't tell a soul I told you – has taken to parking her chewing-gum in books she takes a dislike to. She does it around all the London stores. It's a political act, she says."

"How is Latitia?"

"Pregnant. Not sure whether she's going to have it. I told her, 'Latty,' I said, 'you'd better make up your bleeding mind or it'll be too bloody late'."

"Hurry up please, it's time!" said the reviewer, hoping his quote would fall on fertile – and admiring – ground.

The publicist looked at the reviewer. Blank.

"Still, she's a bloody good reviewer."

Neither the critic nor the publicist realised that at that moment Latitia was floating face-down in a vat of bubbling gum.

Farah frowned, smiled, and got back to her work. It was as she was filling the glasses with wine that she noticed Arthur Whitworth. She smiled across the stacks to him, but his head disappeared.

Arthur was in a state, fearing the worst. Fifteen minutes to go before the start of his reading and not a soul in evidence. Sixty seats! Sixty glasses of wine! It was going to be a repeat of *The Ends of the Earth* launch, and that had been one of the most depressing – ill-attended, empty in all senses – experiences of his life.

Why, he wondered, did he let the publicity department at Cutting Edge arrange these silly events? Why couldn't they do their own publicity and leave him to get on with his work? But then, Arthur recalled how he had written a long letter to Giles Gibbons asking for just the sort of publicity that this reading represented. He wanted to press the flesh, he said. He wanted to meet his readers, he said. To glitter a little.

Still, that was then and this was now.

Farah noticed him again. "Are you attending the reading?" she asked.

"I thought," he smiled, "I might!" Then, thinking the sales assistant knew him, had been making a joke, he asked, "Do you think it will pull in the punters?"

"Hard to say. The author isn't that popular. He's more 'cult'."

Arthur nodded. She didn't know him.

"And the reading conflicts with a big Leeds match, the *Smoking Kills* concert *and* the first much-hyped visitation of the ghost of Annie Walker on 'Coronation Street'."

"Ah, well, umm . . ."

Arthur saw his aunties, Anne and Win, coming into the shop. They kissed him.

"Sign our copies!" they said.

"This is your big day!" Anne said.

"A great day for the Whitworths!" Win said.

"*Another* great day for the Whitworths!" Anne said.

"You're Arthur Whitworth!" Farah exclaimed.

Time passed. The time for the reading came and went. The audience consisted of Arthur's aunties and a man who swayed on the back row holding a glass of red wine in his left hand and a glass of white in his right. As Arthur's time came to read, this audience was suddenly swelled when the entire staff of the bookshop, trying to look as if they had wandered in from the street, appeared as providentially as Guardian Angels, and sat down.

This made quite a decent crowd. But Arthur knew the truth of it. Only Auntie Anne and Auntie Win were deceived and pleased. As he read, Arthur wanted to weep. He glanced up at Farah looking back. He heard the flapping of wings – or was that just blood pumping its way round his decaying frame? When, after the reading, he waited to sign copies of his books, Anne and Win's were followed by all the shop-workers who had already sat through his reading. He was, he knew, signing stock. He was, he knew, being held up – supported like a coffin shouldered by mourners – by these young people who at this hour could have been off doing something they enjoyed.

Still, that was going to be Arthur Whitworth's last reading at a bookshop. That was.

Arthur's aunties, Anne and Win, took him back to their home on the outskirts of Leeds for a fish supper and a good talking-to.

❧ ❧ ❧

The negative reviews – there were several others for *Dying in Style* – caused a few flashes on the surface of the cold, heat-seeking missile of literary London. The editor of *On The Shelf* magazine summed up the deft, and deferential, response:

Sir,

I would concur with your critic that Arthur Whitworth's latest effort is a wholly unworthy product of an imagination that once showed some promise, but I take exception to the critic's pronouncements that such a trashy example betokens the demise of The English Novel.

While it is true that Arthur Whitworth's earlier work was greeted as a lightning-flash of wit and intelligence on our dowdy national scene, his continued use of the thriller genre to peddle his pet hobby-horses . . . class, corruption in the establishment, the nature of treachery, etc., was just that, a lightning flash presaging a downpour of spring rain, followed in due course by summer drought. He was ever, at best, on the sidelines of English fiction. The game, I contend, continues!

Yours faithfully,

Myles Bourke

❧ ❧ ❧

A letter from Misses Anne and Win Whitworth to the Editor of Cyril Parkinson's paper was not printed. It read:

13 Duckworth Avenue,
Leeds

The 17th of December

Dear Editor,

My sister and I think it is absolutely disgusting that you allowed your critic, Cyril Parkinson, to write such a review about our nephew's book, *Dying in Style*.

Arthur Whitworth is a very talented writer. He is also extremely highly strung. Apart from anything else, it was very hurtful to him – and to his aunties – to lay into the book like that.

Maybe we're old-fashioned, but we think it's as true now as it ever was, *if you can't think of something nice to say, say nothing*. You might think about placing that wise advice on the wall above Cyril Parkinson's writing-desk.

We have told the newsagent that we want *The Observer* from now on. We shall also be seeking to persuade all our friends and neighbours to boycott your paper. So don't be surprised if your circulation in Leeds and environs takes a tumble.

Yours truly,

Anne and Win Whitworth

❧ ❧ ❧

The knives were out and flashing crimson for Arthur Whitworth. Alfred Boyd-Ellis, PR consultant, was flattered to be asked to contribute to a slick variation on "The Best Book I Have Read All Year". The trouble was that Alfred Boyd-Ellis had not read a book that year. He had, however, read several reviews of *Dying in Style*; had used these reviews for some in-house training. How, he asked his colleagues, could they rehabilitate Arthur Whitworth after all that ordure had been poured? Answer came there none.

Still, the exercise had not been a complete waste of time:

Without a doubt, my choice for "The Book I Would Give My Worst Enemy This Christmas" has to be Arthur Whitworth's *Dying in Style*, though I doubt I have an enemy upon whom I would wish it.

After that, of course, Alfred Boyd-Ellis had made such an enemy.

❧ ❧ ❧

And, never slow to biff below the belt, or wherever else it could find a vulnerable chink:

Remainders of the Day

Spotted at Peanut Books, Bognor. *Dying in Style* by Arthur Whitworth. £2.99, hardback. Recommended price: £16.99.

❧ ❧ ❧

Who'll Do It Up Cottage
Blubberhouses
Nr Skipton
Yorkshire

Dear Auntie Anne and Auntie Win,

I am sorry it has taken so long for me to write and thank you for your kindness to me when I was in Leeds for that disastrous reading.

Still, I think you're used to having a forgetful, ungrateful nephew by now. I wasn't always this bad, was I? These days, whenever I write a letter, I spend most of the time apologising and excusing myself for not having written.

Partly, I know, it's the writing that is to blame. I spend so much time in company with my characters that I am too tired afterwards for further social contact. And, if that sounds daft to you, I can understand. It sounds daft to me in my saner moments.

Dying in Style was not the success I had hoped it would be. Still what happened *to* the book rather mirrored what happened *in* the book, so I shouldn't complain. Mirror up to nature and all that.

Trouble is, I don't have the will to write since all this happened. I moon about the house, hating my own company but knowing that I am in no fit state to inflict myself on anybody else.

When I come out of this I will be over to see you. Or perhaps you would risk a trip across the Pennines to my place.

Please don't take to heart all those nasty things I said that night. I was feeling suicidal after the hopeless reading.

Love from your faithless nephew,

Arthur

PS In spite of everything, my bed's still dry each morning! So I have come on a bit.

❧ ❧ ❧

Great was the depression in the offices of Cutting Edge Publications. Roberta Coleman, the publicity manager, sat warming her toes in front of the gas fire, glancing down the sales figures, the seemingly endless list of "Returns" for copies of *Dying in Style*. She could hear Giles Gibbons pacing the floor above.

"The critics have killed it stone-dead," she said.

"Don't take it to heart, Roberta," said Morag Aitken, the literary editor. "You win some, you lose some."

Roberta was not to be so easily consoled. She sat back in her chair, stretched, then mussed her short black hair. It fell back in place. She screwed up her thin face, a face that always reminded Morag Aitken of a pixie in a children's picture-book. "I ran myself ragged pushing that book, Morag," she said. "I knew there was a probability the critics would turn on it – just because of the subject matter. It was too much, I suppose, for them to see the book as a way to examine their own consciences about what they do to books or, failing that, maybe even see a funny side."

Morag let out a guffaw. "A bit, a teeny-weeny bit," she said.

"But, apart from anything else, it's a good book."

"It seemed such a good idea at the time," said Morag. "I thought that publishers and writers who had been through death by a thousand critical cuts would buy the book. Evidently not."

"It's Arthur Whitworth I feel sorry for," Roberta Coleman said.

"You always had a soft spot for Arthur, didn't you?"

"Yes, I did. I do," Roberta said. "I know he could be

difficult – Audrey Saunders always says Arthur gives her a hard time – but I never saw that side of him. Odd, isn't it, how people can come to such different conclusions?"

"Maybe Arthur fancies you."

"I can't imagine Arthur fancying anyone, to tell you the truth."

"I'm writing to him now."

Roberta Coleman got up and went to see what Morag was writing. What she read depressed her even more. "Don't send it. Not just yet," she said.

"I've got to, Roberta. Orders from on high. Giles wants rid of it."

"I'm off," Roberta said. "If anybody wants me – which I doubt – tell them I've just popped out to shoot myself."

"Right-ho," Morag said, stroking TippEx over a spelling error to give a personal touch to a word-processed letter. Then, alone with the gas fire, she read back what she had written.

Cutting Edge Publications
2 Mildmay Mews
London E2 7UN
2 May

Arthur Whitworth
Who'll Do It Up Cottage
Blubberhouses
Nr Skipton
North Yorkshire

Dear Arthur

Due to a reorganisation of our warehouse, we are able to dispose of 6,982 copies of the hardback edition of your novel, *Dying in Style*, at the price of £1.99 per copy.

Would you contact Melanie Fairforth to let her know how many copies you would like?

Yours sincerely

Morag Aitken
Literary Editor and Sales Director
Cutting Edge Publications

ᛟ ᛟ ᛟ

Then, quite suddenly, as out of the blue as Death ever comes:

Hello! Neither Cyril Parkinson nor LP Lomax can pick up at the moment. If you would care to leave a message, please do so. After the bleep:

"Have you heard about Arthur Whitworth? Dead, I fear. Could you manage an Obit? 800 words by Thursday? Cheers."

ᛟ ᛟ ᛟ

The following evening in Leeds, a tramp sat in a doorway, drinking British sherry. He watched as a beautiful young woman stapled black crepe around the fringes of a small display window in Waterstones bookshop.

Such a beautiful creature, he thought. And probably not stuck-up either. The sort who would put a pound in his cup, walk on, then return to put in more. And she wouldn't look away, either. She'd pass the time of day with him. Then she'd go off, turning to wave until she rounded the corner. The tramp, a man in his late forties called Jake whose poetry had once shown promise, toasted the young woman with the last of his bottle of VP.

Completely self-possessed, unaware that she was making the tramp's day, Farah Picknett worked for a further hour arranging a tribute to Arthur Whitworth: a tribute made of crepe paper and unsold books.

❧ ❧ ❧

A week later Roberta Coleman, the publicity manager for Cutting Edge, was deep in conversation with a Congolese wine-waiter at a *Guardian* Book of the Year bash in the crypt of St Martin-in-the-Fields. The wine waiter, a man called Patrice Luala from a village ten miles south of Kinshasa, kept recharging Roberta's glass with white wine as he told her in halting English about his treatment by the Congo's Secret Police.

Roberta had gone over to the waiter because he smiled ebony and stars at her when she entered the crypt. He seemed serene, a still tall centre, a well-rooted tree, among the starling chatter. The darting eyes of writers, journalists, critics and publishers out networking, promoting, showing-off, gossiping, smiling and being nice or not nice Roberta had, with a practised eye, taken in straight away. The publicity computer in her brain clicked, prioritising contacts in the crowd. There was work waiting, but the smiling waiter and his full bottle of the Warm South seduced her. Anyway, she was in mourning for Arthur Whitworth.

"So where do you live?"

"A hostel," Patrice replied. "I am a refugee, but they doubt my truth."

"What happened?"

Patrice told her and Roberta felt tears coming to her eyes.

"Are you married?" she asked.

"No, I am single."

They talked some more. They stopped while the award was made, while the winning author spoke. Patrice refilled Roberta's glass, then left her.

Roberta was thinking how odd it all was. An author stood on the stage spouting on about herself. The audience smiled towards her, admiring the dove of success preening mock-modestly above them. What were they thinking? Did they truly admire the author's book or had they – like Roberta – grown tired of reaching for the dictionary every five minutes? And what did all this amount to? The thousands of books in this audience's heads, thousands of characters from print, living, dying, making moral choices . . . but the audience still seemed hollow, brittle as dry reeds. Drop a match and the whole lot would disintegrate in a flash. Was it because literature for most of them was laced with ulterior motives . . . with a living to earn, a reputation to build, an audience to please and amaze? Could literature carry all that, carry on like that, without crumbling to dust, expiring in a flash of sulphurous firework and style?

Patrice was circulating now, the passport of the bottle he carried giving him a welcome. He towered above the throng, his round, neat head slightly inclined towards those he served. He might have been a priest distributing the sacrament. Why, Roberta wondered, could the assembled people not see that Patrice was the best story in the place? She longed to know more, to know him better. She could not understand why the people he served did not feel likewise, why they turned back to one another, excluding him.

Roberta sipped and looked around. There was Cyril Parkinson giggling with that awful man from *The Independent*. She thought of Arthur, his body turning over and over beneath the Irish Sea. Would he have done that to himself if it hadn't been for Cyril Parkinson?

At that moment Cyril, in the midst of having a glass of wine poured for him by Patrice, tilted his head back and laughed. How dare he! Roberta thought. Surprising herself as she heard herself, suddenly she was shouting through the crowd, "Cyril Parkinson! You little shit! How does it feel to have blood on your hands? Are you pleased with yourself? Are you?"

And the publicity manager of Cutting Edge weighed into the crowd, her purse and her fists flying, until she reached Cyril Parkinson. Faced by the height of him, the patrician face, the sardonic smile that rang cool bells of confidence and class, Roberta stopped. Her left hand fisted her purse in midair.

Coolly, Cyril Parkinson grasped Roberta by her thin wrists.

"Silly girl!" he said, "Silly, silly girl!"

* * *

The following morning, the altercation between Cyril Parkinson and Roberta Coleman had made it into the gossip columns of several newspapers. Giles Gibbons called Roberta into his office. He frowned at his publicity manager as, a moment before, he had been frowning at the accounts of Cutting Edge.

"There *is* such a thing as bad publicity, Roberta," Giles said.

"Yes, I know, Giles. Sorry."

"Blaming a critic for criticising is rather like blaming a shark for eating surfers. There's very little point to the exercise."

"No, I know. I'd had too much to drink and I was thinking of Arthur . . . "

"Of course you were. It's understandable. But Arthur Whitworth is no longer on our list. All your best efforts have failed to sell him. Now that he's remaindered himself, taken the coward's way out, you must see that you owe it to the other writers on Cutting Edge's list to do all you can for them."

"Yes, but . . . "

"And last night's little piece of histrionics won't help. We've Harriet Johnson's new hardback out next week. I dread to think what will happen if Parkinson decides to give it a mauling."

"I understand."

"Your outburst was so out of character."

"Yes."

Giles looked down at the accounts. "I don't know . . . " he said.

"Do you want me to resign?" Roberta asked.

"No, I don't. But I *do* want you to write a letter of apology to Cyril Parkinson."

Roberta went hot and cold. "Please, Giles!"

"Write it now, Roberta. And then bring it in here to me."

"I'd rather resign."

"Well, it's up to you. Think about it for an hour or so. If I don't have that letter on my desk in time for the last post I'll know what you have decided. I'd be very sad to lose you. Have another job to go to, do you?"

"No."

"No. I know Cyril is a little shit, but he's a powerful little shit. We just can't afford to be in his bad books."

❧ ❧ ❧

Flat 8
MacArthur Lodge
Inverness Road
Shepherd's Bush
London
W8 3YG
14 May

Dear Mr Parkinson

I am so sorry about my outburst at the *Guardian* Awards last night.

All I can say is that I do not know what came over me. I have been very unhappy since hearing of the death of Arthur Whitworth. I had also taken more white wine than a wise woman ought.

I do hope you will accept my apologies. Perhaps we could meet for lunch or a drink sometime.

Yours sincerely,

Roberta Coleman
Publicity Manager
Cutting Edge Publications

"There's a good girl," Giles Gibbons said.

"I hope he doesn't take me up on my lunch offer, Giles," Roberta said. "I doubt I could keep lunch down facing that creep."

"Did I ever tell you I once rejected a novel by Cyril Parkinson?"

"Did you? Why?"

"Because it was bad, Roberta. All style and no

substance. Like Henry James without a moral stance, strong characters or a sense of place."

"Did he ever find a publisher?"

"Don't think so. I'm not saying that's the reason he was so damning to *Dying in Style*. Negative reviews are expected from Cyril Parkinson. He's the doyen of that end of criticism. I'd just forget it now. Get back to pushing our other writers."

"It's uphill, Giles."

"Don't give up, love," Giles said. "Things'll look up or my name isn't Giles Gibbons."

❧ ❧ ❧

13 Duckworth Avenue,
Leeds

The Press Council,
1, Salisbury Square,
London
EC4Y 8AE
The 16th of May

Dear Sir or Madam,

We are the aunties of the late Arthur Whitworth, a writer cruelly pushed to suicide by the mean and uncalled-for sniping of several critics in the newspapers.

Of course, we know quite well that saying bad things sells papers, but we also know that the lies told about our nephew's novels are the direct cause of robbing us of our last remaining relation, and the wider world of a man who always tried to give his public an interesting and challenging read.

According to our way of thinking, the newspapers have Arthur's blood of their hands. We will go to our graves believing that. Please pass on our complaints to the papers and tell them that we do not know how they can sleep at nights.

Yours truly,

Anne and Win Whitworth

ℰ ℰ ℰ

The Press Council
1 Salisbury Square
London
EC4Y 8AE

Misses Anne and Win Whitworth
13 Duckworth Av
Leeds
24 May

Dear Anne and Win Whitworth

Please accept the sincere regrets of all here at the Press Council about the death of your nephew, the writer Arthur Whitworth.

Unfortunately, it is outside our remit to take action against critics for what is universally acknowledged to be "fair comment".

All I can do at this time is to sympathise with you in your loss.

Yours sincerely,

Gerry Mannering, Secretary

PS I am a great fan of your nephew's books. GM

ർ ർ ർ

Audrey Saunders Ltd
17A Clwyd Passage
London E11 9PS
30 May

Dear Charlotte

Thank you for your fax, covered though it was with crocodile tears for the late Arthur Whitworth. How right you are in asserting that it was completely unlike Arthur to shuffle off causing so little fuss. I would never have expected it of him. Still, one ought to be grateful. No dreary trip to Yorkshire to stand at the graveside, no flowers to purchase. I suppose, as you say, a memorial service might be mooted. I rather hope not. There are few who would step willingly into the pulpit to mouth lying platitudes about him. I suppose I could recycle the one I did for Muriel Simpson but I think we're better keeping very quiet indeed. Let sleeping shits lie, say I! God, he was a common little man!

Yes, I know! The circumstances of Whitworth's death are uncannily similar to the first chapter of *Dying in Style*, where, if I'm not very much mistaken, the dead author's agent gets blown away. Should one worry, one asks oneself? I know life has an infuriating habit of imitating art, but I think we can rest assured that Arthur Whitworth's art will die with him. Amen to that, say I!

Love,

Audrey

PS See you Wednesday!

ꕥ ꕥ ꕥ

But Charlotte was not destined to see Audrey Saunders on Wednesday – nor ever again.

Tape-Recorded Statement. Westminster Abbey. Tuesday, June 6, 8.23 a.m.

Detective Inspector Dyer Speaking to Abbey cleaner, Mrs Millicent Bird:

Mrs Bird, can you tell us how you discovered the body?

I opened the chancel door at 5.30 and made myself a cuppa. Then I got the cleaning equipment out and made my way to the back. I always start at the Great Doors and then work along to the right and into Poets' Corner. But today I had a feeling. I was shivering and it isn't cold and I'm always well wrapped up. Strip down as I go, so to speak. Well, I wheeled my cleaning stuff straight into Poets' Corner. That was when I saw the body. She was lying just as you see her now. Right on Dylan Thomas's Memorial. She could've been asleep lying on her back except for the end of the pen sticking out of her mouth and her teeth biting it and this look of horror . . .

So nothing has been disturbed?

No, apart from me throwing up. Sorry about that. I feel ashamed of myself.

But nothing else?

No.

What did you do after finding the body and being sick?

I called the supervisor and he called one of the vicars and he called you.

Have you ever seen the woman before?

Don't think so. Poor thing!

She didn't go gentle into that good night, that's for sure," said Detective Inspector Dyer, reaching for the "off" button of his tape recorder.

Come again?

❧ ❧ ❧

The evening of the same day, Roberta Coleman was trying to explain the present perfect continuous to Patrice.

Patrice, in an unusual – though perhaps not a unique – position for a student of English, was lying naked beneath his teacher.

"We have been making love," Roberta said.

"We have made love," Patrice said.

"No, that's different," Roberta said, wondering as she spoke how it was different. Thinking up explanations on the hoof, she continued, "We have made love. What have we done this evening? We have made love . . . but now we are washing the dishes. This is different. I think." Roberta wiggled her hips, feeling with delight the full feeling Patrice's ebbing erection was giving her. "We have been making love . . . and we still are."

Patrice thought about that. "I am very happy," he said. "Very happy."

The telephone rang.

Roberta picked it up and heard Morag Aitken, the literary editor at Cutting Edge, speaking.

M: Roberta, it's me.

R: Hello, Morag.

M: What's the matter? You sound puffed.

R: I've been making love.

M: All right for some. Look, love, I'm sorry to call, but there's bad news.

R: What?

M: Brace yourself.

R: Come on, Morag!

M: Audrey Saunders is dead.

R: Dead.

M: Yes, and it looks like murder. She was found this morning in Westminster Abbey. Poets' Corner . . . are you there?

R: Yes.

M: Apparently a pen was found sticking into her mouth.

R: But . . .

M: I know.

R: But . . .

M: It's either a shocking coincidence or . . .

R: Are you *sure*, Morag?

M: Giles told me.

R: Poor Audrey!

M: Yes.

R: I can't take it in.

M: Me neither. Do you know what I thought when I'd recovered from the shock?

R: No. What?

M: I thought of what we'd told Arthur Whitworth . . . you know . . . about publicity.

R: I'm sorry, Morag . . . what did we tell him?

M: That he should do his own.

R: Yes. So?

M: So maybe he's taken our advice to heart.

R: Arthur's dead, Morag.

M: So's his agent.

R: What do we do?

M: What can we do? If I were you I'd get back to making love. I wish I could. How do you find them, Roberta?

R: Poor Audrey!

Roberta put the phone down.

"You have been speaking on the telephone," Patrice said.

"Yes, I have," Roberta said. She got up out of bed and, still naked, walked into her sitting-room. There she picked out her signed copy of *Dying in Style*. Leafing through the pages, she went back to bed, pausing only to marvel at the sight of Patrice lying nude and unconcerned on top of the duvet.

"Here's a comprehension passage for you," she said, squeezing Patrice's right breast. "Listen carefully. After I have finished there will be a test.

'The vaulted ceiling of The Abbey far above her head slowly came into focus. Where was she? The cool hardness of the stone flags beneath her back was pleasant. She felt a delicious lightheadedness suffuse her whole body. This was bliss, staring upwards at the perfectly wrought ceiling. Who had built it? What genius had thought out and sculpted such a marvel?

Still the literary agent did not know where she was or how she had come to be here. And she did not care. As far as she was concerned, this was paradise.

Then a black-gloved hand pinched her nose hard, cutting off air. Heaven became hell as she saw, heading for her gaping mouth, the nib of a stainless-steel pen. A body weighed her down. A balaclavaed face, a gargoyle's face, stared down. She could hear its breathing, smell its foetid breath. The nib pierced her palette in front of her tonsils. She wanted to gag. She bit down on the barrel of the pen but made no impression on the stainless steel. Then, silently shrieking, she watched as the gloved hand twisted the end of the barrel of the pen. A bitter liquid entered her, leaked from the wound in her palette and down her throat. It was a taste a hundred times more evil than anything she had ever experienced. Then the pain started. She looked up, round-eyed, at the vaulted ceiling. She loathed it. She loathed everything. A moment ago heaven. Now, now . . . The dark figure straddled her, stopped her struggles. The gloved hands kept turning the barrel of the pen until it was empty. She died.'" Roberta closed the book. "What has been happening?" she asked.

"Have they been making love?"

"No, they haven't. Certainly not."

"I didn't understand. What has been happening?"

"Somebody has been murdered," Roberta said. "It was the first murder in this book. It's called *Dying in Style*."

ꝏ ꝏ ꝏ

An open verdict was declared at Skipton Coroner's Court, following the death of Arthur Whitworth the thriller writer, whose empty rowing-boat was found capsized in Morecambe Bay in April. Mr Whitworth, a keen sea-angler, was known to have been suffering from depression and a note left on the writer's desk was produced as evidence of possible suicide. However, the coroner, Mr Ian Gardiner, said that he was unwilling to pronounce on the cause of death without forensic evidence. And, in the absence of a body, such evidence was not forthcoming.

ꝏ ꝏ ꝏ

Detective Inspector Dyer enjoyed visiting the Pathology Lab. For there he would meet chain-smoking, sweet-sucking, guilt-ridden Dr Edith Gonne. Dyer's hangover lifted straight away as Dr Gonne's tall, gaunt figure strode towards him along the corridor, a steam train of cigarette smoke fuming behind her.

"What's the verdict, Edith?"

"Prussic acid unloaded from the pen into the soft palette. Come into my office."

Dr Gonne pushed past Dyer and flung open the door to her office. She gestured him to sit in the bald Ercol armchair and offered him a Silk Cut. Dyer took one and watched as Dr Gonne lit a new one from the stub of her last.

"Not given up yet?" he asked, lighting his own.

Edith scowled at the obvious wafting across her desk. "Still waiting for the right moment," said Dr Gonne. "You?"

"I've cut down," said Detective Inspector Dyer.

"Any leads?"

"She was a literary agent apparently. Name of Audrey Saunders."

"That accounts for the method of dispatch."

"Does it?"

Dr Gonne squinted at Dyer. "Think about it. Poetry Corner. Osmiroid pen as murder weapon. The pen is mightier than the sword. All that."

"We mustn't jump to too many hasty conclusions," Dyer said.

"We must at all costs avoid facing the obvious," replied Dr Gonne, implying more than she said, as was often her way.

Dyer noted that Dr Gonne's hand was moving towards the pottery jar on her desk. He held his breath.

"Fancy a sweetie?"

"What have you got?"

Dr Gonne smiled. The smile wrinkled the dry skin of her cheeks. She lifted the lid. A black and white striped sea of Everton Mints looked up at Dyer. He took a couple, opened the wrapping of both and popped them in.

"Two?" asked Dr Gonne.

"It takes two . . ." said Dyer, " . . . these days."

"How's the wife?"

Dyer smiled. "How *are* you?"

"Fine."

"It didn't work, did it?"

Edith inhaled angrily. "What didn't work?"

"Well, you said that living with me was killing you. But you're still at it."

"I've cut down."

"I reckon we could have licked it together."

Dr Gonne, married name Dyer, shook her head. "Timmy, whenever I see you I think fag."

"I know. I'm sorry. I miss you, though, Edith."

"I've gone back to the Church."

Dyer nodded, but didn't say anything. Edith going back to the Church was a bit like Dyer going back to a tobacconist or a gay bar . . . or a church for that matter. It meant something – he was never quite sure what – but it was not news.

"It's helping. I think."

"How?"

"Not sure."

"Were there any marks on the body?" Dyer asked.

"Bruises on the upper arms. I'm still waiting for test results. I have the feeling that the victim was probably drugged prior to the killing. I should know for certain in a day or two."

"Why do you say that? I mean, the look on her face gave me the strong impression that she was very conscious at the end."

"Maybe," said Edith, stubbing out her cigarette, "but

hard to get the victim to Westminster Abbey while fully-conscious. I'd say she was drugged first. A nib buried in her soft palette would have brought her round. Perhaps the murderer didn't expect that."

"I have an answer to that one," Dyer said. "The previous evening there was a memorial service for some dead bigwig in the Allied War Graves Commission. It's possible the murderer and his victim attended that, and then stayed in the Abbey overnight."

"I despair of you sometimes," said Dr Gonne.

"It's just a theory, mind. We're looking at all the closed circuit footage. We might spot something."

"Good luck. Anything on the pen?"

"There's a blurred thumbprint but I have the feeling it's going to belong to the victim. Struggle and everything. There are signs of a powder that is used on surgical gloves to keep them from sticking. Again, we won't know for a day or so. Even when we do it doesn't add up to much."

The pathologist looked at her watch. "Got to go," she said.

"Come back to me, Edith," Dyer said, addressing the ash-tray.

"I can't, Timmy. It's not just the smoking, it's everything. I'm tired of sharing breakfast with one or other of your gentleman callers. And then having to sit there while *you* explain *me* away."

"I'll change everything! I will, Edith. Come back, please! I'm miserable by myself."

Dr Edith Gonne stubbed out her cigarette, reached for an Everton Mint, stood up, patted Detective Inspector Dyer lightly on his dandruffed left shoulder, and left the room without another word.

Dyer sat on, looking at, but not seeing, the ashes on the pathologist's desk.

❧ ❧ ❧

Hello! Neither Cyril Parkinson nor LP Lomax can pick up at the moment. If you would care to leave a message, please do so. After the bleep:

"Have you heard about the awful business. Poor Audrey. Could you manage an Obit? 800 words by Tuesday? Normally, we'd have had one in the freezer, but . . . well you don't expect it, do you? Makes a chap shudder. I heard that she was found with an Osmiroid, the nib of which was buried deep in her soft palette. You'd think the murderer might have stretched to a Waterman. Anyway, The Fuzz think that the pen was used to inject something nasty into her system. Cheers."

❧ ❧ ❧

" . . . Audrey had a nose for talent. Never afraid to take on unpublished writers and set about selling their work – if she believed in it. She will be sorely missed on the London literary scene."

❧ ❧ ❧

"I need a drink," said Cyril Parkinson. He flopped down on the sofa, assured that his statement would bring the drink. He looked around the room, stacked high with books. They had overflowed the bookcases and formed Manhattan skylines against all the horizons of the room.

LP Lomax brought Cyril his drink. "I wouldn't want to go through that again," LP said, clinking his glass against his friend's.

"Who'd have thought Audrey Saunders would have

had such common relations, LP!" Cyril said, taking a sip from his Pernod. "Straight out of the Kay catalogue."

"Who could have done it?" LP Lomax asked. He was opening a small parcel of CDs sent to him for reviewing.

"Search me. That horrid reviewer from *The Standard* kept whispering to me about Arthur Whitworth RIP. If he weren't dead, I wouldn't put it past him." Cyril caught sight of the cube of CDs slipping out of the bubble wrap. "Anything decent?"

"Another *Orpheo*. This is the one with a genuine castrato Romanian. The old Secret Police gave him the voice. It's been the making of him. Might be interesting. Another Beethoven cycle. And a 'live' *Ring*. From Glyndebourne. That's the one I'm in. I coughed all the way through Act 1 of *Die Walküre*. Hope they haven't edited me out." LP Lomax shuffled through the rest of his CDs. "Not much else. All cats on the piano stuff."

"It's odd, though," continued Cyril Parkinson, off on his own tangent. "The murder almost exactly mimics the first in *Dying in Style*."

Cyril got up and searched through his pile of review copies, already bagged and waiting to be dragged off to the second-hand bookshop. He found *Dying in Style* and held it gingerly between thumb and forefinger. Then he sought out the first murder. "Exactly the same, LP!" he said. "It just goes to show, the effects of bad art."

"You don't think Arthur Whitworth could still be alive, do you?"

"I wouldn't put it past him, but I doubt he'd have the ingenuity to actually act out an outlandish murder. I mean, one of the things I couldn't stand about his murders was the way he never explained the method . . . and he never explained it because he wasn't capable of thinking up how such things came about. Too bone-idle to do the leg-work.

No, I reckon somebody's read the book – or, if they've any sense, just the first few pages – and decided to have a go."

"Let's have a look," LP Lomax asked, holding his hand out for the book.

Cyril handed it over.

LP Lomax searched through the book, snorting at one or two of Cyril's comments in the margins. He had to hand it to Cyril: he was a real pro. Not a grammatical infelicity, spelling error, omission, had been left uncircled. He had not merely scanned this book in order to make his criticism; he had studied it minutely prior to shredding.

At last, LP Lomax found the second murder in the book. A critic was poisoned by a drink at a book launch, falling into a dead swoon – more dead than swoon – on a Bakhtiari rug in the middle of a splendid sitting-room in Hampstead. The unfortunate critic had ventured a negative review on the writer's latest novel.

"Fancy another?" Cyril Parkinson asked, wiggling his empty glass.

"I'd go easy if I were you, Cyril," LP Lomax said.

Cyril, misinterpreting what LP Lomax had said, nodded. "You're probably right. Think I'll have a few minutes shut-eye before I go back to the prose-face." Cyril settled himself down on the sofa. "Poor Audrey! I can't say I cared for the woman, but what a way to go!"

Three hours later, LP Lomax came in from his study to see what Cyril wanted for his supper. He found his friend working at his word-processor.

"Review for Sunday?" LP asked,

"That's right, LP, I'm having a marvellous time," replied Cyril Parkinson, "I'm reviewing the new Harriet Johnson."

"Who's she?"

"A Cutting Edge author. She wrote *The Chalk Farm Trilogy*. Hampstead novels, really; they'd just slipped down the hill a bit. Awful turgid efforts. Sold well."

"What's this one?"

"Ah, this one . . . " Cyril said, holding up his copy of *Say it with Flowers*. "Well, the blurb says it's a hard-hitting novel of great wit and humanity. Set in Herne Hill."

"And what do you think?"

Cyril Parkinson did not reply. He pressed "Print" and, as each page stuck its tongue out of the printer, he reached across and handed it to LP Lomax.

LP Lomax read the review. "Ouch! Ouch! Ouch!" he said.

"Quite," said Cyril Parkinson. "That should spread alarm and despondency at Cutting Edge. You don't think I've gone over the top, do you?"

"Of course you have, Cyril," replied LP Lomax, "but you going over the top is what pays the mortgage."

"True," said Cyril Parkinson, "but am I not the most fortunate of men to be able to do what I love most?"

"I'd love to be a fly on the wall at Cutting Edge when the review comes out."

"Giles Gibbons is up to his neck in debt, I hear."

"You think he might go to the wall?"

"He might. He well might," said Cyril Parkinson. "Another drink?"

❧ ❧ ❧

"Did you see it?" Giles asked Roberta the following Monday morning.

Roberta nodded. "My grovelling letter didn't do much good, did it?"

Giles shook his head, a head thick with hangover from a solitary drinking binge. He had started a minute or two after ten on Sunday morning and finished by passing out on the settee in front of Melvin Bragg.

"There was an OK one in *The Mail*," Roberta said.

"You can't console me, Roberta," Giles said.

"And I think I might be able to get *The Catholic Times* to be nice to it. They're bound to like the priest. He's a real poppet and highly moral."

"You're making me feel worse."

"Sorry, Giles." Roberta said.

"I could kill the bugger! I really could!" Giles said. "He's going to ruin me."

"Steady, Giles,"

"Steady! Steady! I'd like to give Cyril Parkinson 'steady'! A steady dose of acid poured steadily down his poisonous gullet."

"You don't mean that," Roberta said.

Giles thought about that. "That review was not only unfair to the book, it was libellous to the author. I wonder should we sue?"

The telephone rang on Giles's desk. Giles answered it. Roberta watched Giles listening. Finally, he passed the telephone to her. "It's for you, Roberta."

Roberta listened to Harriet Johnson bemoaning her review from Cyril Parkinson. At last, taking advantage of the space allowed by Harriet's breaking into tears, Roberta said, "OK, Harriet, it was a bad review. But no publicity is bad publicity. You've got to try and be positive. Don't, whatever you do, let it block you. The one in *The Mail* was great and . . ."

Giles could bear it to longer. He got up and left the office, determining to find a pub that was open and ready to pour balm into a ruined man.

❧ ❧ ❧

The following Thursday, LP Lomax came into Cyril Parkinson's study. He was shocked to see his friend on the floor, writhing in pain, clutching his stomach.

"I've been calling for you!" groaned Cyril Parkinson.

"Couldn't hear. Reviewing CDs. Locked into my earphones. That *Orpheo* was a real disappointment. Almost made me quite like the Solti. What's the matter?"

"Terrible pain in the side. Really terrible."

LP Lomax fetched some aspirin from the bathroom-cabinet. He wondered. He thought it too absurd. He'll be better after something to eat, he thought.

Cyril swallowed down the aspirins and at once vomited them and the water back. He cried out as the spasms multiplied the pain. "Get me an ambulance!" he said.

The ambulance men had to strap down the patient. He writhed, tried to climb the walls of the vehicle with his legs, to invert himself, to bang his head against the window seals . . . anything to relieve the pain. Restrained, there was nothing to distract Cyril from it. He screamed along with the siren.

The young doctors at the Casualty Department at King's College Hospital discussed their screaming patient writhing behind a curtain and restrained by two orderlies.

"Could be withdrawal," said the younger of the two.

"Or acute pancreatitis."

"I smelled liquor on his breath. I think."

"He's in a bad way either way."

Then they heard a statement from behind the curtain, the last statement of Cyril Parkinson's life.

"The drink! The drink! Sweet Hamlet, the drink!"

A sound of choking, a deep sigh. Silence.

"Bloody hell!" from the first orderly.

"Bloody hell is right!" from the second orderly.

The young doctors swished open the curtains, but they had already closed on Cyril Parkinson, critic.

ꝏ ꝏ ꝏ

STRANGER THAN FICTION?

A failed novelist seems to be getting his own back from beyond the grave. *Dying in Style* by Arthur Whitworth bombed when it was published. Our reviewer called it: "A sad book by a sad plonker."

But the recent deaths of Arthur Whitworth's agent and the critic, Cyril Parkinson, point the finger straight at the novelist who, it was thought, committed suicide when he saw what a lambasting the book was getting.

Is Whitworth really dead? We don't think so. We reckon he is trying to resuscitate *Dying in Style* by some real-life killings. Or is that stretching gullibility too far? Watch this space. And watch out for this man!

ꝏ ꝏ ꝏ

"No, you can't smoke," LP Lomax told Detective Inspector Dyer.

"Very well, sir. Sorry I asked. It's just it helps the concentration."

Dyer looked around the kitchen of the flat. "Anything else we should test?"

"You're the expert," LP Lomax replied.

The police had removed all the liquor, the contents of the fridge, even a box of Godiva Chocolates, from the flat.

"Have you lived together long?" Dyer asked.

"We've *shared rooms* together since university," LP Lomax said, wondering where he had seen Dyer before.

"Were you lovers?"

"No, we were not."

"But you are gay, aren't you?"

"Why do you ask?"

"I believe I've seen you in The City of Quebec."

"'The Elephants' Graveyard'? I wouldn't be seen dead there."

"Brief Encounter, perhaps?"

"Briefly."

"The Coleherne?"

LP Lomax snorted.

"Anyway, sir, I think we've established that we have some watering-holes in common. Have you any idea who could have done this?"

"Yes, I have. Arthur Whitworth, the author of *Dying in Style*."

"You sound pretty definite. There are no other possibilities, are there?"

"None. Find Arthur Whitworth and you've got Cyril's murderer."

ぐ ぐ ぐ

"Remember Arthur Whitworth?" Giles Gibbons asked Jim Smart over the phone.

"Don't remind me," the bookbuyer replied.

"Now, Jim, I know you had a bad experience with *Dying in Style* but . . ."

"Could you hold, Giles? I've another call. It might be Mandy."

"Jim, this really . . . "

But Jim had transferred. Giles waited, bending a component of an executive toy on his desk out of shape. The toy had once consisted of two metal struts that balanced needles atop a hardwood plinth. Both struts had magnets on the end and had once played little nudging games with one another, assaulting on the borders of attraction and repulsion. But one strut had taken a tumble and lost its magnet. The other, still magnetised, sat lonely and forlorn, bowed over on its plinth, with nothing to attract. The broken one had turned up that morning, lodged down the side of Giles's office chair. This was the thing that Giles in his irritation bent out of shape.

The lonely intact part of the toy was a powerful image – well, an image anyway – for the publishing industry. The magnet of books attracting no one in particular. It was also, now he thought about it, an apt image for Jim Smart and his one-sided attraction for Mandy, his errant, erring wife.

Still, at this point Jim should be listening to Giles's proposals, should forget sex and the doings of Mandy in order to concentrate on Giles's Great Idea.

Jim came back, sounding even more depressed than before.

"Was it Mandy?" Giles enquired.

"No."

"I am sorry, Jim."

"I just don't know what gets into her."

"No. Look, Jim, have you been keeping an eye on the papers and the television?"

"No, Giles. What with one thing and another."

"Right. Then I'll tell you: I'm about to do a new

edition of *Dying in Style* . . . a huge edition. Not hardback this time. Quality paperback with integral bookmark, wipe-over cover and stitched spine."

"But, Giles, we both got burnt with it last time."

"I'm getting to that," Giles said patiently. "You ought to read your papers, Jim. You really ought. Terrible – wonderful – things have been happening. Hype from heaven." And Giles filled in Jim Smart about the two killings that had mirrored the plot of *Dying in Style*. "There's terrific media interest, Jim. We've had to send out every copy of the novel we can lay our hands on – precious few, I'm sad to say. And the switchboard's been glowing red-hot with requests and enquiries from the public as to where they can buy the book. While naturally it cuts me up to say this: these tragedies are marketing opportunities made in heaven."

"Funny," said Jim. "We've heard nothing at W Crisp."

"You *will* hear, Jim. And I'd like you and W Crisp to be able to satisfy the demand."

"Scuse me a sec," Jim said.

Then, just as Giles had finished a complex and blasphemous expletive, Jim was back. "No," he said, "it wasn't Mandy."

"Sorry, Jim," Giles said.

"I don't know . . . " Jim said.

"How many copies will you take? I'd say 100,000 should do it. For the moment."

"Giles, I worry about you. You could come to grief on this one. Look, can't make any promises. Will make enquiries and get back to you."

"Make it soon, Jim. Make it today. Will you do that for me?"

"Don't know what gets into her," Jim said. The line went dead.

Giles put the phone down. He looked at the wrecked strut of the executive toy lying on top of his fax to the printer. Then he took his pen, signed the fax and called his secretary.

Melanie appeared at the door of his office. Behind her loomed a middle-aged man, big, going to seed, a drooping moustache emphasising a rough unsymmetrical face, a red Gore-Tex jacket and pants bagging at the knees, concertina creases behind. He reminded Giles at once of the picture of Nietzsche on the cover of a much-thumbed, student-days Penguin. He looked for a pile of "Big Issues" under the intruder's arm.

"Melanie, fax this off, will you?" Giles said, tauting his forehead. The implications of the huge print run for *Dying in Style* were making his heart race, his voice tremble. Superman dithering between roles in the phone-box.

Melanie took the fax. "By the way," she said, "there's a policeman outside. He'd like to speak to you."

"Detective Inspector Dyer," Dyer said.

Melanie jumped. "Christ!" she said, "you shouldn't do that to people."

"Sorry, Miss," Dyer said.

"Come in, Chief Inspector," Giles said.

"He's already in," said Melanie.

"Thanks, love," Giles said. "Would you bring us . . . " he turned to Dyer, " . . . Tea? Coffee?"

"Coffee, please. Black. Three sugars."

"Would you bring us two coffees, love? Mine has four sugars. But send the fax first."

"Right-ho," Melanie said.

Giles turned to Dyer. "How can I help you, Chief Inspector?"

"Alas, it's only Detective Inspector," Dyer said. "I live in hope, mind."

"Don't we all?"

"If I might," said Dyer, "I'd like to ask you some questions about two recent deaths. Audrey Saunders and Cyril Parkinson."

Terrible!" Giles said. "Absolutely terrible."

"Did you know the victims, Mr Gibbons?"

"I knew both of them professionally, Chief Inspector. Audrey Saunders represented three of my writers – writers published by Cutting Edge – and Cyril Parkinson I knew through his book reviews. I'd also met him on the promotion circuit."

Dyer nodded. "You published all of Arthur Whitworth's books, didn't you?"

"Yes."

"And Arthur Whitworth was represented by Audrey Saunders?"

"Indeed, yes."

"You know, of course, that the two murders were almost identical with the first two described in *Dying in Style*?"

"I do. It's quite uncanny, isn't it? Like the plot of a novel, in fact?"

"Would you mind if I smoked?"

"Not at all, Chief Inspector," Giles said, though he did mind rather. Still, he took a pottery bowl, emptied out some paper-clips and passed it over to Dyer.

"I won't dirty your ash-tray, sir," said Dyer, a besieged smoker sensitive about small inessentials. He took from his pocket a large Golden Virginia tin. This he opened, revealing the ash and stubs of about twenty cigarettes. He lit up, while Giles stared in disbelief at the pyre, the memento mori, in the tin. A match flared. Its sulphurous smell reached him, followed a moment later by a whiff of tobacco expelled through Dyer's huge nose.

To distract himself, Giles asked, "Have you any theories as to who's behind the murders?"

"Well, let's put it this way," Dyer replied. "If Arthur Whitworth was alive we'd have some tough questions to ask him."

"But Arthur's dead." Giles shook his head sorrowfully, "Another tragedy. A great loss."

"He's a great loss to this investigation, Mr Gibbons."

Melanie came back in, placed Dyer's coffee down next to the Golden Virginia tin, recoiling at the sight of it. Then she put Giles's cup on his musical mat. It played *The Blue Danube* in a tinny hi-tec tinkle. Giles smiled a *sorry-about-that* though, in truth, he was rather proud of his musical mat, a gift from a Swiss at the Frankfurt Book Fair.

"Roberta wants to know," said Melanie, "do you really mean 250 K? You know, for the fax?"

"Yes," said Giles. "Thank you Melanie."

"It's an awful lot," Melanie said.

"Thank you, Melanie."

The door closed.

"Of course," Dyer said, "we can't rule out Arthur Whitworth. No body has been found. Still, in the meantime we also have to consider who else might have something to gain from the deaths of these people."

Giles decided to come clean at once. "Cutting Edge has a great deal to gain, Chief Inspector. There are signs that there's going to be a big demand for *Dying in Style*. It's not certain, of course – nothing is in this game – but it's looking hopeful. We're ordering a big print run in anticipation."

"In anticipation of what, sir?"

Giles Gibbons picked up the wrecked strut of the executive toy and bent it. It broke. Dyer noticed, but didn't say anything. "Just in anticipation."

Dyer still didn't say anything.

"You've got me feeling guilty now. Like an innocent man passing all those customs officers in the green channel. Guilt by association, I suppose."

"As long as you're an innocent man, then you've got nothing to worry about, have you?"

"No, but you hear such tales," Giles said.

"I do wonder why you published *Dying in Style* in the first place, Mr Gibbons?"

"We thought it was a good read."

"But if what I hear is correct, it's pretty hard on publishers, critics, and all that. I mean, didn't it offend you? Didn't you feel it might offend a lot of your friends?"

"Not in the least, Chief Inspector. To tell you the truth, the book had the ring of truth. We are a bit like that. Arthur knew exactly what he was writing about. Anyway, everything that Arthur Whitworth wrote offended someone. He was that sort of writer. He took the thriller genre and used it to ride his hobby-horses. His first novel attacked 'teacher abuse' – his term. *The Ends of the Earth* gave car manufacturers and anti-ecology MPs a bad time. *Ashes on a Dead Man's Sleeve*," and Giles couldn't help his eyes wandering to the Golden Virginia tin, "killed off the world's tobacco moguls. He asphyxiated them in a variety of ways, if I remember rightly. Then there was *Bankers' Draft*, in which Swiss bankers were done away with. The victims received bank statements showing that their moral capital was way overdrawn. Corrupt money from drugs and the third world and . . . "

"That's all very well, sir, but . . . "

"I'm just making the point that Arthur Whitworth had lots of targets. He used his novels to tell a story and to inform the general public about what he saw as evils in the world. We thought it was quite droll when he submitted a novel about the world of books."

"But it didn't sell?"

"No. It was a great disappointment to us. Still, that happens, you know. Publishing books isn't that different from throwing darts at a board; you hope that a few may hit the target."

"But you think it will sell now?"

"We have hopes, Chief Inspector. It's an ill wind. I'm sure that sounds callous but . . ."

"It's the way of the world."

"It is, rather."

"I quite understand, sir. You don't by any chance have a copy of *Dying in Style*, do you? I think it's essential reading for the conduct of this investigation."

Giles Gibbons looked doubtful. "You couldn't wait until next week, could you?"

It was Dyer's turn to look doubtful.

"Very well," Giles Gibbons said, "maybe I could find you an uncorrected galley from our first print run. It has the full text, but it may have some errors still in it. Would that do?"

"Thank you."

Dyer stood up, putting the lid on the Golden Virginia tin. "You don't have any theories yourself about who might be behind these deaths?"

"None, unless it's a fan of Arthur Whitworth's books. You never know what hands a book will get into, do you, Chief Inspector?"

"No, I don't suppose you do." Detective Inspector Dyer replied. He placed the Golden Virginia tin in the pocket of his Gore-Tex.

❧ ❧ ❧

That evening, alone in the messy Highbury flat he had once shared with Dr Edith Gonne, Detective Inspector Dyer arrived at the last page of *Dying in Style* and laid it, and his red pencil, aside. He squeezed his eyes, wondered whether he needed new glasses. No, not until the present ones were too scratched to see through. He wasn't going to let the buggers get him before the built-in obsolescence of their product had well and truly obsolesced. £69.95 for a few bits of wire that must be worth 50 pence max. Disgusting!

Dyer held the book up. He looked at its bulk, the wrinkles along the spine that he had caused. Not a bad achievement for a half-day. More productive than wandering the streets, swallowing a skinful, meeting eyes that meeting his wandered off to more hopeful, more youthful, vistas; watching the rest of the world pairing off. There had to be an argument for reading, for seeing sense and giving up on The Search. What was he searching for, after all? It was all so meaningless, wasted so much of the diminishing time left. If he gave that up, think of the time he'd save, the money, the angst. And Edith might come back to him.

He surveyed the ash-tray. His Golden Virginia tin was full again. They'd have to go, too. Giving up: so much to bloody give up at fifty to try and make it through to sixty. Maybe he should read Whitworth's novel about the tobacco industry.

Dying in Style was still held aloft, momentarily forgotten. He came back to it. Not a bad read, he thought. More to it than the critics had allowed. Mind you, you couldn't expect critics to take to the book. The author had obviously had no time for the breed. Apart from the succession of gory deaths he conjured up for them, he had painted a world of seedy hype, of deals between media moguls, of nepotism, a literary version of payola. No, not surprising that the hand, bitten by Arthur Whitworth – the hand that fed him when it felt like it – had slapped back.

Still, the author of that kind of book would have been ready for such attacks, wouldn't he? He couldn't have expected to get away with it, could he? That would have been plain naive.

Thinking of Edith, Dyer fumbled for a cigarette, lit it and telephoned the CID in Morecambe.

"No body?" he asked.

"None," said the detective sergeant on the other end.

"Pity."

Dyer watched the smoke swirling around the room. A blue U-shaped valley of it swayed in front of him.

"You've alerted shipping to be on the lookout, have you? You keep reminding them?"

The sergeant said they had. Coastguard too. But it was needle-in-a-haystack stuff. "The currents are all wrong for washing him ashore. Anyway," he concluded, "he's probably underwater now. He might or might not rise to the surface."

"How do you mean?"

"It depends."

"On what?"

"The body could get lodged under a rock, caught in weeds. Or it might get eaten up by fish. A picked-clean skeleton will sink. With no fatty tissue to swell and turn it buoyant. Lots of variables, you see."

"What do you think? I mean, could someone have taken the rowing-boat out and then swum back to shore?"

"It's not impossible. Unlikely, though. Currents make it a bit on the iffy side. I'd say Arthur Whitworth's dead. I feel sorry for the poor bloke myself."

"For why?"

"*Dying in Style* would sell like mad up our way. People who haven't cracked a book in years are looking for it. No copies to be had anywhere. My wife's reading bits in her paper. She's waiting for the murder of a literary editor now. Then, she says, she'll read on."

"It's pretty rum."

"You can say that again. Any other leads?"

"No."

Dyer phoned Scotland Yard. He told them to warn all literary editors. "Don't give them the wind up, Charlie. We can't stretch to protection for each and every one. Just tell them to mind their backs."

Dyer lit another cigarette, lay back on the sofa and wondered who would be next. Then, seeing that the night still had some life in it, he put on his leather jacket and went out to see if things were hopping at The Elephants' Graveyard.

ꟷ ꟷ ꟷ

"We'll take that hundred thousand," Jim told Giles.

Giles Gibbons silently punched the air. The sudden action jarred his shoulder. He had to pause to rub it before writing a note to Roberta Coleman on a Post-It. Roberta read the note, and beamed.

She made off down the fire-escape of the Cutting Edge offices, across a dank yard and into the warehouse.

The new edition of *Dying in Style*, pallet-loads of it in units of twenty copies each, sat wrapped in tough plastic reaching from floor to ceiling. They dwarfed the rest of the stock in the cavernous room that had once been a coach-house.

Patrice, with no other work in prospect, had been recruited by Roberta. He was boxing consignments, sticking labels on and piling them up to await delivery to bookshops.

"I need help!" he said.

"I'm here to help," Roberta replied. "Where's Morag?"

"She delivers books with her car. Urgent, she said."

"Well, she'd be more useful helping here."

Patrice nodded and got back to work.

Roberta had persuaded Giles to take Patrice on for as long as the panic continued. Two days into the arrival of the new edition of *Dying in Style* there seemed to be no end to it. Patrice could have been kept busy just selling books to people coming in off the street. Each night they went back to Roberta's flat and passed out without giving one another a second glance.

Roberta looked at the sea of books. She thought of Arthur Whitworth. How cruel that he could not witness this! Still, it happened all the time. It was almost one of the givens that the artist had to pass on before he was appreciated. But this was a little different.

She wondered about it. But only for a second. The lorries from W Crisp were due in an hour to take away one hundred thousand. She looked at herself backed by all this moving product. A small, a fragile, young thing achieving, magnifying. Tinkerbell with a mobile phone. Then Roberta changed the imaginary channel; she saw herself momentarily as the star of an up-market perfume ad. With Patrice, stripped to the waist, as the love interest. This was wonderful! This was living! But . . .

Roberta tried to banish doubt by shifting stock.

❧ ❧ ❧

"God! I'm next! I know I am!" wailed Fidelma

O'Mahoney-Gunton, the literary editor of *The Evening Sentinel.*

Following the murder of Audrey Saunders in the manner minutely described in Arthur Whitworth's novel, Fidelma had telephoned Cyril Parkinson to express her anxiety.

Cyril had had little time for Fidelma O'Mahoney-Gunton. The feud went back some years to an incident when Fidelma had sent several excerpts of Cyril's review of a Saul Bellow novel to "Pseuds' Corner". All had been printed, but so had Fidelma's name.

"Some shocking types are writing these days, you know," Cyril had said, seeking to wound two birds with one barb. He'd put the telephone down.

But with the death of Cyril Parkinson the connection between the novel and the murders was made by all. Literary London and, indeed, the Great British Public, ran to their bookshops to seek out copies of *Dying in Style*.

There had, of course, been none.

"It must be me! He's got me to a tee!" continued Fidelma. She was addressing her PA, Gervase Taunton. Gervase was re-reading Chapter 3 of *Dying in Style*.

"You're over-reacting, love," Gervase said. "The third murder is the literary editor of a London evening paper, it's true. It could be AN Wilson, I suppose."

"Does AN Wilson have a male PA? Does AN Wilson appear on 'Late Review' dressed in red lycra and lime-green boas?"

"I've never seen 'Late Review'," Gervase said. "Look, love, it's fiction!"

"Fiction like fuck!" said Fidelma O'Mahoney-Gunton.

"Well," said Gervase, having come to the end of the death scene, a death which took place on camera on "Late Review" when the bolt from a crossbow had been shot through the temples of the literary editor as she was in mid-flow demolishing the musical version of *Waiting for Godot*. "Maybe you shouldn't go on 'Late Review' for a week or two."

The literary editor thought about that. War was declared. Opposing armies – Vanity and Fear – fought to the death.

"It had some nice touches," continued Gervase. "I like the way Mark Lawson pushed his glasses up his nose to express his horror when the bolt hit. And the way the producers do a close-up on you . . . I mean the victim. It's just what they'd do too. Way after the watershed, isn't it? You know, I really rather enjoyed *Dying in Style*. To tell you the truth, love, I was a bit upset when everyone trashed it. It made me wonder about my taste, if you get me."

"If I don't go on, they'll have won," said Fidelma O'Mahoney-Gunton. "And I might not be asked again. God, I hate them all!"

Gervase nodded, thinking about that. "Who, love?" he asked at last.

"Everyone. Writers, mainly. God, I hate writers!"

"Why, love?"

"Because they write books, that's why. They keep on writing books. On and on. Crap. Crap. Crap. And it all ends up on my desk. Buggers!"

"So are you going on 'Late Review'?"

"Yes."

◆ ◆ ◆

Two days later the literary editor of *The Evening Sentinel* was nodding with enthusiasm as an Ulster poet poured scorn on a better poet's juvenilia. These proceedings were brought to an end by a slight bang – more like a pop – that seemed to emanate from under the chair of Fidelma O'Mahoney-Gunton. The literary editor slumped, dead.

Dr Gonne's post-mortem revealed that a tiny Semtex charge attached to a cunning gizmo set into the steel plinth of the swivel-chair had sent an arrow through the seat of the chair, through the intestines, heart and, finally, brain, of Fidelma O'Mahoney-Gunton.

❧ ❧ ❧

"All this is selling books, I hear," Edith Gonne told Dyer the morning after the post-mortem on Fidelma O'Mahoney-Gunton. "What's that on your neck?"

"Nothing," Dyer said, pulling up the collar of his Gore-Tex.

"It's a love-bite, isn't it? Honestly, Timmy! At your age!"

"I know," Dyer said. "Tell you the truth, I don't remember a thing. I was at The William and the next thing I remember is waking up."

"Where?"

"Where do you think?"

Edith nodded and put out her cigarette. "You ought to think about what you might pick up."

"No lectures, Edith. If you'd come back, I wouldn't do these things. It's loneliness that drives me to it."

Edith had heard that one before. "It's lust, Timmy; it's poor old human nature, Timmy."

"Don't you miss me?"

"Not much," Edith lied. Then she compounded the lie with another. "Mother makes a fuss of me."

"Come back! Go on!"

"And what's in it for Edith?" Edith asked. "A *mariage blanc* might be all right as far as it goes but I want a faithful *mariage blanc*. I want a smoke-free, stimulating environment, no messing about. And that means *no mortal sin*!"

Dyer took out his cigarettes and reached for one.

"Don't smoke it, Timmy," Edith said. "This is a test. If you don't smoke it, I'll know you might mean it."

"Edith . . . " Dyer played with the cigarette as Giles Gibbons had played with the strut of his executive toy. "I'm in no fit state . . . " He put it in his mouth and lit it.

"Hopeless!" Edith said. She looked through her notes. "That's three murders, Timmy. Feeling the pressure, are you?"

"We're doing everything we can. I've finally persuaded Scotland Yard to take the *Dying in Style* theory seriously. The lads in Morecambe have put an all-points-alert out for Arthur Whitworth. They're running an old interview with him on "Crimewatch" this week."

"His publishers must be over the moon," Edith said. "Couldn't they be behind it?"

"It's a bit obvious, Edith."

"Yes, but it's so obvious it might be dismissed and they might be so subtle that they know that."

"We've absolutely nothing to go on."

"The Semtex charge could point to terrorist involvement. It was quite a sophisticated little charge that did for that woman with the awful dress sense."

"The props department at the BBC have no idea how the chair got tampered with," Dyer said. "Still, they showed me the chair they used in 'Mastermind' and let me have a glance in at the 'Top of the Pops' studio. I think I passed Robert Robinson on the way out. Can't be sure, but I think it was him."

Edith made a sound in her throat that boded no good. "Who done it in the book?"

"The author of the book. He's writing it from prison,

very happy to have a bit of peace to write, though we only get to know that in the end. I was quite surprised by that ending, to tell you the truth."

"But isn't it a bit obvious if Arthur Whitworth is the culprit? I mean, wouldn't he cover his tracks?"

"He has, Edith. He's 'dead' and we can't find him. He's done a great job."

"How about a devoted fan of the book?"

"We've checked all the libraries . . . those that are on computer anyway. There are a few dozen real devotees, no more than that. Most probably devour anything and everything in the 'Crime' genre. Two of the fans are Arthur Whitworth's aunties in Leeds. They're well known for touring the libraries and taking them out again and again. For the PLR, apparently."

"What's PLR when it's at home?"

"It's Public Lending Right. The money that writers get when their books are borrowed. A penny or two per borrowing."

"Real devotion from those aunties," Edith said. "If I were a writer, would you tour the libraries, Timmy?"

"My every waking moment."

Edith pulled a face between sweet and sour. "So who's next?"

"A publicity manager for a publisher. If it follows the book."

"Can't wait!" said Dr Edith Gonne.

"Come back to me, Edith? Do I have to get down on my knees?"

"From the look of those pants," Edith said, "you've already spent a fair amount of time on your knees. In mucky places. No, Timmy, I think I'm better off at Mother's."

❧ ❧ ❧

At Jim's insistence Giles met him at the Waterloo Sauna.

"It'll do us both good," Jim had said, sounding not the least bit like Jim.

"You sound quite like your old self," Giles told him, though this was not in fact true. Jim's old self was the self that had been pessimistic and neurotic ever since Giles first approached him about *Dying in Style* – ever since their first-ever meeting – come to that. This was something new.

"Yes, I think I am my old self again, Giles," Jim said.

"Don't tell me now; tell me when we meet."

"Right-ho!"

In fact, Giles had already exhausted the possibilities of the Waterloo Sauna before Jim happened along . . . He had sampled the sauna-box and, as always, hated the way the heat seemed to sear his lungs, making breathing a trial, bringing him to the brink of a boring, near-death experience. Still, it was supposed to be good for you, a bit like reading nineteenth-century Russian novels. Two elderly *habitués* of the place were talking car-boot sales.

Giles took a cold plunge and then sat in the recovery room computing book-sales in his head. That was cheering. *Dying in Style* was shifting wonderfully. Another printing of a million had been ordered. He shuffled million about his mouth with his tongue, caressed it like a nipple. He felt himself stiffening.

"There you are!" Jim said.

"You look different without your glasses."

"Mandy says I ought to try contact lenses," Jim said, with a smile.

"She isn't back, is she? That *is* good news. I told you she'd come back."

"She says she doesn't know what gets into her. It's a primitive urge, she says."

"But you wouldn't have her any other way, would you, Jim?"

"Wouldn't say that. If I could have Mandy without the worry I'd feel better. Still, be lost without her."

"Books shifting OK?" Giles asked.

"Sold out," Jim said. "Had doubts as you well know, but . . . never seen anything shift so fast."

"We're reprinting. The Rights Department is up to their eyes sorting out translation rights. The American edition hits the streets next week."

"That's great news, Giles."

"Yes, it is, Jim. Cutting Edge looked like it was going under before all this. It's a great relief, but it's also terrible."

"Yes. Shocking. By the way, Mandy gave *Dying in Style* the thumbs-up. She read it on the plane to Sri Lanka."

"Mandy is seldom wrong in these matters."

"Never wrong, Giles. By the way, sorry I'm late. Was off sorting out some financial matters with Mandy."

"Anything interesting?"

"Insurance. Mandy thinks we're both under-insured, what with her wandering off – though she says that's all in the past – and me in a stressful job. Of course, saw her point right away."

"Don't over-extend yourself, Jim," Giles said.

"She's worth it."

"Of course."

"Fancy adjourning to the sauna?"

Giles didn't, but he followed Jim through the pine doors that led to hell.

Inside the two *habitués* were still deep in conversation.

However, it had shifted to a more interesting topic as far as Giles was concerned.

"I think the dead writer did it," said the one whose testicles hung down over the edge of the pine perch.

"That doesn't make sense," said his friend, whose belly started from his overhanging dugs and finished balanced on the pine.

"Why not?"

"Because he's not going to be able to get at the royalties, is he? Not if he's dead and that."

"But if he's doing the murders, he's not dead, is he? Stands to reason."

"But if he's not dead and he's doing the murders, he's not going to get at his money, is he?"

"No, but maybe the money isn't important to him. Maybe it's revenge he's after. Revenge is sweet and all that."

"But he got his revenge by writing the book. Read it, have you?"

"No."

"You ought. It's bloody good, especially the way things are turning out."

"You know what I think?"

"What?"

"I think if the writer chap didn't do it then maybe the publisher did it. He's making money hand over fist."

"The police are useless, as usual. Did you see the bloke in charge of the investigation? A right berk he looked. Mumbled and stuttered and talked about matters proceeding satisfactorily. Satisfactorily! I ask you! With people dying like that! Shocking! Did you see the woman cop it on that BBC 2 programme?"

"No."

"Me neither.

"Think I'll take a plunge."

"Me, too."

The two men left.

"See what I mean?" Giles said.

"Amazing testicles on that bloke."

"Don't start, Jim."

"No, of course not. But I know for a fact that Mandy's partial to a good pair. Can't supply them, I'm afraid."

"You're perfectly adequate."

"Yes, I'm *adequate* all right. But *adequate* doesn't cut the mustard with Mandy. She says that big testicles on a bloke are like big tits on a girl; they're a turn-on."

"I can't see what earthly difference a large pair of bollocks makes."

"Yours are large."

Giles sought to cover himself up with the inadequate towel.

"Can't you shift Mandy's thoughts to higher things?"

Jim looked more like his old self again. He stared back at Giles, all sweaty and despondent. "Don't think so," he said. "Mandy's in one of her 'sated' periods. Know because she goes all domestic. But if I know my Mandy the urges will be back. She can't help herself."

Giles shook his head.

Jim nodded sadly. Then, quite suddenly, he brightened. "By the way, Mandy wants to have everyone at Cutting Edge round for a slap-up do."

"Whatever for?"

"It's Mandy's way of telling me that she wants to be a dutiful executive wife. You have to hand it to her for trying."

"Yes, yes, indeed!" Giles said.

"We'll fix the date when we've cooled down. Mandy also said to warn what's-her-name . . . your publicity woman . . ."

"Roberta."

"Roberta. Mandy reckons that she might be next."

"Does she? Well, that's a relief."

"How do you mean, Giles?"

"Because if you're telling me, it means you don't think I'm the murderer. Lots of people do, you know."

"The thought never crossed my mind, Giles."

"Shall we take the plunge?" Giles said. "After that I must get back to the office. I've got product to shift. Mountains of it."

❧ ❧ ❧

Edith Gonne arrived back at the flat to find her mother deep in conversation with Miss Mullin, the priests' housekeeper from her mother's parish. They greeted one another and then Mrs Gonne gave Edith one of her looks.

"I think I'll take a shower," Edith said. She left them to it.

Standing under the miserly jet of water Edith wondered about the latest twist in the soap opera of Miss Mullin. Two or three times a week the housekeeper visited her mother to unburden herself about events in the parish.

Miss Mullin was not a happy woman. It went back to the day when the bishop assigned a new curate to the parish. And that new curate had been an Anglican before his flight to Rome. And that new curate had a wife and grown-up family.

Via her mother, Edith had learnt of the unfolding crisis. The presbytery had been divided into two flats; Miss Mullin forced into a small boxroom next to the kitchen. Then the wife of the new curate had started inviting the parish priest upstairs for posh meals that had corrupted his taste-buds, made him dissatisfied with the bacon-and-cabbage diet that had rolled out of Miss Mullin's kitchen for thirty years.

On top of that, changes had been made in the liturgy at the curate's insistence. Out to the garden shed had gone the plaster statuary; out the Cassio organ played with little talent but much enthusiasm by Mary Coogan, spinster of the parish. And in had come bells and smells and hard tunes that nobody could get their tongues around and off to the next parish had gone the likes of Mary Coogan. And in had blown a troop of snobby ex-Anglicans.

And Miss Mullin was feeling like a spare part and was always on the brink of buying a single on the Sea Cat and going to live with the sister she hated in Ballinacorriga, County Mayo.

Edith's thoughts turned as she turned in the shower, colliding painfully with her mother's hand-rail: everything was shifting. Nothing holding still. She had come back to religion to find it greatly changed, and not for the better. Wanting certainty, wanting respite from the cruel realities of snuffed-out life, the pointlessness of the cadaver, she had hoped to find it back in the old Church. Her mother was pleased she was back; pleased, too, she had left Timmy who, she never tired of telling her daughter, she'd seen through from day one. But it was like being back in a place you have dreamed of loving for decades, a place in which you have had the most momentous and moving experiences of your youth: it was not – of course it wasn't – what your imagination had conjured up.

She dried herself on a hard, overwashed grey towel. She caught her naked self in the mirror. She wasn't shocked. She was used to herself: thin, angular, bony. Maybe her breasts were drooping a mite further; there could be a little extra flesh around her protruding pelvic bone – due to no fags and too many sweets. But, nevertheless, Edith felt tears welling up. No babies had passed through her, and now none ever would. That's what you got for trying to turn a queer back facing front.

She commanded herself to butch up. She heard her mother saying goodbye to Miss Mullin. She got into the clothes she had stripped off ten minutes before. She badly wanted a fag.

"So what's the news, Mother?" Edith Gonne said, rejoining her mother in the lounge.

"Miss Mullin is obsessed with some murders," her mother said. "It's good in a way; it's taking her mind off the parish. You know what Father Kelly's done?" She waited for Edith to respond. Then she inhaled momentously and said, "He's joined a Wine Society! *A Wine Society*; that just about sums it up."

Edith nodded. "What murders?"

"Those publishing murders. Miss Mullin is waiting for a publicity person to get killed, she says; says she can't go back to Ireland until it's all finished with."

"I don't undertand."

"Well, it's taking her mind off her troubles and, once Miss Mullins leaves the presbytery I've a feeling Father Kelly will go completely off the rails."

"I suppose so," Edith said absently. *Who's on the rails? What are the rails?* she thought.

ℴ ℴ ℴ

The victim of the fourth murder in *Dying in Style* had indeed been a publicity manager by the name of Rachel Collie. The unfortunate Rachel had been electrocuted in her Power Shower.

Roberta Coleman had watched the edition of "Late Review" in which the unfortunate literary editor had been killed. Within minutes, her telephone was ringing. The tabloids asked her how it felt to be next on the hit list.

"I'm absolutely terrified!" said Roberta Coleman.

"Are you going to seek police protection?"

"Naturally," replied Roberta. "I'm unable to go into any details about the measures I'm taking to protect myself. Everyone in publishing is worried. I can say, however, that your call has been forwarded to a secret safe house."

This was both true and untrue. While Roberta Coleman was, indeed, away from home, she was simply staying with her friend and colleague, Morag Aitken – Arthur Whitworth's editor – in a flat across the road from her own.

"That should get them going," said Morag Aitken. "I think we deserve a drink!"

"Right-ho," said Roberta Coleman. "I could do with one. All the work. Patrice. Also, I am a little bit anxious."

"What is there to be anxious about, Roberta? You and I both know that all this has nothing to do with Arthur Whitworth."

"Do we?"

"Of course we do! For starters, you and I both knew Arthur Whitworth. He might have been OK – and only OK – at thinking up plots, but he was no murderer. He didn't even have the guts to go on 'Kaleidoscope'."

"That's not quite true. He did go on once, but that chap with the estuary accent froze him out in favour of one of his Oxford chums."

Morag shrugged.

"It's a horrid coincidence, isn't it?" continued Roberta.

"Arthur Whitworth is *dead*! To tell you the truth I've been wondering whether one of us at Cutting Edge might be the killer. I mean, Roberta, this is a publicity wheeze made in heaven!"

"Do you think Giles did it?"

"Wouldn't have the energy!"

"It's playing into his court, though."

"It is, isn't it?" Morag said.

Morag handed Roberta her drink. "You betcha!" she said, "A million sold in two weeks. It's almost been too much trying to keep up with demand. The Rights Department is under siege. We can thank all the fuss for saving Cutting Edge. Did you hear that some Japanese computer company is trying to buy rights on *Dying in Style* to make a computer game?"

"No . . ."

"We've had several calls from Hollywood. Giles just says 'maybe' and they add three noughts for the film rights."

Roberta drank. "It's a high price to pay for shifting a book, though. Audrey Saunders was a good friend of mine."

"I'm sorry, love," Morag said, "I'm just trying to accentuate the positive. It is really frightful what's been happening."

"I've asked Patrice to move in with me."

"Is he going to?"

"Not sure. He's very proud. But you should see where he lives. It's a whole different world out there."

"Couldn't you push the security aspect? Men like to feel useful – or they always did when I knew any."

Roberta frowned, bit her lip.

"Look, if you want to stay here, you're very welcome. Also, after what you said to the press, it might be better for you to lie low for a while. You know, until it all blows over."

"But what about the office?"

"We'll manage. At the moment we're a one-book-operation. And the publicity for *Dying in Style* looks after itself."

"Everyone's hoping it'll be me next!" Roberta said.

"Nobody's hoping any such thing, Roberta! How could you think that of us? While it's perfectly true that the deaths have made a big difference to us, we wouldn't have had it happen like this for the world!"

Roberta, perhaps naively, believed her friend. Any mixed motives at Cutting Edge were completely understandable. After all, she was feeling them herself. It was wonderful that a book she had despaired of had come back from the grave. The people she spent her life phoning, faxing, sending review copies to, pleading with, were beating a path to her door, selling the book for her. Yes, that was good. Much more than good. Perhaps too good.

"I think I'll take a holiday," Roberta said. "Do you think Giles will let me?"

"I think Giles will be delighted. From all points of view your putting your feet up adds to your publicity. So, while you're off doing nothing, you've never been working harder, if you get me. If it'll make you feel better, you can get Giles to give you a few manuscripts from the slush pile."

Roberta nodded. She had one more drink with Morag and then went to bed. She washed herself at the basin, eying the electric shower behind her.

In bed she wondered. If by some stranger-than-fiction fluke, Arthur Whitworth was behind the murders, might she draw some comfort from the feeling that she would not be on Arthur's list? After all, she had always done her best to publicise his books. She had gone to quite inordinate lengths to gain attention for them. She always sat engrossed with his latest hardback on the Tube. As she did this she felt certain that her reactions to the book were pushing it into the heads of her fellow commuters. She turned the pages at great speed, her facial expressions running the full gamut of "good read" emotions: smiles, horror, wide-eyed amazement, quiet satisfaction. Her fluent body-language communicated *buy this book that a gorgeous young thing on the tube is having orgasms over*! Two journeys a day, varying her route, for two weeks, reading a text she knew perfectly well in order to spread the word was good work, wasn't it?

When she went into bookshops she always, feeling like a shoplifter, rearranged Arthur Whitworth's books into more prominent positions. When the dire reviews came out for *Dying in Style* she got her computer-whizz of a brother to print up garish posters. Then, using her mountain-bike, she pedalled around putting up the posters in prominent places throughout the capital, next to the pop-concerts, rallies, and incomprehensible Arabic notices, in the hope that people would see one and have their memories jogged. All this quite apart from the endless phoning and faxing and information-packing and lunches and networking and pestering of reps. She had, in short, always done her best for Arthur Whitworth.

Partly this was due to the fact that publicity was what Roberta Coleman was paid for; it was also what she loved. Publicity was like living the Lottery. Every working moment, every action, could come up with a winner, could land the slithery serendipitous fish of media attention. But there was more. She had rather liked Arthur Whitworth. They were from the same part of the country. She could identify and sympathise with his gaucheness, his pathological shyness, his vulnerability. She shared these feelings, though in her case they were buried beneath a neutral accent and a Metropolitan veneer.

Roberta believed in Arthur Whitworth's books. They were a good read. Also, and this appealed to Roberta greatly, Arthur Whitworth was never merely content to tell a story. His books took on issues. They sought to make a difference. She liked the idea of this shambling, hopelessly inept bachelor sitting in his cottage with his roll-ups and his fishing tackle trying to make a difference.

Of course, that was hopeless from the publicity point of view. It was like Brad Easton Ellis said, on the – now late – "Late Show" . . . Roberta turned over in bed, trying to remember what Brad Easton Ellis *had* said; something to the effect of his being a writer and not pretentious enough to think writing made a difference. Roberta hadn't liked that. How did Ellis *not* know that he hadn't made a difference, hadn't, in his case, been the cause of murders taking place? It could not be proven, but . . . and then Edmund White a few weeks later, asked how he would like to be remembered, replying "As a stylist". Christ! While the world dies, while people starve, and hunger and degradation stalk the planet, to seek to be remembered as *a stylist!*

When Arthur Whitworth was drowned, only Roberta tried to persuade Giles to have a memorial service.

"There's no family. We're all he had."

"Don't think so, Roberta," Giles had said.

Don't think so, Roberta . . . she repeated Giles's words like a mantra. They lulled her towards sleep, reassuring her somehow. But then she was awake again, staring at the ceiling. She could hear Morag preparing for bed. Was it that which had brought her back? Or was it the thought that, if Arthur Whitworth was alive and re-enacting the plot of *Dying in Style*, it would mean that he was mad as a hatter anyway? And, if he was mad as a hatter, what part would logic or, indeed remembrances of kindness past, have in his crazed world-view?

Don't think so, Roberta.

She heard Morag enter the bathroom. Silence and the flush of the lavatory, an old-fashioned high tank. Then silence again.

Roberta lay on. As the time passed she began to suspect the silence. But, she thought, that's part of it. I must sleep.

More time passed. She got up, just to make sure, put on her dressing-gown and walked to the bathroom.

"Everything all right in there?"

No answer.

"Morag!"

No answer.

Roberta Coleman knocked, then opened the door. She screamed. Then, just as she was, she ran from Morag's flat and along the road to the police station.

After telling the bald facts of what had happened to a woman pc, Roberta Coleman became hysterical. The police doctor was called. He sedated Roberta and she was taken to the Rape Suite to sleep.

❧ ❧ ❧

"Has anything been touched?" Dyer asked the policeman at the door of Morag Aitken's flat.

"Nothing, sir. We've switched off the electricity, though."

It was one in the morning.

Dyer went into the flat, borrowing the policeman's flashlight. The beam caught rows of hardback books, a wall crowded with paintings. A hi-fi system. He stepped into a picture-lined corridor off which the bedrooms and bathroom of the flat led. More pictures. Posters of several National Theatre productions, an English National Opera poster for "Wozzeck". Dyer, wanting a cigarette, turned into the bathroom.

Morag Aitken's body lay on the tiled floor. All but the left leg was in contact with the tiles. That leg lay half in, half out of the bath-tub, the knee bent over its rim. Blood ran from a head-wound, doubtless caused by the fall back resulting from the shock.

Dyer returned to the flat door.

"Just as a matter of interest," he said, "who thought to have the electricity turned off?"

"I did, sir," said the policeman.

"Good thinking, constable. What made you think of doing that?"

"That's easy, sir. As soon as the young lady at the station mentioned that she was in publishing, I had a shrewd idea how the victim had died. Read about it in today's paper, didn't I? In advance, like."

Dyer nodded. He could recall the scene himself. The publicity manager of the murderous author's publisher who had failed to sell his book had come back drunk from a party. Thinking to try to sober herself up prior to doing some work, she had taken a shower. And that was it.

"Is the deceased in publicity?" Dyer asked.

"Don't know that, I'm afraid, sir."

"What we need is an electrician."

"One's on his way, sir."

"Well done, son. You haven't any theories about who could have done this . . . you know, icing for the cake and everything?"

"Yes, sir. I have given the matter some thought,"

replied the policeman who, even to Dyer's used-to-blue eyes, seemed little more than a child. "Either the writer, Whitworth, isn't dead and is trying to sell his novel by making everyone interested; or, he is dead but has an accomplice or a fan who wants to make fantasy reality; or, it's someone who has something to gain from a lot of fuss surrounding the book."

"Fuss?"

"Well, by all accounts, the book wasn't selling. It was that which was supposed to have driven the writer to suicide – if he's dead that is. I don't know whether he had any relatives who might stand to gain. According to the paper I read, he was reckoned to be a bit of a recluse."

"So who stands to gain?"

"I don't know how the business works. But it seems to me that the publishers are doing rather well out of it."

"But one of the *victims* – and the poor thing isn't yet cold – works for the very publisher who stands to gain. What's the company again?"

"Cutting Edge is, I believe, the name, sir."

"What's your name, constable?" Dyer asked.

"Keeley, sir."

"Been in the force long, have you?"

"Three years, sir."

"So you're . . . "

"Twenty-four and a half, sir. I joined a bit late. Tried plumbing first."

"It didn't suit?"

"It suited me long enough to get qualified. But when I started doing it day after day . . . well, you know."

"No, I don't," said Dyer. "I'd love to have taken up a trade. It must be nice to be wanted. I wonder if plumbing would suit me?"

"You could give it a go, sir."

"Too old," Dyer said, almost to himself.

"You're only as old as you feel."

"That's old enough," Dyer said. "Plumbing wasn't for you, then?"

"Just didn't suit, sir."

"And bobbying does, does it?"

"Down to the ground, sir."

Dyer shook his head. "You're a lucky man. Have a first name do you, PC Keeley?"

"Desmond, sir."

"You're a Des, are you?"

"Desmond, sir. To tell you the truth, I wouldn't mind getting into your line of work."

"Studying are you, Desmond?"

"I'm working for my sergeant's exam, sir."

"Here they come," Dyer said, hearing the siren approaching. "Married, are you, PC Desmond Keeley?"

"No, sir."

Dyer thought. Dyer fantasised. "I've got a few plumbing jobs need doing. You don't do a bit of moonlighting, do you?"

"I don't see why not, sir."

The police van drew up to the kerb with a shriek of brakes. The siren stopped. Banging of doors.

"Right then," Dyer called out, "where's the electrician? It's hands-on men we need."

❧ ❧ ❧

Chewing, Dr Edith Gonne emerged through the swing-doors of the autopsy room.

"I knew you'd be here," she told Dyer.

"Electrocution, was it?"

Edith nodded. "I have met with things dying, you with things new-born. Who's your friend?"

Dyer looked behind him, where PC Desmond Keeley stood, in civvies, holding an open notebook.

"This is PC Keeley. He's been seconded to me."

"Cradle-snatching again?" Edith asked.

She walked past them into her office. There were flowers on the desk.

Dyer and Keeley followed her in. Keeley stood in front of the door while Dyer sat down and took out his packet of cigarettes. Edith pointed to a notice.

"You haven't, have you?" he asked.

"This is my second day. I'm on the gum."

"Again?"

Edith chewed and gave details of injury, time of death. "The blow to the head might well have killed the poor thing," she said. "She hit the floor with terrible force. Did you find out what caused electrocution?"

"As far as we can see, the wiring leading up to the electric shower had been exposed, the cover cut, the insulation drawn back. It only took a few drops of water . . ."

"Any leads?"

"A few."

"The papers have given the investigation – and that means you and your friend – a bit of a roasting this morning," Edith said with some satisfaction.

"I'm dying for a fag," Dyer said.

"Have a sweetie instead."

Dyer reached for a sweet. "It's not the same," he said.

"You ought to try the gum. It's working for me. Today is the second day of the rest of my life."

"I must write that down."

"Do," Edith said.

"Write that down, would you, Desmond?"

"Right you are, sir."

"Don't do everything he tells you to, constable!" Edith said. "Innocence is a rare commodity in this world."

Keeley looked suitably embarrassed. He dropped his clear blue eyes, scratched a non-itching unfurrowed brow.

"You don't have the slightest idea who's doing this, do you?" Edith said.

"A pattern is emerging," Dyer said.

"You mean the pattern that every last tabloid-reader had tumbled to after the first murder? Come on! You can do better than that!"

"That is one avenue of enquiry."

Edith pursed her lips. "You're hopeless, Timmy," she said. She looked at her watch. "Must rush."

ᘛ ᘛ ᘛ

"Where to now, Detective Inspector?" Desmond Keeley asked.

Don't know. Don't care. What I want is early retirement. Days at Bethnal Green Turkish. Getting off on rubbing down ruined heterosexual bodies. Resenting the young Fruits with many an F and a Blind. Nights with Edith. Slippers. Not giving a toss who done it. I don't give a toss who done it. Why do they have to do it round me?

"Now let me see," Dyer said. "I'd better interview the friend of Morag Aitken. While I'm doing that, I'd like you to go and see what the lads have come up with at Audrey Saunders's office. They've been buried knee-deep in paperwork for weeks. Come back to the station at twelve – I should be finished by then – and we'll have a spot of lunch and talk it over."

Curling up with a young constable in front of the telly.

Plying him with Special Brew until he turns to putty in my hands and becomes a consenting adult. Yes! Yes! Yes!

"Fat chance."

"Sorry, sir?" Keeley asked.

"Nothing, constable,' Dyer replied. "Just thinking out loud."

⁂

"Do you feel able to answer some questions, miss?"

Roberta Coleman nodded.

Dyer switched on the tape recorder. He spoke time and interview subject into the machine.

"You've had a terrible shock," he said. "Were you very close to Miss Aitken?"

"We worked together at Cutting Edge. I live – lived – almost opposite her. And we were friends. I suppose we were quite close."

"Why were you staying at Miss Aitken's house?"

"I'd have thought that was obvious. I was scared."

"Because of the book?"

"Yes."

"Did you know the late Arthur Whitworth well?"

"I knew him as well as I know most authors. Perhaps a *bit* better. We come from the same part of the country."

"Where's that?"

"I'm from Ripon."

"Did you like his books?"

"I did, yes."

"And, from what you know of him, do you think he might be responsible for . . . for what's been happening?"

"He was very disappointed with the reception given to *Dying in Style* – as I was. The book got some shocking reviews. I'd never seen anything like it. Everyone turned on it, starting with Cyril Parkinson. Still, it can be like that. Once one critic draws blood, the rest gather round like jackals to outdo the one before in vitriol. That's what the book was about."

"So you don't like critics?"

"Not much. I definitely don't like the way some of them slaughter books."

"So you think there might have been reasons – other than literary reasons – why the critics put the boot into *Dying in Style*?"

"There could have been lots of reasons. Arthur Whitworth punched LP Lomax, Cyril Parkinson's friend, at a literary gathering. That can't have helped. Also – and this is just my own pet hobby-horse, though I probably shared it with Arthur – the literary establishment in this country tends to come from a small number of public schools and Oxbridge colleges. The 'old boy network' is strong. They share dogmas about what makes good literature, dogmas that are beyond the concerns of most readers. They review their friends, lionise them. Arthur Whitworth just didn't fit in. A provincial budgie with a distinct, somewhat grating, voice. He was just made to be pecked."

Dyer was silent. "It all sounds depressingly familiar," he said. "Call me naive, though, I'd have expected . . . I don't know . . . *better* from bookish types. Par for the course in other lines of work, but *books* . . . " Dyer paused, pulled his nose. "I don't know."

"I'm painting a bleak picture, I know. It's not all like that. But human nature doesn't change. Critics have a living to earn. If, say, the editor of a literary magazine writes a novel, it would be a very brave critic who would write a negative review of that novel. But there are critics whose reviews are always helpful to the writer and the reader, even when they're negative. Writers can learn from these reviews. But you did ask me about Arthur Whitworth and he did provoke the worst. Especially *Dying in Style*."

"Were you really scared last night, miss? I mean, before the terrible events?"

Roberta thought about that. "No, not really, not *seriously* scared. It all felt like a game. Sounds terrible I know, what with people dying. I suppose I thought that if Arthur Whitworth was doing all these murders, he wouldn't murder me."

"And you think Arthur Whitworth is responsible?"

"No, I don't. I think Arthur's dead. Anyway, I don't think it was in character. *Dying in Style* probably got the whole thing out of his system."

"The book's selling well as a result, isn't it?"

Roberta smiled for the first time. "Yes, all this has been great for Cutting Edge. I suppose that's what I meant before when I talked about being excited. I know it's horrid of me but all this is great publicity." Roberta paused. "Do you mind if I say something really horrible?" Dyer nodded assent, not knowing what to expect. "In spite of Morag's death – and Morag was a good friend of mine – I'm still excited. A side of me – a quite horrid side – *loves* what's happening. Murders are much better at shifting books than selling them with packets of cornflakes. It's an idea made in heaven."

"Or hell?"

"Or hell. You don't have a cigarette, do you?"

"I might be able to manage that. Do you mind if I join you?"

"Is it OK to?" Roberta gestured to the notice.

"Just this once."

Dyer lit her cigarette, then his own. They inhaled together.

"I don't usually," Roberta said.

"Me neither," Dyer lied.

Roberta nodded knowingly.

"Have you any theories about who might be doing this?"

"Well, by rights it should be me. Or Giles. We're the ones who stand to gain."

Dyer nodded. "You'd also be the first ones – after Arthur Whitworth – to come under suspicion. It is odd, though . . . "

"What's odd?"

"You being with Morag Aitken when she was killed. While it does tend to indicate that the murderer wasn't after you – how would he have known you were going to stay there? It's quite a coincidence that you were there."

"You don't think . . . "

"I'm just thinking out loud. To tell you the truth, I'm a bit lost."

"In an existential sense?"

"I'd tell you that if I knew what it meant. I'm nothing like the clever copper in *Dying in Style*, am I?"

"No, you're not. Don't forget, though, he was murdered in the end. His little vice did for him. You ought to watch yourself! Still maybe the difference between you and him is all a matter of style."

"No, miss, there are substantial differences between us. Tell me, did Arthur Whitworth get on with Morag Aitken? She was his editor, wasn't she?"

"Oh, yes, I think so. Morag gave Arthur his first break. She stayed loyal to him, even after some really bad reviews and disappointing sales. Morag was convinced *Dying in Style* would be Arthur's "break-through" book.

She was really miserable when the knives came out . . . " Roberta looked at Dyer. "Figuratively speaking, of course."

"How's Cutting Edge doing?"

"Before all this?"

"Before all this."

"It wasn't looking good. What with the Nett Book Agreement going, the proliferation of "home entertainment', and the way the Arts establishment have been slagging off the English Novel – Cutting Edge's bread and butter – it all looked a bit bleak. Giles lost a lot of money on his try at breaking into the audio-books market. We were only hanging on by the skin of our teeth. Rumours of restructuring and down-sizing were in the air. And down-sizing at Cutting Edge would have meant us disappearing."

Dyer looked at his watch. "Right, I think that's about it for now. Who's next, do you reckon?"

"According to *Dying in Style*, it's the Director of Pile It High! who sold the top ten fiction list for half the cover price."

"So someone in the book trade."

"If it follows the book."

Dyer nodded and made some notes. He turned off the tape recorder. "Right, Roberta, I think it's time we got you home."

"No fear! I'm disappearing!" Roberta said.

"Will you leave me a contact number?"

"If you'll give me one more cigarette." She held it in her hand. "After this one, I'm stopping," she said.

Dyer took one out of the packet. "Now might not be the right time."

"There's never a right time, is there?"

Dyer thought about that. "No," he said, "there isn't.

Roberta pulled on her cigarette. "Look, I don't suppose this is the time to ask, but I have a problem. Nothing to do with what happened . . . " And Roberta told Dyer about Patrice's situation. "Is there anything you can do for him? I know he's genuine. They can't send him back. They can't!"

"It's not really my line. Between you and me and the gate-post, I'd advise him to lie low. Keep him away from any building with a royal coat of arms on the front."

Roberta nodded. Then, without any warning at all, surprising both Dyer and herself, she broke down.

⁂

LP Lomax sat alone in the flat he had shared with Cyril Parkinson for fifteen years. He was listening to a new recording of *Dido and Aeneas*, with French orchestra and soloists. He would, he had decided, give it a star for the way the French accents of the singers masked the dire lyrics of the piece. But that was about it. He craved for his Kirsten Flagstad recording . . . or maybe the Janet Baker. And he would tell his readers so.

In a quick and impulsive move – for LP Lomax – he clicked off the recording, searched the shelves of his considerable collection of CDs, and located the Flagstad. This he slipped into the player, clicked it to the track he wanted, turned the volume almost to maximum, and sank back into his chair.

He listened to *When I am Laid in Earth* once, letting the tears come. Then, just as it was ending, he pressed the repeat button, fixed himself a gin and tonic and sat back down.

When I am laid . . . am laid in earth . . .

Cyril had been laid in earth for over a month. His death

a mystery as far as the hopeless, tobacco-smelling policeman was concerned. What was happening to Cyril's body now, beneath the cold earth of Mortlake Cemetery? Perhaps the damp had yet to penetrate, the first worm to find a way through. Would corruption start from without or within? What was the start of the rot? What was happening down there? All Cyril's style, all his substance, rotting to nought . . . that's what was happening.

May my wrongs create no trouble in thy breast . . .

Cyril might have echoed that. Just possibly. But the manner of his passing, and its perpetrator, would have caused him to demand resolution and revenge. LP felt trouble in his own breast. He had nobody. Nobody! The murderer had taken everything from him.

Remember me! Remember me! But forget my fate!

Impossible, too. How could he ever forget those last minutes? The terrible death behind a curtain while the NHS jittered? No, the aria was moving all right, but the spirit of Cyril Parkinson was rising up to demand exactly the opposite of the sentiments expressed . . .

The telephone rang. LP Lomax straightened his tie and answered it.

"Chief Inspector Dyer. Might I come round?"

"Do," said LP Lomax. "I hope you have some progress to report."

"That's *Dido and Aeneas* you're playing, isn't it?"

"God! Not another cultured copper! I can't stand it!" LP Lomax told Chief Inspector Dyer.

"Sorry, sir," said Dyer. "It won't happen again."

❧ ❧ ❧

Desmond Keeley drove Dyer to LP Lomax's flat. The traffic on the Marylebone Road held them up.

Dyer was studying photocopies of letters taken from Audrey Saunders' offices. They didn't add up to much. Correspondence to and from Arthur Whitworth, together with a few private letters – sent as faxes – to friends, which mentioned the late author. You could have said that Audrey Saunders was two-faced. Still, it was not really surprising that she did not have much time for Whitworth. His letters, dating back to his first novel, were uniformally carping. Hardly a "thank you" for services rendered. Just demands for more publicity, more work, more effort. It was odd. This petulance seemed to conflict not only with Whitworth's books but with everything Roberta Coleman had said.

"If Arthur Whitworth was still alive, Desmond," said Dyer, "this would be an open-and-shut case. Are all professions like this, full of bile and angst and that?"

"I've been thinking about that," Keeley replied. "I suppose when you write books and they get criticised in the papers, it's a bit like one of my performance assessments being printed in the papers. Fine if it's good, I suppose, but a bit hard if it's insulting. There's a lot of work in a book I should think. You can understand how things might get out of proportion."

"I know all that!" Dyer replied, "It's just a bit . . . I don't know . . . disappointing. I mean, isn't literature supposed to increase our understanding of the world . . . make it a better place? Or am I hopelessly out of date?"

"Search me, sir," Keeley said.

Dyer had been trying to trace the movements of Audrey Saunders on the day she was killed. She had put in a full day at the office and then, straight from work, she had gone to a launch party for another author on her books. People interviewed had seen her there. Quite happy and animated, drinking orange juice. She had bowed out about eight, saying she had work to do before bedtime. But, as far as could be detected, she had not gone home. Messages on the answering-machine had not been listened to. Of course, it was possible that she had been too busy to listen to them. Still, Dyer held to his opinion that the literary agent had been accosted between the launch party and her home. The Abbey was carefully locked at closing time and did not reopen until the cleaners arrived at five the following morning. Edith Gonne had given the time of death as between midnight and four. So, in all probability, she had been taken to the Abbey before it closed.

But all this was peripheral to the main point. Thus far no clues, apart from the glaring one of the book, pointed to a murderer. No fingerprints anywhere; no fibres. Nothing.

In the case of the Cyril Parkinson death, a bottle of Pernod spiked with poison was the only evidence. What was striking Dyer very forcibly was that all the victims had lots of enemies. How could the production of books engender the making of such enemies?

❧ ❧ ❧

"May I sit down?" Dyer asked LP Lomax.

"Of course."

"I'll be frank with you, Mr Lomax, we have absolutely no leads – apart from the obvious. We've issued a full description of Arthur Whitworth. I was wondering if you might have had any ideas since we last spoke."

"I said I'd phone you."

"That means no, does it?"

"Find Arthur Whitworth and you've got the man. I told you that at the time, Inspector, and you just repeated that he was dead."

"You don't like Arthur Whitworth, do you?"

LP Lomax smiled sardonically.

"Why did he hit you?"

"I've told one of your colleagues."

"Tell me."

"I was standing alone, looking at a display of new fiction in the shop. I don't like these affairs. I only went to give Cyril some moral support. Anyway, this chap comes up to me and, without a by-your-leave, started ranting about the amount of work all those novels entail and how critics are the scum of the earth. And I said, "There are an awful lot of silly novels about. They don't come cheap. Perhaps the reader needs warning." And Whitworth said critics were all corrupt. I said that some of my best friends were critics. "Like who?" he asked. "Cyril Parkinson," I said. And he hit me."

"Is that all?"

"That's all."

"And you didn't know the identity of Arthur Whitworth at the time?"

"No."

"Cyril had given Arthur Whitworth some very poor reviews in the past, hadn't he? I mean, before *Dying in Style*?"

"That's true. Cyril hated the books."

"Now why was that?"

"There was something pretentious about Whitworth. Using the thriller form to mount a very creaky soapbox . . . and not writing particularly good plots."

"Is that your opinion or Mr Parkinson's?"

"Cyril's. I've not read any of Whitworth's books. I trusted Cyril's judgment."

Dyer nodded. "Why didn't he ignore them if he disliked them so much?"

"Search me."

"But you think Arthur Whitworth nursed a grudge, do you?"

"It looks like it, doesn't it?"

"It does," said Dyer. "I've been thinking a bit about a writer's lot since starting on this case, Mr Lomax. It's a rather lonely life, writing stories. In Arthur Whitworth's case it was completely solitary. He had to be dragged down from Blubberhouses by his agent for that party at Hatchards. Speaking as a complete outsider, of course, I can see how the balance of the mind gets disturbed. After all the work, the book gets published. Good reviews must be wonderful . . . but bad reviews must hurt like hell. And the judgment is so very public."

"They choose to do it, Mr Dyer," said LP Lomax. "Nobody asks them to write books."

"No, of course not. Still, speaking for myself – and my young constable – we've been rather enjoying Arthur Whitworth's novels. We've been reading them as part of the investigation. They're real page-turners and I, at any rate, keep finding things in them to make a chap think."

"So?"

"So when we read the books and then see Cyril's bad reviews we're not sure what to think. Once or twice I've felt a bit insulted on the author's behalf. My own behalf, too, for that matter. It makes me feel daft for liking them. Does that sound daft?"

"It's a matter of taste, of opinion."

"Yes, but it's an opinion magnified by publicity. I've looked through a good many of Cyril's reviews. Not one that I saw had a good word to say about any of the books under discussion. That paper has the highest circulation Sunday readership. A few million – potentially – read what Cyril wrote . . . "

LP Lomax looked at his watch. "Mr Dyer, I . . . "

But Detective-Inspector Dyer was not going to be stopped. He leaned back in his chair and began talking, as if to himself: "I remember when I was a kid I'd take the District Line to school. I must have been around twelve. I saw a scrawl in big paint letters on a wall by the line. It said, "Tom Pender of 13 The Drive, Wembley is Queer." I remember at the time thinking how cruel it was. But it stayed there year in year out. It became part of the scenery. You knew you were three stops from school, two stops from home, when you saw it. Quite often the train would stop, held up by signals, for minutes at a time. I never understood why Tom Pender – or his mum – didn't come along and rub it out. And giving the poor bloke's address. The hurt is in the detail."

"So?" asked LP Lomax.

"I'm just thinking up motives. From the reviews I read, it might have been any of fifty authors – or their mums – who killed your friend. You've no idea how the bottle got poisoned, have you?"

"None."

"Right then, Mr Lomax. I'll be off."

Dyer stood up. "What are you reviewing?"

"Dido and Aeneas."

"Good, is it?"

"Not very."

"And you're going to say that with some certainty?"

"Yes."

Dyer nodded. "Certainty's a great thing," he said.

"Certainly is," said LP Lomax, aiming a look at Dyer which stylishly expressed barely concealed contempt.

⁂

Jim and Mandy Smart
Invite all at
Cutting Edge
to celebrate the
Return from the Grave
of
Dying in Style
by
The Late Arthur Whitworth
Eight Til Late at 176 Avenell Road, Islington N5
on Tuesday next. Regrets only.

"A bit tasteless, isn't it?" Roberta said, when Giles read the invitation to her over the phone.

"It is a bit. I expect Mandy's behind it," Giles said. "She's probably trying to show Jim she means well."

"Who'll you get to go?"

"Well, Roberta, I was hoping you might, for a start. I've roped in Patrice – he's doing sterling work in the warehouse, by the way. Melanie's going, and one or two reps."

"But I'm supposed to be in hiding. I can't just show up as if nothing's happened."

"Can't you do a Salman and waltz in unannounced? You could bring that policeman with you. It would be a way of meeting up with Patrice, too. He's pining for you, Roberta. By the way, why didn't you tell me he was a doctor?"

"It didn't seem relevant. He's not allowed to practise. Look, Giles, I'll think about it. It would be nice to see everyone. But at Jim and Mandy's? Remember last time?"

"I do, indeed," Giles replied. "Still, he's done marvellous work at shifting *Dying in Style*. We've got to keep him sweet. Did I tell you we're relaunching the rest of Whitworth's novels? Jim will be invaluable at seeing they catch on."

"I'll think about it," Roberta said.

"Have you read Arthur's new one yet?"

Roberta looked at the pile of manuscripts she had been given prior to holing up. "No, not yet. Haven't been able to face it. You know."

"Take your time," Giles said, in a tone that meant exactly the opposite. "Hopefully, see you Tuesday."

❧ ❧ ❧

Five weeks earlier, in the middle of Morecambe Bay, Arthur Whitworth had been surprised to find how buoyant he was. It had taken him an hour of nightmarish thought to rock the rowing-boat sufficiently, with enough conviction, to overturn it. He had made several attempts but as water came over the gunwales each time, he drew back at the shock of it. That cold was what he would be in for. Cold doubled and tripled by the knowledge that it was the last sensation he would ever feel before panic, suffocation, blackout and death. Each time he stopped rocking the boat he sat clutching the oars, pitying himself, mewing like a desperate animal.

Floating on the smoothly undulating water, blowing through his fists, Arthur remembered the terror of cold and wished he had a pen. Virginia Woolf had once lamented that she deeply regretted her inability to describe her own death. Reading that under very different circumstances in his cottage, Arthur had thought it a precious, silly thing to think, let alone consign to paper. But now he could understand and sympathise with the sentiment. The emotions had been so real and raw when he had capsized the boat . . . drops of cold firing his brain, taking him back to a warm fireside in the now-deserted cottage, to times when he had been really happy. That August day when, new to teaching, he had opened the A level examination results in English and seen that every single one of his pupils – even Withenshaw – had achieved a decent grade; the arrival at the summit of Ben Nevis that first time; his first prize-winning cod; the launch party for his first, enthusiastically received, novel; all the glory days of his fifty years had stood out so finely, like a red rowing-boat on a grey icy sea.

Contrasting that with the present, with the present's hopelessness, was worth communicating. Perhaps Virginia had experienced similar intense emotions as the stones carried her under the River Ouse.

Past happiness and present misery started Arthur Whitworth rocking the boat with added manic intensity. Water rushed in on the starboard side. He could have stopped then, as he had before. But, letting out a thought-drowning roar, he kept the tipping motion up until the boat – the boat he had so loved – threw him away. He could still recall the hurt of the lurch, the abandonment of him by the sturdy boat.

One abandonment deserved another. The cold vanished. Arthur had let himself go limp, as limp as a sleeper turning deeper into a billow of cool duvet on a sunny morning, to await the feeling of drowning. His head was still full of the good things. The wretched reviews for *Dying in Style* hardly impinged. Funny, that. But the thought brought back Cyril Parkinson's review. Cyril Parkinson who was always grudging – even when the rest had been extravagant in their praise. The words of the review, read only once, came back verbatim: *No flowers. By order. Putrefaction truly Bruegelesque . . . If, perchance, some enemy were to present you with this opus*

. . . as a gift! . . . send it back, throw it on the fire, put it in a sack loaded with stones . . .

Arthur lay face-down in the water and willed himself to sink. He held his breath until he could hold it no longer. Then he tried to breathe the opaque water. He coughed and spluttered it out. He recovered himself, wondering what to do, how to do it. Land was invisible. It was only a matter of time – *but how much time?* – before exhaustion made what he was trying so hard to achieve an automatic response. He exhaled, thinking that emptying his lungs might release him from his wretched buoyancy. It did no such thing. The water seemed to be carrying him, refusing to take him in. Rejecting him. Rejecting all his work. All his pomps.

Don't invest all your self-confidence in your job, a wise old bird had told him once. Arthur lay on his back and looked at the leaden sky. *I did, Alf, I did,* he told his dead friend's shade. Alf Wakefield had taken pride in mining. Then, when he found himself shut out, he took pride in pigeons and allotment. *Always have something in reserve; nothing lasts forever.* And Arthur had promised to write that down and pin it on the wall above his writing-desk. He had not. Writing had come along to replace teaching as his life's work. If that went, everything went. Daft. Daft, but there you are.

The rowing-boat was now about two hundred yards away. In theory he could swim back to it and wait for help. But it was a theory only. One way or another the time had arrived, his time had arrived, It had to come some time. Scrolling the flickering months on his electronic datapad, the year changing every six seconds into the future, past the millennium and on . . . 2010 . . . 15 . . . 20 . . . somewhere there, on one of those dates that came and went, each one taking hundreds of thousands of fragile humanity with it . . . somewhere there was his death day, the start of his disintegration. The day had bleeped for him a little earlier than planned. Nothing exceptional in that. Birds flew into jet-engines, gunmen went berserk, joy-riders ploughed through bus queues; death came when it would, just as it had come for him.

Or had it?

Arthur's bottom, lower in the water than the rest of him, grazed something. Or had something bitten him? Had a shark, a gnashing critic, a carping commentator wandered from warmer climes to savage him? Arthur Whitworth thrashed about in a panic. He found, to his surprise, that his arms touched sand. He looked around. Water was passing him out towards the west, towards Ireland, like the current of a river. He stood up; his legs gave way beneath him and he sat down in the water like a toddler on a hearth-rug. He wiggled his toes, shivered, stood up again.

Looking landwards he saw a fringe of green. The water passing him, no more than two feet deep now, was draining away towards the west. He stood, squinting through seawater or tears, and he thought he saw a band of yellow between himself and the faraway green of land. He sat down again, and concentrated on the water pushing past him.

He started to bellow like the baby on the hearth-rug. He was shaking with emotion, shivering with cold. The tide in Morecambe Bay was ebbing and in a matter of an hour he would be beached. Cocklers, bait-diggers, people with shrimping-nets, the odd cantering horse and above-it-all rider would in an hour or two be where he had been attempting to take his life.

Odd. *Taking my life.* The need to do so had faded. He did not know how. Suicide, he now understood, took careful planning. Virginia had managed things better with her pockets filled with stones. A real pro was Virginia. Arthur, on the other hand, had not considered the minutiae. He was not much of a swimmer, so he'd thought that it would be easy to sink, even though hard to splutter for a while and force unconsciousness onto himself, but at least possible. But something kept him buoyant. His incipient beer-belly, perhaps? Or an unconscious ache to go on with his life? He stood up again and several bands of yellow sandbanks led like the slats in a gate to the line of green. Where was that green?

He walked towards it, cold now, the wind on his sodden back. He saw a lighthouse, or was it a chimney? If it was the Sefton Light then Monica, the deputy-head – now retired – of his old school, lived alone just below it. Monica would take him in, give him a warm, let him work things out even if working things out simply meant mugging up on how to do the job right.

But he stopped, the Irish Sea still lapping his ankles. He couldn't turn up at Monica's after so much time had passed. And not now; not like this. She knew he came to the bay to fish and, knowing that, knew he never dropped in. Maybe she put his neglect down to his being a reclusive writer. He put it down to the embarrassment of times when he had postponed a visit. Monica was not the only one he had neglected since taking up writing. But Monica had deserved neglect least of all. To turn up now! Now that he was once more dithering on the edge! Now that he could make use of her again! That was impossible.

He reached the sand and went across it to the sea wall. There he sat, contemplating his fate. He was beginning to feel the cold. What, though, was the alternative to visiting Monica? He had no money on him. His car, with the keys still in it, was parked miles away. Monica would help him as she had helped him in the past.

Arthur Whitworth walked up the steps and trudged along the promenade, like a snail. A hundred yards from the door of Monica's cottage he started praying that she would be in.

ꕥ ꕥ ꕥ

"I've never been so stuck in a case before," said Detective Inspector Dyer. "It's staring us in the face that Arthur Whitworth's behind these murders. The whole country believes it; even Ed Stourton on that talk-in got very irate with that old woman who said that, alive or dead, she couldn't believe Arthur Whitworth had done it. She knew he couldn't have from his books. Ed Stourton quoted chapter and verse to demolish her. I'd give my pension for a clue."

"Steady on, sir,"

Constable Keeley, armed with a rusty expandable wrench, was tugging at a stuck section of Dyer's u-tube under a peculiar bathroom basin which sat next to the fridge in his kitchen. "If you'd given me some notice I'd have brought my tools from home," he said.

"Just do what you can, Desmond."

"That won't be much. How long have you had this er . . . arrangement?"

"It was here when Edith and me moved in. Neither of us were much for decor and that. A kitchen and bathroom combined didn't worry us. At least the lav is separate."

Tugging at the wrench, Constable Keeley replied, "But this is a bit more basic than decor. How long's it been blocked?"

"A year. Maybe two," Dyer replied. "Still, to be fair, it isn't really blocked; just sluggish."

Dyer lit a cigarette and gazed out of the kitchen window

over Highbury Fields. He noticed that Edith's parking-spot was empty. Even after two months people still avoided it because of the doctor parking-sign. He'd used it himself once or twice. How long before the neighbourhood got the message that Edith was not coming back?

A sound of metal grating on metal, a groan from Constable Keeley. Dyer turned to see his plumber fall heavily on the floor. His left shoulder caught the side of the sink unit, making the pyramid-high stack of dishes judder and fall back into the three-day-old washing-up water.

"Done it!" said Constable Keeley.

"Are you OK?" Dyer asked.

Keeley pushed around to view his shoulder. He rubbed the spot. "Just a flesh wound," he said.

"You're bleeding, Desmond," Dyer said. "Let me see."

Desmond took off his shirt.

God, you're gorgeous. "I'll put some TCP on it," Dyer said.

"Don't worry about it, sir."

"You don't know what you might pick up."

"No."

Dyer fetched TCP from under the sink. He applied it to Keeley's shoulder. "Does that hurt?"

"It stings a bit."

"You've got a lovely shoulder, constable."

"Thanks very much, sir."

"Is the rest of you that lovely? Are you so perfect all the way down?"

"Can I put my shirt on now, sir?"

No, you can't. You want to make progress in the force, constable? Get those pants down. Show me what you've got. Let the seedy fellow who can give you a leg up get his leg over, gobble you up. "Put your shirt on, Desmond."

Keeley did so. In a trice he was back under the sink,

like someone in an earthquake under a table, unscrewing the piping. He took off a section of u-tube and held it over the swing-bin whose swinging section lay amid balls of dust between sink and cupboard.

"Disgusting!" he said.

Dyer, pacing, misinterpreted. Then he was peering at hundreds of filter-tips pouring out of the pipe and spattering the old coffee-filters, detergent packets and Bulgarian wine bottles of the swing-bin. "That's what was causing it, was it?"

"That's about it," Keeley said. "It *is* a bit disgusting, sir, you have to admit."

"I admit it, Desmond," he said. He looked at Desmond. "Sorry, son," he said, regretting, trying to express it. Then he was back to the surface. "Me and Edith, well I suppose we put the fags out under the tap and then stuck the filters down the plug-hole."

"Your sin will find you out, sir."

Dyer nodded at the truth of that. "You've great gifts. Great assets, Desmond," he said.

Before Constable Keeley could blush again, the telephone rang.

Dyer answered it. He listened, saying nothing. Then he put the phone down with a grunt of goodbye.

"That was the chap with the red hair . . . "

"Sergeant Drury."

"Sergeant Drury. Nothing to report on the publisher chap . . . "

"Giles Gibbons."

"Nothing to report. Good as gold, apparently. Leading Sergeant Drury one hell of a dance. Flogging that book, shouldn't wonder. I wonder if I should get Drury onto something more useful."

"Like what, sir?"

"You tell me, constable."

"He does lovely kitchens. I've seen what he did for his missis. They live off the Holloway Road. He did all the joinery himself."

"This'll do me. If Edith comes back I'll think it over." Then Dyer was back to looking out of the window. A car was parked adjacent to Edith Gonne's parking-space. It started to manoeuvre, as if to park in it, then thought better of it and drove off. "I suppose there's a chance," Dyer said.

"How long have you been married, sir?"

Dyer had to ask Keeley to repeat the question. "Since a couple of years before you were thought of, constable."

"No kids?"

Dyer gestured about the untidy flat. "Can you see any evidence? Photographs? Letters?"

"No, sir."

"No kids, Desmond." Dyer looked away, back to the parking place. "As you've probably intimated from tonight's pathetic attempt at Doctors and Patients, I wasn't the marrying kind, Desmond. I lived in this flat with a policeman I met at the Hendon Police College. Eight years we were together as young bobbies, fielding the questions about when we were going to take the plunge. We ironed one another's shirts, studied for our sergeants' exams, took turns making meals and a whole lot more that I won't trouble your innocent head with. Two salaries; we thought we'd put in our time and go off to live in the country." Dyer stopped, still looking at the parking-place.

"So what happened?"

"Patrick – that was his name – was killed in the line of duty, as they say. He was chasing a suspect through Central London. The car went out of control and crashed into a lamppost. Patrick was in the passenger seat. His colleague stepped out of the car without a mark on him."

"Sorry, sir."

"I was the colleague, Desmond."

Keeley said nothing.

Dyer continued: "It was the funeral that brought me and Edith together. I mean, picture the scene. There Patrick's family were, the chief mourners, and there I was with the best thing in my life broken in the coffin at the front of the church. And feeling as guilty as hell. And no one saying anything to me. Lots of loaded looks of course. No mention of me from the pulpit. We'd both known Edith a bit in a professional capacity. She was new to pathology then, of course. She came up to me outside the church and hugged me. I loved her for that and I've loved her ever since. In my way. Sound daft?"

"No . . . but . . . "

"But what?"

"I was thinking of the accident."

"It wasn't my fault. The brakes were faulty." Dyer paused. "Anyway, Edith proposed to me. And that's been it."

"Until she walked out?"

Dyer turned from the window. "Thinking about Giles Gibbons, though; he'd probably have hired killers to do his dirty work, wouldn't he? It doesn't come expensive. And he'd have one hell of a lot to gain, you have to admit."

Keeley, not for a moment missing a step in Dyer's change of subject, said, "He's making money on *Dying in Style* hand over fist. America's got the bug now. Selling like hot cakes and there's a nightly bulletin on the major networks about what's happening here. They're waiting for the next murder."

"I know, Desmond. Aren't we all?" said Detective Inspector Dyer.

❧ ❧ ❧

Mandy Smart, dressed in a sarong bought in a Jaffna shop – a shop that a bomb had since blown away – had spent the whole day in preparations for her party. She wanted to make amends for wandering off. Gazing at the display of tasty titbits she had prepared to pass around to her guests, she felt content. She wondered what could possibly have got into her to wander away like that, to hurt dear Jim, to cause everyone such worry.

Then, like a cloud of content rolling off the searing sun, she was edgy again. She was on the beach on the Jaffna Peninsula, the only foreign tourist, and the people showering attention on her. It brought everything back. For a moment the skewered sausages, the smoked salmon wrapped around gherkins, the dips, the crisps, the deep-fried mushrooms . . . seemed such a waste of time. Why, if her funds hadn't run so dangerously low she could be on that beach now, sunning herself, helping to improve the English of the fishermen and soldiers who wandered by. What was she doing here when she could be there?

The Sri Lankans had loved Mandy Smart. She had gone there anonymously, of course; nobody had known that she was a Page Three Girl, though they could perhaps have suspected. When the sun set over the mangrove swamps, Mandy would retire to her beach-hut, and await the coming of friends. All through the night, every night they came. Great big Tamils who parked a gun in the corner before coming to her all rude and rapacious; gentle youths with flowers behind their ears who took her with much tickling. The sea lapping. Cooling off. A shadowy figure. Hotting up. Exploding.

She sighed. Avenell Road could not compete with that.

Jim's career was all well and good but she would swap it all for a beach-hut in Jaffna.

After that, what was all this? Vanity and a waste of time. She thought of it, again, though it hurt and made her yearn. Yes; she had told them, I shall return. I shall return with medicine and language-learning tapes and everything I can carry that Mothercare stocks. I will come back to you as both whore and benefactor. The milk of human kindness I shall give to you. Like some new goddess for your pantheon. Be patient, my dears!

"Be patient!" Mandy told herself. "My time will come again, just as Arthur Whitworth's has." She heard the key turn in the front door. Jim came in, accompanied by Giles, Patrice, Melanie and a crowd of cronies from W Crisp. Giles hugged Mandy and Mandy winked at Patrice over Giles's shoulder. Patrice looked over his own shoulder to see who the wink was for.

Jim looked at the colourful display on the table. "What a picture!" he said. "All your own work?"

"All my own work, Jim!" Mandy said, releasing Giles.

"Come and look at this, guys and gals!" Jim called.

Over to the groaning technicolour table they trooped.

"Did you get caterers in?" asked Jim's secretary, Cheryl.

"No, dear," Mandy replied, "a few packets of Philadelphia and a lot of imagination."

"It looks too good to eat!" said the manager of the Holborn shop.

Mandy smiled, fixed drinks, told people to tuck in – after all these were only the hors d'oeuvres.

"There's more?"

"There's a Sri Lankan curry waiting in the kitchen. Served on banana leaves," Mandy said. "In Jaffna you just chuck the plates out of the window so the cows can get the benefit. Now that's what I call civilisation. See to the drinks, Jim."

"Is that where you were? For your holidays?" asked Cheryl.

"Yes, I did several cookery courses," said Mandy.

"And I've been getting the benefit. As you can see," Jim said, patting his non-existent paunch.

"It's a great idea to have a party for *Dying in Style*," said the accountant. "Not everyone would have thought of that."

"It's a bitter-sweet occasion, isn't it?" Mandy said. "I read *Dying in Style* while I was away. I loved it. Then when I got back and found what had happened, well . . . " Mandy touched her cleavage and the room went quiet, " . . . I was completely devastated. In Jaffna we'd launch candles onto the ocean, but this is the next best thing."

"Do you miss Jaffna?"

"A little. But I was missing Jim like mad."

Jim smiled and bit on a salsa-spread crisp.

"Drinks, Jim!" Mandy said, a sliver of ice in her voice. "Now I wonder if I could find a volunteer to help me dish up the curry."

And Mandy made straight for Patrice.

"Giles, I . . . " Jim said.

"What, Jim?"

"Nothing."

Roberta arrived just as things – with the absence of Mandy and Patrice in the kitchen – were getting difficult. Conversation had started to flag. Jim was looking tense, worrying about Mandy and what might be getting into her.

"You came!" Giles said.

"I thought about it and then I thought why not," said Roberta. "Where's Patrice?"

"He's in the kitchen helping Mandy dish up."

"I'll just go and say hello."

"Roberta . . . "

"Is the kitchen this way?"

"Roberta . . . "

"Shan't be a tick," Roberta said.

Roberta disappeared through the door. It swung to behind her but before it had settled in the "closed" position the door opened again and Roberta strode through, past the party and out of the front door. It was slammed.

"What got into her?" said the accountant.

"No idea," said Jim. He looked about him. "I think I'd better go and lend a hand."

Everyone watched Jim disappear into the kitchen. The door fanned shut. It stayed shut. All watched the door. After a long moment it opened and Mandy, with Jim close behind her, announced that dinner was served.

Everyone said how wonderful and trooped through the door where steaming portions of curry and rice lay on banana leaves. Mandy was still standing close to Jim. Patrice was sitting with his head in his hands. Had anybody been able to see behind the happy couple's togetherness they would have been surprised to notice that Jim had his wife in an armlock.

"Tuck in, everybody!" Jim said.

By this time, the country and the wider world were all agog to see who would be murdered next. Three weeks had passed since the last victim, yet interest had not waned at all. Quite the contrary. A part of people – even quite good and decent people – ached for Arthur Whitworth to kill somebody else and get away with it.

Perhaps it was the mixed motives of those obsessed with the book and its realisation in real life that kept so muted complaints about the lack of police progress on the case. Daily, Detective Inspector Dyer expected to be hauled in and then dragged across the carpet by high-ups. Thus far, this had not happened. The story was unwinding. True, there had been a bit of a hesitation in the proceedings, but to end it with an arrest and a prosecution before the fictional murders had been enacted in reality was something that struck those excited by the happenings as akin to injustice.

After all, as an editorial in *The Times* asserted, it is a basic characteristic of human nature for us to want to know how our stories end. We ache for an after-life partly at least so that we can sit in front of the celestial Sky TV and click between goings-on, godlike, in the world we have left. Whether it be the fate of Ulster, Bosnia, Burundi or the woman behind the bar in a soap opera, it strikes human beings as the height of injustice not to know how things turned out; to be ripped away from the action without knowing The End.

The clues that Detective Inspector Dyer had been able to glean – and they were few and far between – all pointed to Arthur Whitworth as the killer. Dyer had pestered the CID in Morecambe for weeks for news. To no avail.

Bodies were washed up and minutely examined. Sad bodies, a shredded patch of what they had once been, bloated and cured by too much time in brine; bodies reduced to picked-clean skeletons and washed into trawling-nets, bodies whom the unfortunate finders and keepers found hard to imagine ever having trailed behind a loved one or wheeling a trolley in Tesco; bodies that seemed dead as a nail. But none was Arthur Whitworth's. All those with the head attached had teeth of some sort and Arthur Whitworth's dentist had asserted that the only records he held on Arthur Whitworth were the records of his last National Health dentures.

A disappointing July waxed into a blistering August. Minute forensic details on the victims returned from Dr Edith Gonne – who was still off cigarettes and on religion – and gave Dyer and Keeley days of work, but produced no results. They lost Sergeant Drury, who was assigned other duties. Several days on the run Dyer took Desmond Keeley home to see to his plumbing.

⁂

"Mandy, it's Giles."

"Giles. Nice to hear from you. I'm sorry about the bit of bother . . ."

"I'm ringing to thank you for a wonderful party. It was so thoughtful of you and Jim to put it on."

"It was nothing. You know what a fan I am of Arthur. I'm really sorry about . . . you know . . ."

"Are you and Jim er . . . all right again?"

Mandy did not answer right away. Then she said, "Do you really want to know, Giles?"

"Yes, I do. You're both very dear friends, and Jim . . ."

"I hate him," Mandy said.

"Ah," Giles said. "I'm sorry to hear that."

"I told him right from the start I was a free spirit but . . ."

"You don't happen to know where Patrice is, do you?"

"Why do you ask?"

"It's just that Patrice was working for us at Cutting Edge. He was doing good work there. I'd like him to come back, but he's just disappeared."

"Patrice drops in," Mandy said. "He doesn't have a bean. I've been helping him out . . ."

"Does you credit," Giles said. "Next time you see Patrice, could you ask him to get in touch, Mandy?"

A pause. "All right." Then Mandy was shouting, "I've got to get away, Giles! It's driving me nuts here. If I had the money I'd be in Jaffna. I have so much to contribute there."

"Indeed," Giles said.

"It's not only *that*. I know what you think. I know what Jim's been telling you. But it's not just that. I went to Jaffna looking for romance, it's true; but I want to go back to help, to teach, to *give*!"

"I hate to think of you feeling so low, Mandy," Giles said. "I wonder if I might be able to help."

"If only you could, Giles!" Mandy said.

Giles coughed before proceeding. "It seems to me that what you need is a quiet time to think things through. I have a country place in Nottinghamshire. It's been on the market for a while. Now that Cutting Edge is back on the up – so to speak – I can afford to keep it and live there again. But, wouldn't you know it, I've so little time. Just the odd weekend."

"Yes?"

"Well, I was wondering if you might like to go and stay there for a while. It's empty. It needs living in. The countryside around is rather lovely. I might drop in from time to time, but you'd be perfectly free to work out where you go from here."

"But you'd tell Jim . . . "

"I wouldn't tell Jim, Mandy. Jim is his own worst enemy. I'd like to see you both happy."

"I'd love that, Giles. I really would."

"Right, then," Giles said, "just name the day."

"I will, Giles. Thanks."

"Don't mention it," Giles replied, "Don't forget about Patrice, though, will you?"

"He's coming round today."

"Jolly good," Giles said.

ර ර ර

Arthur Whitworth watched the unfolding of events in company with Monica Gardiner. He had arrived at her door, puffed and bedraggled. Monica Gardiner, after squinting for a few moments at the damp apparition on her doorstep, recognised the ex-head of English at St Mary's Comprehensive and bothered him inside her neat cottage.

"Arthur," she said, "what's happened?"

Then as Arthur tried to explain – and he wasn't going to hold anything back, the sight of her reminded him that he never could – Monica took him into the bathroom, produced a man-sized dressing-gown out of thin air, ran the bath and told him to come out when he was ready.

Arthur Whitworth, whose empty rowing-boat had already been found by fishermen, lay in the hot water. Tears came to his eyes and rolled down his round cheeks. It seemed like a miracle. It *was* a miracle. To be back in the element that had been intended to do for him, to smother his sad life, and then to find himself in this deep aromatic bath with weeping white tiles and "PM" wafting in from the kitchen. Perhaps he had died and this was heaven, he thought, only half in jest. Maybe heaven was as mundane as this. Maybe it was as simple and domestic as life on earth without the strife of street and cranium.

He soaked himself for half an hour, then got out into the warm bathroom, towelled himself dry and put the dressing-gown on.

Back in the kitchen, a mug of tea warming his palms, Arthur told Monica everything. Monica, he saw – and she saw too – was just as she had been with him in the corner of the staffroom during one of his crises. As the story of the *Dying in Style* fiasco tumbled out: the way the critics' words had burrowed like weevils into his brain and would give him no relief, sapped his strength, strangled all ideas, took his life-force from him. Monica could remember listening to how the Fourth, Fifth and Lower Sixth at St Mary's had managed the exact same thing all those years ago.

"You haven't changed, Arthur," she said.

Arthur Whitworth had taken the earliest of early retirements from teaching. The profession he had entered at twenty-three with such high hopes had turned into a work of frightening drudgery. He shook as he entered the gates of St Mary's each morning. As he left them in the evening, he breathed a sigh of relief mixed with a sense of foreboding at the thought that the following morning he would have to return to the buildings that tortured his spirit, lashed his fragile ego, made him despair.

It had happened by degrees. He could not explain the way the attention span of the classes slowly but surely shortened, the easily calmed hubbub turning into a barrage of antagonism; the obtuseness, the glad-to-be-ignorant attitude which he could not penetrate with the force of his enthusiasm. That enthusiasm became the butt of his pupils' humour, turned into a stick to beat him with.

Monica had said things would get better. But, when Arthur Whitworth started weeping during a class on *The Merchant of Venice* and had to be led out in tears from a – for once – silent class, she knew and he knew the game was up.

An arrangement was made and Arthur Whitworth left

teaching. He bought his cottage near Blubberhouses and started writing *Teacher*, his first novel. Monica had soldiered on at the school. They occasionally met and as the years passed it was Monica's turn to recount her woes. The form-filling, the Office For Standards in Education inspections, the bureaucracy, the scapegoating of teachers . . .

"Early retirement?" Arthur had enquired. He was then in the middle of writing his fourth novel. He was managing. Nothing marvellous, but he was making enough. His confidence was biffed, even then, by the odd bad review, but, compared with the teaching experience it was easy enough to take. That was before the knives came out for his novel about environmental issues.

"I'm thinking about it," Monica said. "I may be able to get a note."

"How do you mean?"

"Medical retirement. I've got a weak heart, Arthur. It runs in the family. All the aggro isn't helping; putting it mildly, that is. My doctor's on my side."

When her mother died of a stroke the following year, Monica looked into it, found that – even without enhancement – she could manage. She handed in her doctor's note. She waited. When permission came through – and the governors had been only too pleased to be rid of her, her seniority made her too expensive – she bought the cottage by the sea near Morecambe and, sending a few close friends a change-of-address card, started her new life away from it all.

Arthur had visited her at the cottage several times in the early days. They talked about old times. It was like the staffroom again, but with no terrors on either side. Then the frequency of his visits had declined until it was impossible for him to break the ice he felt would have formed.

"Well," Monica said, "it's over now."

"It's good to see you. Seeing you makes everything better."

"It is not good for man to be alone," Monica said.

"You need a bit of solitude to write."

"But solitude gives way to loneliness once the day's work is over," Monica said. "Amn't I right?"

"You're perceptive, Mon. You always were, of course. You're probably the one who should have done the writing."

"Maybe I am writing," Monica said, gesturing to an Amstrad with a cover over it, on which was written "North Lancashire Education Authority". "I've joined a group. They like my stuff." She stopped, looked at Arthur in his dressing-gown. "However, Arthur, I'm not particularly perceptive about loneliness. I wasn't able to anticipate it. I've been experiencing it of late. Moving to this cottage and that; it's not been the unalloyed delight I'd worked it up to being in my imagination. I should have learnt from my mistakes in that flat in Morecambe I moved to after Mum died – views and no people – and I came to hate it. Then, a few months later, I make the same mistake all over again."

"It's called human nature," Arthur said.

"It's called being right daft."

"Part and parcel," Arthur said. "I worked myself up into a state about my books. I put everything into them – all my life experience, my self-esteem, everything. I thought I needed to cut myself off. It wasn't a wise thing to do. It meant that when some critic put the boot in – and I know I'm not to everyone's taste – it really got me lathered up. *Dying in Style* was the result. I wrote myself into a corner. You know, I thought they wouldn't dare biff it; they'd just have to take it on the chin, like writers have to, and wait for the burn to stop throbbing."

"But they didn't?"

"Did you see the reviews?"

Monica nodded. "But if you'd gone through with what you were planning, they'd have won. Like the nasty minority of terrors at St Mary's won. I wished you'd come to me earlier, Arthur."

"I'm here now, Monica."

"Yes, you are, aren't you? You will stay a while?"

"If I'm not imposing."

"I'll fix us a nice dinner. I did a good shop at Asda today. We're all set for the duration."

"I ought . . . " said Arthur, thinking of the swamped boat, a side of him wanting her rescued too.

"Ought . . . should . . . such sad little modal auxiliaries, I always think. They kill the joy of the present moment stone-dead, Arthur."

"Let's not talk of killing," said Arthur.

"Quite right. Let's not."

And Monica Gardiner went off happily to the kitchen to cook for two, leaving Arthur Whitworth to nod off on the sofa, knowing that for the first time in ages a meal was going to be put on the table for him.

❧ ❧ ❧

"I've seen some lightning visits in my time, Roberta," Giles said, "but that beat all."

"I could kill her, I really could."

"I should have taken more care of Patrice. It all happened so fast," Giles said.

"Nobody's to blame except that rapacious cow. Mind

you, it might have been a good idea to brief Patrice about what she's like. No sign of him, I suppose?"

"None. We've had to get some students in to help out," Giles said.

"What about Mandy? Mandy, I ask you."

"Jim's in a state. They had a big row during the curry meal – and it was a hot one, I'd never tasted hotter. It was all going on around us. "What gets into you, Mandy? What? Can you tell me please?" While we all tried to balance the banana-leaf plates and the heat of the food burning us inside and out. I tell you, Roberta, it was one of the worst occasions I've ever attended, and that's saying something."

"Patrice hasn't gone back to the hostel. He was supposed to check in with the police today. Bet he didn't. I could kill him, too!"

"Talking of killing," said Giles, "we've sold translation rights to China – the People's Republic no less. Six-figure sum deposited in the Hong-Kong-Shanghai Bank. Part of the Midland, did you know that?"

"Yes," Roberta replied.

"It came as quite a fright to me. What a world, eh? Still I suppose it's safe. Trouble is . . . "

"Yes?"

"It's going a bit off the boil here. Over a million isn't bad, but if it . . . you know . . . kept up just a bit longer . . . "

"Another murder, you mean?"

"Sound horrid, don't I? I don't mean to."

"It's only natural, I suppose. I've had the thought myself. I keep stamping on it but . . . well . . . you know . . . "

"Too right," Giles said. "Where are you, Roberta?"

There was a pause on the other end of the line. "The police," Roberta said at last, "won't let me say."

"Understand. Understand completely," Giles said.

"You wouldn't mind my sort of telling the press, would you? I'd just say you're holed up in the country, terrified, that sort of thing. They pester me the whole time and it would be lovely to have something to tell the buggers. I could lie and say you're abroad."

"Feel free. Look, Giles, I hope you don't mind my lying low."

"You lie as low as you like, Roberta. *Dying in Style* has been doing its own publicity. We've already put Cutting Edge back in the black. It was touch and go for a while there, you know. Everything else is jam."

"That's good news."

"That's bloody great news. Cheers!"

"Bye."

Roberta put the phone down and looked around the one big room of the cottage in Suffolk. It had been loaned to her by her sister-in-law, and had been built at the bottom of the garden of a much larger hall house just outside Semer. Roberta's brother and his wife used the hall house for weekends, Roberta's sister-in-law having been left it on the death of an aunt. This meant that for two weeks – forgetting the wretched return trip to London – she had been alone there, apart from two scant weekends. The loneliness of the place was getting to Roberta. She wanted to see how her flat was getting on, to visit Morag's parents who had always been good to her, always asked to be remembered to her . . . to be in London and walk its streets. To find Patrice. Never much of a one for the country, she felt she had had her fill of it this time.

She went back to her desk to read the manuscripts Giles had given to her to crit. There were several hopeful books there, books which she felt might find a readership in normal, more bookish, times. There was also a copy of Arthur Whitworth's new one. Although she knew that it was probably the only one Giles was interested in, she had held back from reading it.

A queer part of her felt that, if she read the manuscript, some alchemy would bring Arthur Whitworth down on her to make her the next victim. What if she hated it, though she had never hated a novel by Arthur? What then?

"I don't believe Arthur Whitworth is behind all this," she thought. "I don't. It's just not in character." And as she thought it, she felt she might melt the murderer's heart. And when she thought of the melting heart, it was Arthur's.

Still, there had been nothing for a fortnight. Perhaps whoever was behind the murders had made his point. Deciding to face her fear full on, she opened the typed manuscript. She read:

An evil act never concerns merely those most intimately involved. Like a cancer it spreads its menace to all who brush against it, whether they hear about it in the laundrette, in a paper or on "The Six o'clock News'. A child molested and killed, also kills the freedom, even the childhood, of many thousands of children. They find themselves reined in, denied the comfort of fearful strangers, the everyday experiences that made our own green remembered youth so idyllic and carefree.

Peter North knew all this. He had listened, watched, read, enough stories of evil: beheadings, dismemberings, garrottings of innocents. He had shaken his head, even wept a tear or two, gone on his way defiled. When he found himself in the midst of committing an act of great evil, he determined that it would go no farther. His crime would remain undetected and, hence, the infection would be buried as deep as a body in a fever-cemetery.

A typical opening for Arthur Whitworth, that was. Nailing its colours to the mast, laying down straight away what the book was about. Roberta read on for half an hour. Then she set down the typescript and paced the room.

It was publishable all right. At this point Arthur Whitworth's laundry list would be publishable. Morag would probably have taken the red pen to some of the author's asides – Morag and Arthur had always battled over that – but in the circumstances that was neither possible nor necessary.

She paced. She thought of Patrice. She wanted him there. Wanted him. Perhaps she had not explained enough to him. She had disappeared from his life, leaving him with a job of sorts and the promise that she would be back. But when Mandy Smart came along, did he jump for a bit of possible security, security Roberta had started to supply, but then, distracted, withdrawn? Well, she wouldn't know the answers to any of it hiding in Suffolk.

"I want to go home!" she told the ideal sunset, the birds bathing in the pond outside the window, the waves of ripening wheat.

The telephone rang, making Roberta jump. For several rings she hesitated about picking up. Who, after all, had her number, except the police. She did not think she could face more bad news.

Ten rings, and still on it went. Roberta remembered that the caller might be her sister-in-law. The late rings of the phone seemed to register the caller's panic. She picked up.

"Roberta?"

"Patrice!" she said. "Where have you been? I've been phoning the hostel, but I can't make myself understood."

"I am not there," Patrice said. "It is dangerous there. The Immigration were looking for me there."

"Why?"

"My application is rejected."

"Why didn't you tell me?"

A silence from the other end. "I didn't know if we are still friends."

That was true enough.

"So where have you been?" Roberta asked.

"In the street," Patrice replied.

"In the street?"

"Yes."

"Sleeping?"

"Yes," said Patrice. "I have been sleeping in the street."

She saw him in a trice, lying in Ryman's doorway, one of those from whom she averted her eyes, wrapped in a sleeping bag, speaking too eloquently of suffering going on all around her in the shadows. Guilt rose up. "Look, Patrice, I'm coming back to London. Can you meet me at my flat at . . . " She looked at her watch, a Rolex given to her by Mum and Dad for her twenty-first – *With that Rolex I could . . . could have . . .* " . . . say, nine?"

"Nine this evening?"

"Yes, nine this evening. It will take me that long to get back."

A silence from the other end. Then, "Thank you."

"I'll be there by nine. If I'm late, just wait there. Will you do that? I . . . I'm so sorry, Patrice."

"Thank you," Patrice said.

It was only after Roberta had rung off and started to pack that the thought occurred to her. How had Patrice got hold of her number?

She called a taxi to take her to Ipswich Station.

Two and a half hours later she was hailing a taxi for the ride from Liverpool Street Station to Shepherd's Bush.

She was going to be late. It was already five to nine.

She prayed Patrice would stay put. Then the taxi was travelling along the Strand. It stopped just after The Savoy. She watched the evening crowds crossing the road, moving along the pavement; behind them people lying in sleeping bags in the shop doorways. She bit her knuckles.

The taxi edged its way towards Shepherd's Bush. As it turned into Roberta's street at 9.25, she found herself craning round the driver to see if Patrice was waiting outside the flat. She couldn't make him out. She got out. Paid the driver. The cab made a daring U-turn back up the road, leaving Roberta looking around for Patrice. There was no sign of him.

Roberta stood on the street for a minute or two, wondering what to do. Had he understood her instructions? Had pride risen up and made him prefer a shop doorway to the flat of a faithless friend? Had the police caught up with him?

She opened her front gate. A figure appeared from behind the hedge and made her jump.

"I have been waiting for my teacher since half an hour."

"Patrice!" She took him in her arms, smelled his unwashed body, the damp of his clothes. She sought out his mouth but then, seeing Patrice under siege from Mandy Smart, seeing herself in that siren role, she drew back. "I thought you wouldn't come," she said.

He shrugged, then gestured to his small bag of belongings sitting, like a mongrel, at his feet.

"Let's get into the flat," she said.

Roberta unlocked the front door. "After you," she said, rekindling a language game,

"No. After you," he said.

She went in and pressed the time-button for the dark

stairs. They started the ascent, Roberta pressing light onto the cold tiles at each landing.

As she ascended she was deciding the future. This flat would be their nest, Patrice's sanctuary. She would not go back to Suffolk. No, she and Patrice would stay here quietly. She would protect him from harm. She would scratch and bite and kick any official who dared try to remove him. They would love one another, forget the outside world and everything to do with *Dying in Style*.

They reached Roberta's door. "Don't worry about anything, Patrice," Roberta said. She unlocked the door, and pushed it. "Welcome home," she said.

"After you," Patrice said.

"No. I insist."

Laughing, Patrice walked ahead of Roberta into the flat.

The door seemed to resist his push. Nothing he could put a finger on. Then Patrice saw a taut piece of string leading from the door, across the hall to . . .

A deafening roar from both barrels of a shot-gun, lashed to the stripped pine chest of drawers. Patrice had time to lift one hand to try to protect his face, before the pellets demolished it, then pepper-potted his front with holes that instantly bloomed crimson.

His lifeless body was thrown back onto the concrete behind the WELCOME mat. It carried Roberta with it. She, feeling a searing pain down the left side of her face, in her left hand and arm, was crushed beneath her dead lover's weight.

She lay there for a long moment, detached, wondering. Then as the echo of the shot-gun reverberated in her head, the wet dripping of warm blood onto her face brought her to. She began to scream.

ꙮ ꙮ ꙮ

The ambulance with Roberta Coleman hysterical inside had just turned into the gates of St Mary's Paddington when Dyer arrived at the flat. He got out of the car and looked across the road to Morag Aitken's flat, where he had met and recruited Constable Keeley a few weeks before.

Dyer was panting when he reached the top floor of the building. Between fourth and top floor he was aware of drops of moisture hitting him. Only when he arrived on the final flight and the light gave him sight did he see that drops of blood speckled his mackintosh.

A sheet donated by a neighbour – and drenched with blood – covered the body of Patrice. A sergeant from the local police station stood to attention. Dyer crouched by the sheet and gently lifted the hem.

"Jesus wept!" he said.

He replaced the sheet, thinking of his interviews with Roberta Coleman some weeks before. How confident she had been that all would be well for her. Lying low was all she had needed to do.

Keeley came to the door of the flat and said, "A booby-trap. Gun-trigger connected to the doorknob. I'd say they were entering together and for some reason the African chap went first."

"How's Roberta Coleman?"

"I think she may have got a pellet or two in the face and some on the left side. It was hard to tell. She was covered in blood but probably a lot of it belongs to the deceased."

"I feel responsible, constable," Dyer said. "We should have . . ."

"You're not responsible, sir," said Keeley. "The murderer is responsible."

“Rest in peace!” Dyer told the bloodied remains of Dr Patrice Luala, refugee.

ꙮ ꙮ ꙮ

Later Dyer and Keeley sat in Dyer’s office.

“A teacher of mine, Father Coogan, used to say to me, ‘Boys, do you want to know what the great wickedness of the age is?’ And we’d say, ‘Yes, sir!’ though we knew full well. Father Coogan was always saying it. Can you guess what he said, Desmond?”

“Sex?” Desmond tried.

“Try again.”

“Greed?”

“No.”

“Laziness?”

“You’re getting cold.”

“I don’t know. How many vices are there?”

“‘Publicity, boys!’ That’s what Father Coogan said. We used to think he was out of his Catholic mind. I was a sceptic even then. But the longer I live, the older I get, I see that Father Coogan was probably right.”

Constable Keeley didn’t speak.

“Think about it, son,” said Dyer. “Terrorists blow up innocents for publicity; we’re told what to look like, what to buy, what to worry about. Truth is massaged by great engines of publicity. These great juggernauts brainwash the population in a way that perhaps religion used to. At least religion had a greater good in view, a bit of transcendental vision, a hope against hope. Publicity has only its perpetrators’ good in view. Those who need its sacraments wait in line for the light to fall on them and lift them with its grace. They’ll do anything for it. Take away publicity and people would live easy integrated lives.

They'd consider one another's strengths and weaknesses, admiring those who work quietly for the community's good, keeping the reprobates in line. They'd find their honour, their self-respect, in their neighbours. But publicity distorts, destroys perspective. Those reduced by not being in the limelight have their virtue stolen from them by those who are magnified by the Great Lens. Publicity is pitiless. Its lens magnifies prior to burning up the chosen ones."

"Not sure I get you."

Dyer lit a cigarette, inhaled and contemplated it. "Absurd, isn't it?" he said. "You're too young to remember how it was. When I took up these things, Desmond, publicity pushed them as going with a great life-style. Beautiful people puffed on them in the mountains, by cool streams. Beautiful women followed the chap puffing on a fag. Now, thirty years later and a hopeless addict, I still partly see cigarettes in that light. The human psyche, Desmond! So easily got at! So easily moulded! Take this case: a writer who needs publicity to shift his books gets bad publicity. Books fail to shift. Writer 'dies' and brings his book to life in order to get saturation publicity. Good or bad, it doesn't matter. But think of the people who get blown away in the process. And the motives and morals turned upside down! Even Roberta, poor thing, told me that she half hoped for another murder. She could not in all honesty come out and say, 'We at Cutting Edge spend days and nights on our knees praying to every god who may or may not be that there is not another murder'. She couldn't because this is ultimate publicity. If ever they have a patron saint of publicity managers – apart from the Angel Gabriel – Roberta Coleman ought to be at the front of the queue. A martyr to publicity, she is."

"Martyrs die, don't they, sir? Miss Coleman is still alive."

"I'll have to go and see her. God, I hate this job!"

"That's all very well, but what do we do now?"

Dyer considered. He was seeing himself approaching Roberta Coleman's hospital bed. He could see no farther. At last he said, "I think we go and find Arthur Whitworth."

"Easy to say, sir," replied Constable Desmond Keeley.

"I'll say it again, then. I think we go and find Arthur Whitworth. Pack a bag, Desmond," said Detective Inspector Dyer.

ꕥ ꕥ ꕥ

Arthur and Monica shared the only bedroom in the house that first night. The only bed, too. There was also a put-me-up sofa bought from *The Observer* in a mad mood and then regretted at leisure, but it was Arthur who asked to share the bed.

That first night they had been as chaste as two angels or two aged teachers who had shared moans and coffee mugs too long. They drank wine with their meal that night, then a succession of brandies. They talked about old times, the highs and the lows of teaching and their fifties in the nineties.

"Why did you never marry?" Arthur asked her.

"You've asked me that before, Arthur," Monica replied. "There was Mum and there was work and there were no offers. And that's just for starters."

"Michael Ring was mad for you." Michael Ring was head of physics at St Mary's.

Monica spluttered into her glass, but didn't say anything.

"I wish I'd married," Arthur said.

"You still could."

He shook his head, though he couldn't tell for the life of him why he was shaking his head. *I'm dead!* he thought. Then, taking a sip of the brandy, feeling it passing through his very live system, he realised again, *I didn't die! I'm here!*

He slept for thirteen hours. Monica brought him breakfast in bed, though by that time it was three in the afternoon. He ate, got up and had another bath, listening to Monica playing the piano in the hall outside.

That day they did not turn on the television or a radio. Once Arthur suggested that it was time for him to get back home, tell someone what had happened, do the right thing. But Monica, happier than she had been in months, pleaded with him to stay with her quietly – for both their sakes.

When, a couple of days later, they came to from their strange idyll, Arthur Whitworth's obituary had appeared in *The Telegraph*.

"I don't think the fellow liked me much," Arthur said. "I wonder who they got to do it?"

She was amazed at how unperturbed he was. Perhaps it was just like one of the twists in his novels; perhaps he lived in the imagination with such happenings welling up like clouds from water, then swirling, swirling, until their actual occurrence in real life did not bother him, did not perhaps seem as real as plots and the actions of his characters.

He went very silent. They watched the news that night, but no mention of his death was on either national or regional bulletins. It hurt Arthur a bit, somehow . . . not much, but a bit. To have missed the details of his own demise, the reaction to his death. Had there been one? What, if there had, was the twist, the spin, given to it? Had his photograph, perhaps the dire one on the back of

Dying in Style, flashed up while sundry acquaintances spoke of his bitter attitude to being a second-ranker.

"Who should we tell?" Monica asked, as the news gave way to more nonsense.

"I don't think we tell anyone, Monica." Arthur replied, looking at the dot on the blank screen wandering up the tube, then finally disappearing.

"What? No one?"

Arthur Whitworth was busy plotting. There might be a novel in it. There might be a whole new direction in it. "Would you mind if I stayed with you a while?"

"But, Arthur?"

"Just a couple of days. I only want to see the reaction to my own death; to see how the story ends. You can understand that, can't you? It's a once in a lifetime experience, if you see what I mean."

Monica was not sure that she did. Still, she had been happy to have him with her; would be happy if he went on staying with her. The solitary life did not suit her. To lose – without much regret – a busy life of school, parents' and governors' meetings, examinations and staffroom had been enough. The further cutting of human contact was too much altogether.

"I can't say I really understand, Arthur. I can't say that. Still, if that's what you want, we can live quietly for a few days. Just you and me. That would be nice. This is really lovely . . . really cosy."

"Thanks, Monica." He took her slim hand in his fleshy one and pressed it.

Half an hour later Monica drew the curtains of the lounge, though the sun, a golden ball over Morecambe Bay, still had two hours before it hit the skirting-board of the horizon.

❧ ❧ ❧

Detective Inspector Dyer postponed his entry to the ward in which Roberta Coleman was because, on passing the door, he had noticed a middle-aged man and woman seated by her bed. These he took to be Roberta's parents. He also noted the bandage covering one side of the patient's face.

He returned with heavy heart to the nurses' station and interrupted a nurse frowning into the face of a computer screen.

Dyer read the nurse's name-badge and asked, "Staff-Nurse Martin, can you tell me how Roberta Coleman is getting on?"

"Are you a relative?"

"I'm a police officer."

The staff-nurse pursed her lips, ran a mouse-pen along a name on her screen. The name and half a page of information disappeared. The screen blanked for a second, to be replaced by another name, more information. The nurse swivelled in her chair to face Dyer. "She's comfortable," she said.

"I noticed the bandage on her face. Is that serious?"

"It isn't life-threatening," the nurse replied, "but it's serious."

"Might I see her?"

The nurse stood up. "Roberta's parents are with her now."

Dyer nodded, but did not move from the spot.

"Have you any form of identification?"

Dyer handed her his police identity card. The nurse eyed it with suspicion. "I doubt you'll be able to get much sense from her," she said. "She was very disturbed when she woke up from the operation. We had to sedate her."

"Operation?"

"Several shot-gun pellets were removed."

"Of course." Dyer didn't know what to say next.

He was about to say he'd wait when a man's voice behind him said to the nurse, "We'll take a break now, nurse."

"Right you are, Mr Coleman."

Dyer turned to face Roberta's parents. He saw her in both. The father, about his age, well-preserved, of regular habits. The mother petite, ageing well. This, judging from the look of them, was the first tragedy ever to face them. Still, what did he know?

"I'm terribly sorry about what happened to Roberta," Dyer said.

The father nodded, and started to turn away.

The mother smiled. "And you are . . . ?"

"Detective Inspector Dyer."

"I believe Roberta mentioned your name. Before all this. You interviewed her after Morag's death, didn't you?" said the father.

"I did. You have a very plucky daughter, Mr Coleman."

"What we don't understand," said Mrs Coleman, "is what she was doing returning to her flat. With the man who . . . "

She could not complete the sentence.

"We thought she was staying in Suffolk," said Mr Coleman. "We thought she was under police protection."

"Roberta told us she was well-protected," said Mrs Coleman. "She told us not to worry . . . "

Dyer nodded, still not knowing what to say. He looked up from counting the grey tiles at his feet to find himself meeting Mr Coleman's eye. The man's cold stare made him return his gaze to the floor. "Your daughter's out of danger, I hear."

Mr Coleman suddenly exploded. "If you call losing the

sight in her left eye *out of danger*; if you call holes up and down her side *out of danger*; if you call being completely traumatised out of danger . . . then I suppose you're right. But she should never have been put *in danger* in the first place."

"Now, Edward . . . " said Mrs Coleman, placing her hand on her husband's right arm.

Mr Coleman turned to the nurse. "We'll be back in half an hour, Nurse," he said. He linked his wife's arm and without another word they walked away down the corridor.

Dyer watched them go. "Might I go and see the patient now?" he asked the nurse.

The nurse nodded, already in the act of turning back to face the computer screen.

❧ ❧ ❧

"Who is it?"

"It's Detective Inspector Dyer, Miss Coleman. Do you remember me?"

"Are you still lost?"

"More than ever."

Roberta said nothing for a long moment. Then, "Come closer, Mr Dyer. I can't see you."

Dyer did so, until he could see himself in Roberta's seeing eye. "He's dead . . . Patrice . . . he's dead, isn't he?"

"Yes, he is."

"They wouldn't tell me, but I knew he was dead. I can still feel him falling on me. Where is he?"

"Now you mustn't worry about that now. You must concentrate on . . . "

"Where is he?"

"He's in the police mortuary."

Roberta nodded. "Don't let anything happen to him, will you? Don't let them send him back to the Congo."

"No."

"You promise?"

"I promise."

"He came here to escape from danger."

"I know. I'm sorry."

"It's all my fault!" Roberta said, and a tear leaked from her eye.

"No," said Dyer, "it was my fault. It was completely my fault. I should never have allowed you to go off."

"Why did you, then?"

"It seemed the right thing to do at the time," he said. "I honestly didn't think you were in danger."

"Neither did I," Roberta replied. "Not really. Not seriously. Even after Morag's death it still seemed just a game. I was drunk with the excitement of it all. It's sick, isn't it? I'm sick, aren't I?"

"Of course you're not. You must rest. I'll come and see you again."

"No," Roberta said, "don't go. You're a policeman, aren't you? You're sorry for not having protected me before, aren't you? Protect me now."

Dyer sat down in the chair Roberta's father had been sitting in.

"That's good. Now what shall we talk about?"

"The nurse said you wouldn't have much to say. You ought to be resting up. You've had a terrible shock."

"Tell me about yourself."

"What do you want to know?"

"Are you married?"

"Yes."

"Children?"

"No."

"Couldn't?"

"Didn't."

"Regrets?"

"I've had a few. But then again . . . " Dyer said, trying to lift with a put-down line.

"It's funny. Around the Cutting Edge offices we'd more or less decided you were gay."

Dyer laughed.

"Why are you laughing?"

"It's funny. It's true, I am. But nobody thinks I am."

"Why not?"

"Well, look at me."

"Melanie – that's Giles's secretary – thought you were cuddly."

"Umm . . . "

"It's not so much the look of you, it's the way you look at other people: that dishy side-kick of yours, for instance."

Dyer went along with the banter, though he was aware as he did so that Roberta was elsewhere. Her voice had entered a higher, frantic register. Tears were falling from her eye, down the conduit of an incipient smile-line, over the precipice of her prominent chin, down her neck, to form a tiny pool in the hollow at the base of her throat. Her talk, so odd in someone in her situation, came from some well-practised surface. She was performing, winning him round. She was on automatic and probably running on empty. This was her sales pitch, her burrowing through the soil of indifference to the light of publicity. But another side of Roberta, he knew, was burrowing farther into the dark.

Suddenly, in mid-sentence, Roberta cried out. Her cry echoed in the room. She stopped, shocked at the sound, then seemed to be listening.

"Take it easy, love. You've had . . . "

But she turned away from him, moaning, mewling.

The nurse was beside him. "You'd better go now," she told Dyer matter-of-factly.

He stood up and turned to walk away. Then he stopped, hearing Roberta's voice.

"Detective Inspector," Roberta said, "don't let Giles Gibbons near me. Please!" She spoke in her normal voice, quite matter-of-factly.

"Right you are," Dyer said.

Outside the hospital entrance Dyer rang to request a police guard for Roberta Coleman.

⁂

The cleaner was dusting around Dr Edith Gonne when the telephone rang. Edith picked up the receiver and said, "Yes?" all bossy.

The cleaner, whose name was Mercy Staunton, had never answered the phone in that way; she didn't consider it the well-brought-up thing to do. Still, she knew Dr Gonne of old; knew that she cut up dead bodies and never got much thanks for anything. Her patients were past giving her boxes of Roses, making her feel appreciated and all that.

"What do you want, Timmy?" Mercy heard, as she rubbed at a coffee-ring on top of the word-processor. That would be Detective Inspector Dyer, Dr Gonne's husband. He was nice. Mercy couldn't see how they had got hitched in the first place, couldn't see what he saw in her. She ought to know her luck. There weren't many men who would put up with it.

"I'm still not smoking," Edith said, exhaling a plume of smoke in Mercy's direction. Mercy could not resist looking up to try and catch Dr Gonne's eye in the lie, but she was looking down at her full ash-tray, twirling the livid red end of her cigarette into a point.

Mercy smoked; she was a martyr to them. But she never said she didn't when she did. She wished she didn't, mind. Not doing it would eke out the housekeeping better, maybe allow her to drop one of the four cleaning jobs she did. But giving up didn't work for her. She lashed out at the kiddies, shouted and felt shocking.

"Sixty-four pellets were removed. Any one of about fifteen could have been fatal on their own. Three through the eye for a start. Nine through the heart and lungs. Liver shot through. No, it does not make me give up on the notion of a compassionate God, Timmy."

Mind you, Mercy thought, she had never known a pathologist who didn't smoke. It went with the job, like miners and miners' lung. They smoked because they could not take the stink if they didn't anaesthetise their sense of smell. That's what the last pathologist had told her. He'd died in the act of sewing up a suicide.

"The body can stay in the mortuary as long as is necessary. I haven't the faintest idea what will happen to it . . . If he was here illegally, I expect the problem would be handed to the Congolese embassy. I don't know, Timmy. Why are you so concerned over a body? It's the living you should be protecting. No, you're not making much of a job of that. No leads? . . . You're looking for Arthur Whitworth? In Blubberhouses? No, Timmy, I can't come back. Not this time."

Sad, that. But expected. She was too strong and he was too weak. Or something of the sort. It stood out a mile. Probably she needed taking in hand – probably a side of her wanted that like anything. But Timmy Dyer wasn't the man to do it. Offhand Mercy couldn't think of a man who *could* have done it.

Dr Gonne rang off. She looked up, saw her cleaner for the first time. "Men!" she said, "What would you do with them?"

"Search me," Mercy replied. "Mine walked out. Disappeared in a puff of smoke. That's why I'm here, I suppose."

"I didn't know that."

"You never asked, Dr Gonne."

"I'm always a bit distracted."

You're always miserable, Mercy thought. "Busy, I expect. A lot on your mind and that."

"Sorry? What did you say?"

"Nothing. No leads in the *Dying in Style* case, are there?"

"What makes you ask?"

"Well, it's interesting. I'm interested, along with the rest of the country. I haven't read the book, but they're serialising it in the paper and I feel like I've read it from all the stuff on the telly and in the papers. Do you think Arthur Whitworth did it?"

"I've no idea, Mary,"

"Mercy."

"Mercy. No idea."

"Go back to Inspector Dyer, Dr Gonne."

"What? What did you say?"

Mercy turned away and started dusting again. "Nothing," she said.

❧ ❧ ❧

Constable Keeley walked into the bar of The Stalker which, he supposed, might have been Arthur Whitworth's local in Blubberhouses. The six or seven men crouched at the bar like crows on a fence stopped talking and looked at the door. Keeley had known that would happen; it was that sort of place. He hitched up his pants – it felt like the thing to do – and approached the bar trying to think of something neutral to order.

Deciding to ask for the local bitter, he ordered a pint of it and remarked on how good the weather was. The publican grunted something about drought. When he paid and the man came back with his change Keeley asked if he could have a word.

"What about?"

"About Arthur Whitworth."

"What's it worth?"

"You've been asked before, have you?" Keeley asked.

The publican, a thin man with a fat temperament that hung off him in folds, turned to the still-silent bar, and shouted, "He wants to know about Arthur Whitworth!"

The gents at the bar covered ears, let out collective sighs. One slumped his head down on the bar and started to snore.

"You ought to have got a tape made, John!" said a young, well-chinned man wearing a patchwork cap.

"Ask him what it's worth!"

"Already have," replied John,

"I'm a police officer," Keeley said, "from London."

John straightened up. He seemed sobered. Keeley felt his self-confidence rise.

But then John turned to the bar, thumbed towards Keeley: "A police office. From London!" he called out.

More sighs, shaking of heads. The same man collapsed his head on the bar. It made a thud that quite alarmed Keeley for a moment before he came back up smiling.

"I wonder if I might ask you a few questions. You know, alone."

"We've no secrets here," John said. "What I can tell

you is easily told. Arthur Whitworth never came in here. He bought his booze at The Mace."

"So you can't tell me anything about him?"

"I didn't say that, did I? I just said he never came in here. From what I saw of him he was OK. Some people thought he was snobby, but I'd say he was more on the shy side myself."

"Do you think he was the type to commit suicide? I mean, did he seem highly strung?"

John, looking uncertain, peered at a washed glass for streaks.

"He used to be my teacher," offered a customer in the corner whom Keeley had barely noticed.

"Did he?" Keeley walked over to the man, a man not much older than himself. "Mind if I ask you a few questions?"

"Does that mean we're free to get back to our pints?" asked one of the crows.

"By all means," Keeley said, then he added in a way he had seen policemen – on the television mainly – speak: "for the moment."

There were muffled repetitions of the phrase from the crows, followed by laughter.

Keeley mounted the bar-stool next to the young man. The plastic top had been ripped at some point and mended with ducting tape. Keeley was never without ducting tape himself.

"Have you been asked all this before?" Keeley asked.

"You haven't asked me anything yet."

"No, but about Arthur Whitworth in school. My name's Desmond, by the way."

"Winston. I don't come in that often. Once a week. Thursdays usually. Like today."

"Pay-day?"

"Dole-day."

"I see. Are jobs hard to find round here?"

"Decent ones are. I only got two O levels: English language and literature . . . that was in the days when they had O levels."

"What did Arthur Whitworth teach you?"

"English."

"Good teacher, was he?"

"He got results. Look at me. Trouble was he couldn't put up with bad behaviour."

"And he had bad behaviour to put up with?"

Winston shrugged. "Quite a bit, yes. Kids can spot a weakness in teachers a mile off. Arty was hopeless at discipline. We gave him a hard time."

"But you still managed to pass the English exams?"

"Almost all of us did. Don't ask me how. He just kept at it. Sometimes the row got so bad that you couldn't hear him. Still, something must have gone in."

"But he wasn't popular?"

Winston thought. "You know, he *was* popular. Most of us really had a lot of time for Arty."

"So why did you act up?"

"I've heard some daft questions in my time . . . "

"It seems fair enough to me."

"Don't all kids of that age act up? We couldn't help ourselves. Looking back it all seems . . . I don't know . . . wicked. We liked him, but we just had to play up."

"What sort of things did you do?"

"Imitating his voice, farting, throwing things. Mind you, there was one kid in the class who made the rest of us look like bloody angels. He was the sort of ringleader like. He had the class wound about his little finger. I suppose without him it wouldn't have got so bad."

"What's his name?"

"Hector Parris. Arthur often used to say that he was well-named."

"Why?"

"That's what Hector used to ask. I can still see him. 'Why, sir?'"

"And did Arthur ever tell Hector why?"

"Not in so many words, no. He'd smile and with a shaking hand – his hand always shook in our class – he'd plonk his foot down on the teacher's stool and point to the heel."

Keeley nodded, as stumped as the class had been. "Did you ever see him cry?"

"Yes. He was real close to it quite a few times, but he cried just the once. And that was it. We never saw him again after that."

"What brought it on, do you remember?"

"Yes, I remember all right. It started off same as usual. Hector Parris was larking about. We'd been reading through *The Merchant of Venice* with different kids playing roles. Parris had caused trouble. The usual thing. Then he started swearing; fuck this and bugger that and on and on. Arty stopped the reading and said, 'Parris, you take over as Portia. Act so and so, scene so and so,'" Winston stopped, drained his pint.

Keeley signalled the barman for refills.

"Thanks," Winston said. They waited, Winston's account put on hold until the arrival of the pint. Keeley thought of Roberta Coleman in her hospital ward with Sergeant Drury guarding her. Sergeant Drury said he was dreading the removal of the bandages from Roberta's face. All the police guards were. They had really fallen for Roberta. Though they had only seen half her face, she had won their hearts completely.

"Cheers!" Winston said, and he took a long gulp from

his new pint. "I can remember feeling as if something was in the wind. Arty never asked Parris to read because if there was one thing Arty couldn't stand it was hearing literature crucified. And Parris always put on a show. And he came out with everything in this really flat monotone. Like a dalek. And it drove Arty nuts. Anyway, that's why I was all worried when Parris was asked . . . "

"What did he read?"

"Portia. Like I said," Winston replied, "the trial scene. As he read, I could see Arty shaking more and more. Then his hands went up to cover his eyes. He sat down at the teacher's desk, still covering his eyes. But he couldn't cover the sound – and I can still hear that sound – of weeping. Finally, even Parris saw that he'd gone too far. He stopped. The class was silent. We looked up at Arty. He took his hands from his face and was staring back at us. A shocking moment – and it *was* shocking. I don't think any of us had ever seen a man looking like that. Not in real life. On the box maybe. But not in real life. I'll never forget it." Winston shivered slightly and reached for his drink.

"But what did Parris do to bring it on?" Keeley asked.

By way of reply, Winston came close to Keeley: *"The fucking quality of mercy is not bleeding strained. It droppeth like shit from fucking heaven upon the shit-house beneath."*

Keeley smiled weakly, and drew back. "Charming," he said.

"Anyway, we never saw Arty after that, not to speak to. We heard he took early retirement. That's what the head said."

"And you've never seen him since?"

"I have seen him, yes," Winston said. "I saw him in Skipton once; helped him carry a carton of wine to his car."

"How did he seem?"

"Fine. He asked about the class. There was only one thing odd, I've remembered it since because it was so odd . . . though maybe not."

"What was so odd?"

"Well, seeing as Parris had been buried that day and seeing as the case had been big in the town, it was odd that he didn't mention it."

"You mean Parris is dead?"

"He topped himself. His mother found him hanging in the barn."

Keeley considered. "When was this?"

"A couple of years after Arty left teaching."

"And he'd turned to writing by then?"

"Yes, his first book was out."

"Have you read it?"

"No."

"That's odd."

"Maybe," Winston said. "I always thought I'd get round to it, but whenever I think of Arthur Whitworth I think of him blubbing. I thought that reading one of his books would make me feel worse, specially one called *Teacher*."

"Why do you think Hector Parris topped himself?"

"No idea. Maybe he was a bit of a star at school but when he left and had to work all isolated on a hill-farm with no one but the sheep to impress, he got depressed. His uncle had done the same thing . . . you know . . . way back."

"Hanged himself?"

Winston nodded.

"And what about you? No idea about jobs?" Keeley asked, suddenly anxious to get back to the B and B and tell Dyer what he had heard.

"I might go down to London and have a look around."

"Why not apprentice yourself to a plumber. It's not a bad life. You meet interesting people."

Winston looked at Keeley.

"I used to be a plumber."

"But you're not now?"

"No, I'm not now," Keeley replied Then, thinking of Dyer back in the double room of the B and B, he said, "It's a hard old job climbing the greasy pole in the police, though. Be a plumber."

❧ ❧ ❧

The days passed quickly for Arthur and Monica. At first she kept hinting that they would have to tell the authorities he was still alive; that all this could not go on. Every day made it worse. But Arthur replied that it was all too interesting to stop in its tracks. She, chuffed by company and cuddles in bed and kitchen, building castles amidst the flowery wallpaper that covered all walls of the cottage, went along with it. Arthur was an artist after all.

There were times when Arthur would become distracted. Again she put it down to his artistic temperament. He'd sit in the easy-chair that had been her favourite before he arrived and look through the PVC double-glazing to the sea. She did not know what he was thinking.

Arthur was thinking how peculiar it all was. Things were starting to unfold exactly as he had plotted in *Dying in Style*. True, the obituaries were not as he had imagined they would be. Perhaps Audrey Saunders, his agent, was not relieved to see the back of him. But what made him so reluctant to call a halt – to change at one stroke the scenario and pronounce himself living – was precisely the thought that had come to him when close to death in Morecambe Bay. Then, the thought of extinction had been hard because it stopped his story stone-dead. Now, like Mark Twain, another writer whose death had been brought forward in error, he could watch "from the other side" the unravelling of his own story. He might as well have been sitting on a cloud watching life on earth as in Monica's cosy armchair watching the sea.

Daily, he sent Monica out to buy all the papers. While in WH Smith she was ordered to see if any of his books were in stock. That first day she came back with one paper containing an obituary – generous but anonymous – and the news that two copies of *Teacher* were on display.

Arthur nodded, not quite knowing what he had imagined. A special, crepe-surrounded, display? Weeping and gnashing of teeth among the doilies and cassettes . . . intimations of literary immortality?

But that was pushing his story past the line of credibility. Better be a pessimist. Whenever Arthur Whitworth had entered a bookshop when "living" he would think, if his books were on display, that they would never sell. If they were not in evidence, that they had never darkened the doors of the shop in the first place. In bookshops, too, came other subtle or not-so-subtle intimations of vices he had not thought himself a prey to. Special displays given to other writers: posters, stacks, whole windows full of one book, had made him feel – momentarily but profoundly – an envy melding into hatred. Of course, he stifled the emotions; told himself that it was unworthy and petty, but he could not stop them bubbling up.

This had never happened to him when he was a teacher. This had never happened before publicity became his master and he its poodle.

Then one day Monica came home loaded with groceries and the day's papers – full of the death of Audrey Saunders in Westminster Abbey.

"Who was she?" Monica asked, looking over his shoulder, watching his red neck draining of blood.

"My agent," replied Arthur Whitworth, "and a character in *Dying in Style*."

Smoothing a crumpled antimacassar as she moved around the sofa, Monica sat down beside Arthur. "Do you mean your agent's dead, or the character from *Dying in Style*, Arthur?" she asked.

"Both."

"You mean the woman found in Westminster Abbey was your agent?"

"Yes."

"And a character in the novel?"

"Yes. I based the literary agent on Audrey Saunders."

"Based?"

"Yes. Based," Arthur replied. "God, what am I going to do?"

Monica took his hand. Arthur looked at it there. It was uncanny. This was exactly how it had been in the past. She thought about what to say, as Arthur read the news reports of the Audrey Saunders's death. It was strange how his guilt came bubbling up to the surface. Surely an over-reaction; surely this must be a coincidence. Still, it was quite clear that Arthur did not see it as a coincidence.

"Arthur," she said, "people die, you know."

"It doesn't say *how* she died. But foul play is suspected."

"I honestly don't see the problem. Maybe it was naughty of you to model this character on your agent, but that's about the extent of it . . . " she paused, " . . . isn't it?"

"No, it isn't! I wrote *Dying in Style* in order of get at the people who were doing me down. It was a devilish prayer for vengeance. I was livid with Audrey for not doing enough for me, for not backing my books. There were times when *I wished her dead*. I murdered her in the book and now she's been murdered in real life."

There was a knock at the door. "Don't answer it, Monica!"

"What do you mean, 'don't answer it', Arthur!"

"Well, give me time to get out of the way."

Monica paused as Arthur darted into the bedroom, clearing away all evidence of his presence as he went.

She answered the door, thanked the delivery-man for the parcel, a dress from the Kay catalogue unless she was very much mistaken.

Sitting on the sofa, Monica unwrapped the package. Yes, it was the dress. She called for Arthur, but there was no answer. She waited.

Arthur Whitworth was lying on the floor, next to the bed. He turned and saw balls of fluff underneath it, next to an Antler suitcase. That didn't go with Monica somehow. Or maybe it did. He had pigeon-holed Monica as "tidy and efficient spinster". But was that right? What was right? Could you ever really know people?

There was Audrey Saunders, dead and in a morgue somewhere, her pretty body violated by some pathologist. He had, because of the job she did for him, decided upon her character. But what really did he know? What was the fluff under the bed in Audrey's case? It did not come near to describing Monica, his Good Samaritan. He suddenly saw Audrey Saunders rushing from her agency to man a helpline, take over as a volunteer at the Oxfam shop, demonstrating with a candle for *Amnesty*. He laughed at the thought. Totally out of character! But what did he know? What did *he* know? What did he *know*?

The twinges he had when writing about people lifted from real life were turning into a great body-enveloping pain. No, he would never in his wildest dreams have wished such a fate on Audrey, but at the typewriter he felt free. Had some crazed reader – and judging from the sales there weren't many readers crazed or otherwise – taken it into his head to turn fantasy into reality? No, it was too daft. Nobody would swallow that if it were a plot. Still . . . " And Arthur Whitworth clicked from reality and began thinking up fiction.

Monica, in her new dress, pleased with the look and fit, knocked at the door offering tea.

"Coming, Monica!" Arthur Whitworth called, like his old self.

ஃ ஃ ஃ

"It's odd, you have to admit," said Constable Keeley to Dyer.

"Read me that bit again," Dyer said. He was drinking neat whisky from the plastic cap of his shaving-foam can.

Keeley took up his copy of *Teacher* and read:

"'Wondering why me, are we, Haddock? Wondering why Teacher got you to do that odd dictation of a suicide note? Wondering, perhaps, if this is all a dream. No, you're not dreaming, Haddock. The place you stand is where our revered headmaster stands, high above a sea of students. The skipping-rope around your neck is hessian; thin, true, but thick enough I have no doubt to carry a Haddock away from dull mundanity to the realms of the afterworld. Death is but a push away, Haddock. Teacher will push you, make you drink from the celestial cup of endless morphia. You are not dreaming, Haddock.'

'Please, sir!'

'"Please sir!" A petition to move the gods to tears. But not Teacher, Haddock! You will die and shortly too. But I would not send you to your eternal fate without telling you why you go: you are going to die, Haddock, so that the rest may live. Education is important. You have been stopping the majority from receiving it. You have bullied, brayed, barged the days away, and your misdeeds have wasted many thousands of hours of this school's time. You have killed many futures stone-cold dead. Teacher has told you of this many times over the years, has he not?'

Silence.

'Has he not?'

Silence.

'Has he not?'

'Yes, sir!'

'"Yes, sir!" Respect! Such a strange jewel to find in a Haddock's mouth. Any last requests? Within reason.'

Haddock launched forth on a stream of language. Teacher, soon tiring of it, ascended the stage of the assembly hall, marched to the headmaster's podium and pushed Haddock from it into the yawning space that lies between the knowing and the unknowing . . . the teacher and the pupil . . . the living and the dead.

Then, placing the note that Haddock had written for him during detention on the floor of the headmaster's podium, Teacher left Haddock swinging."

"Mmm, you read well, Desmond," Dyer said. "Ever thought of taking up teaching yourself, have you?"

"Never gave it a thought, sir."

"Read the whole novel, have you?"

"Every word, sir."

"Are there any other murders?"

"The Minister of Education and several members of the inspectorate."

"And does Teacher . . . does he have a name?"

"No, sir. He's known as 'Teacher' throughout."

"Does Teacher get his just desserts, Desmond?"

"No, sir. He gets away scot-free and takes early retirement. With enhancement."

"Enhancement, yet?"

"Yes, sir."

"So is it a satisfactory read? I mean, Haddock – and he sounds like a proper little shit – gets rather more than one might consider appropriate."

Keeley interrupted, "Haddock was a real swine, sir. He was a bully and a sadist. To tell you the truth, I was really chuffed when he got what was coming to him."

"Was this before or after you interviewed the chap in the pub . . . what's-'is-name?"

"Winston Boswell. Before, sir."

"But knowing what you know now, what do you think?"

"It's a bit of a coincidence."

"You know, I think it's about time we interviewed some of Arthur Whitworth's colleagues. We know he didn't have any friends after he 'retired'. But he must have had a few at that school where he taught. What was the name again?"

"St Mary's Comprehensive, sir."

"Ah, yes, St Mary's. I think we'd better call in at St Mary's in the morning. What do you think?"

Desmond Keeley nodded. Then he went into the en-suite bathroom to take off his clothes, put on his pyjamas – tops and bottoms – and get ready for bed.

❧ ❧ ❧

Earlier that same evening, Dr Edith Gonne approached the foot of Roberta Coleman's hospital bed holding a pot of violets. Roberta was sitting up in bed, reading the day's paper.

"It's Roberta, isn't it?" Edith said.

Roberta looked nonplussed.

"Don't worry, dear," said Edith. "The policeman cleared me at the door. I'm Edith, Detective Inspector Dyer's wife. He asked me to pop in to see you."

"That was kind."

"I won't stay long; you probably get more visitors than you want. Judging from the flowers. Mind if I sit down?"

Roberta gestured Edith to sit in the bedside chair.

"I'm terribly sorry about what happened. Still, the nurse tells me you're well along the road to recovery."

"I'm leaving hospital tomorrow, I think," Roberta said.

Edith nodded. "As well as being Timmy Dyer's wife, I'm also a pathologist. Timmy mentioned that you were worried about your friend, the African man, Patrice Luala."

"Yes," Roberta said. "I know it's a bit late to be worried, but I don't want him – his body – to be sent back to the Congo."

"It's all arranged," Edith said. "His body can be released whenever you want. Just say the word. I've brought you all the paperwork."

Edith reached into her bag and took out several sheets of paper. "I think you'll find everything is in order."

Roberta took the papers off the coverlet of her bed and read them. The tears started. "I'm listed as next-of-kin."

Edith took her hand. "I know, dear," she said. "I know."

Roberta reached for a tissue and rubbed away the tears, then blew her nose. "You've taken a weight from my mind," she said.

"Good."

"Tell me," Roberta continued, "were you the pathologist who . . . ?"

"Yes. I know it's probably no consolation, but Patrice died instantly. He wouldn't have known anything about it."

"It's all my fault."

"It was the fault of whoever did the murder, Roberta. Nobody else's," Edith said sternly.

Roberta nodded, sniffed, then cuffed her wet face with the sleeve of her nightdress. "How long can you keep him . . . the body?"

"We can keep him for as long as necessary. When you've decided on arrangements – and take your time – he can be released into your care."

"I don't want undertakers," Roberta said. "I want to do everything myself."

"How do you mean?"

"I was Patrice's only friend in London – a poor friend – but Patrice told me once how he'd buried his brother. He and a few friends carried him to the graveyard and dug the grave themselves. He couldn't understand the way the English give their loved ones over to strangers. The big cars. The expense."

"Tell me about Patrice."

Roberta told Edith what she knew. It did not take long. Then she was back to the subject of funerals. "We once published a book about DIY funerals. You need a coffin, a Ford Transit or a large Estate, a grave or cremation service and a place to store the body prior to burial. You're looking after Patrice. All I have to do is find everything else."

"I've a Volvo Estate, if that would help."

"You've already been so kind."

"When you're ready, I'll help you with the funeral in

any way I can. Apart from anything else, it will be a learning experience. If Timmy goes on the way he's going, I'll have to bury him."

"You've read *Dying in Style*, have you?"

"No."

"Oh," said Roberta, "I thought you had."

Then the conversation turned to Detective Inspector Dyer.

Finally, just before Edith left, Roberta told her about her pregnancy.

Two hours later, Dr Edith Gonne, blessing herself, was walking out of Westminster Cathedral, battling against the wind blowing across the piazza to light a cigarette. Just as she seemed on the point of succeeding, a beggar came up, asked for spare change, and was wafted away by Edith. The light went out with the distraction. Edith cursed and walked on.

It was not until she had sheltered in the doorway of MacDonalds on Victoria Street that she managed to light her cigarette. Then, drawing deep of the smoke, she turned and walked towards Westminster.

As she passed the Army and Navy Stores, it began to rain, then abruptly stopped. Edith lit another cigarette from the stub of the old one. A woman walking past her in the opposite direction gave her a killing look. Edith looked straight back, imagining the woman, grey, flaccid, exposed – lost to everything she had covered and primped and powdered and creamed and cared for – to Dr Edith Gonne, pathologist, and her slicing implements.

Dusk was well advanced by the time Edith passed Westminster Abbey. The floodlights turned the building more golden with each pulse into night, each step she took.

Nights were drawing in again. It might soon be time to call Timmy and tell him to come back for the winter. After all, she was back on the fags as bad as ever, her addiction to nicotine compounded by the squares of nicotine-impregnated gum she chewed, often with a cigarette in her mouth at the same time. She needed diversion and Timmy Dyer provided diversion on long winter evenings.

Edith arrived at Westminster Bridge and wondered whether to cross the zebra and proceed back to her mother's along the Embankment on the north side. That way, St Paul's – always a pleasure – would lie ahead of her. But seeing the long line of traffic, thinking of Mother waiting, asking about Miss Mullin, she decided to cross the bridge and walk along the Embankment close to the National Theatre and away from the hubbub.

Miss Mullin, priests' housekeeper for all her adult life, daily mass-goer, visitor to the poor and sick, unoiled, unsqueaky cog in the Catholic wheel, had been found in the gas-filled kitchen of the presbytery the day before. Her ticket for the Sea Cat, purse full of Irish punts, small suitcase, had been found sitting forlornly in the hall next to the front door.

The parish priest called Edith. Edith went round and had gone into the kitchen where Miss Mullin sat, her hat still on, rosary wound around her gnarled fingers, a peculiar look – half pain, half pique – on her slack features.

What can she see now? Edith thought. This was her habitual thought when faced with corpses. Despite decades of work with her enquiring scalpel, the body held tight to its mystery. She could cut and saw and delve all she liked, the body denied access to *something*. Something fought off all enquiry. Cause of death it yielded up easily enough, but cause of life lay hidden.

Edith prayed for hovering souls while cutting up leaden flesh.

"You'll have to phone the police, Father," Edith said.

Father Kelly shuffled. "I know. Of course. But I was wondering . . . this is going to sound dreadful."

"They'll be discreet," Edith said.

She had hit the right button.

"A terrible thing to happen."

"Why did she do it?" Edith asked.

"I blame myself," said the priest.

Miss Mullin had given Edith's mother a daily account of her decision to leave and go back to Ireland. She had told the priest, who said little, save to enquire about her period of notice. Edith had heard of Miss Mullin's doubts that she could pick up her life in Ireland; that she would know people there; that she could not bear the idea of living with her sister; that no provision had been made for her pension.

Well might the priest blame himself! Of course he was going to feel guilty. Good. Miss Mullin's body lay in the mortuary waiting for her in the morning. She would not, she decided, perform an autopsy. She'd sign the papers, have a word with the coroner and let the undertaker send her home on the Ryanair flight to Knock Airport. One more obscure martyr.

Edith had mused her way to the centre of Westminster Bridge. A man was standing alone, looking up-river past the Houses of Parliament towards Chelsea. He had a large stereo headset on, connected doubtless to a small stereo player. Was he a tourist receiving a dose of history? A fan of classical music heightening the experience of watching the gold-lit architecture with a bit of Elgar? An airhead scrambling his brains, destroying his hearing, with Gonne-disapproved-of pop?

Edith was passing behind the man, had already almost forgotten him, when she heard the sound of sobbing. In comparison to the traffic noise, the buzz of the city, the sobbing was nothing to speak of. She walked on a few paces, then stopped.

Before she had considered how unlike her this was – remembering Miss Mullin – Dr Edith Gonne was behind the man and had asked, "Is everything all right?"

The man did not turn. The sobbing continued. Of course, he could not hear her with the headphones on. "Is everything all right?" she repeated, louder.

The man still did not turn. Instead, oblivious to her, he lifted one leg up onto the bridge rail. Then he seemed to jump upwards and the other leg was up, so that his left leg was akimbo while his right knee knelt on the rail. Edith reached out and took the man's arm. He turned at the touch and for a moment they looked into one another's eyes. The man opened his mouth to speak but at that moment lost his balance and fell, though Edith made an attempt to hold him.

She heard no splash. The traffic continued as if nothing had happened. Perhaps nothing *had* happened. One more death. Edith Gonne looked past the lights into the water. A pleasure steamer was passing through one of the arches of the bridge. People on deck were dancing. They did not seem to have seen the man fall. Only she, Edith, had seen.

She stood for a long time looking down. She said a *De Profundis*. Then, coming to herself, she ran back to the Palace of Westminster to get help from the policeman at the gate.

The river police were alerted. Edith gave the police her details and continued her walk back to her mother's flat in Bloomsbury, taking a route that avoided the Thames.

Weary, she passed Miss Mullin's presbytery and said a

prayer. She might go there to Sunday mass the following Sunday just to hear what the priest would say. Then she might back out of the church – and The Church – yet again. One way or another, it had been an eventful evening. She would have to tell Timmy all about it.

❧ ❧ ❧

Dyer was having a mug of Nescafé in the staff room of St Mary's Comprehensive at breaktime the following morning. The head of English, Peter Hall, had handed him the mug telling him how honoured he was because it had been Arthur Whitworth's. Dyer looked at the pottery mug, which held close to a pint, and read the legend painted under the glaze: *Ex libris: Arthur Whitworth.*

"Very nice," Dyer remarked. "Do you keep it in a glass case?"

"No," replied Peter Hall, "it's got to take its chances with the rest. Left on the draining-board. It's a popular mug, probably because it holds so much."

"Have you seen anything of its owner since he retired?" Dyer asked.

"In the flesh, no," replied the teacher, "I saw him on the television once. Read a few things about him."

"Do you know his books?"

"Yes, I've read them all."

"What do you think of them?"

"A good read."

"Nothing more? Would you say they're built to last?"

"Arthur was no Hardy. I think he would have been the first to admit it."

"You think he's dead, then?"

Peter Hall looked at Dyer. "Yes. Is there any doubt?"

"But what about all the fuss over *Dying in Style*?"

"I don't take any notice of that."

"Don't you?" Dyer asked. "We do, Mr Hall."

"Well, it's your business. We've got an OFSTED coming up." Peter Hall made a gesture to include the whole of the glass and cement structure that was St Mary's Comprehensive. "This is my domain. A great big sepulchre to white. Personally, I don't think Arthur would hurt a fly."

"Well, his books have caused several flies to be spattered to the wall, Mr Hall."

Peter Hall did not react.

"Right then," said Dyer at last, "can you tell us any members of staff who did keep up with Arthur Whitworth?"

"Monica – she was the deputy head – and Arthur were quite close."

"Was, you mean she isn't here any more?"

"No, she retired some years ago. Ill-health."

"Would anyone have her address, do you think?"

Peter Hall shouted across the staffroom. "Anyone know Monica's address?"

"Who wants to know?" asked a young woman with a ponytail. She was sitting in the corner of the staffroom smoking and blowing the smoke away from the man in the armchair next to her. Then she wafted her hand about, scooping up any wisps of smoke that might approach her silent colleague's nostrils.

Dyer approached. "Detective Inspector Dyer, miss," he said.

The man in the armchair looked at Dyer, then up at his smoking colleague. "They've come to get you, May," he said.

"Nice to see a school with such a liberal smoking policy," Dyer said to May, feeling his pockets.

"She's a law unto herself that one," said the teacher in the armchair. "The last of the fumers."

May looked at the teacher mock-angrily.

"We'd miss her if she wasn't here, though," he continued.

"Would you have Monica Gardiner's address?"

"What for?" May asked.

"I'm not at liberty to divulge that information, miss."

May burst into laughter. "I'm sorry. My class have been writing playlets and one or two have policemen in them. Last night, just as the 'Late Book' was finishing on the radio I drew a red line through exactly what you just said on one of my kids' plays. Then I wrote in big angry red letters, 'CLICHÉ! PEOPLE JUST DON'T SPEAK LIKE THIS ANYMORE'. But they do. They do. God!"

The teacher in the armchair looked at Dyer. "Poor May is within a hair's breadth of complete spiritual, intellectual, physical and moral breakdown . . . especially moral. I blame OFSTED myself. Nobody should be placed under such stress. It's more than flesh and blood can bear."

"I blame the teachers, Gord," May said.

"Mind you," said Gord, "there are some shocking parents about . . . off to the pub."

"And 'Top of the Pops' can't help," May said, dropping her cigarette into the lukewarm Nescafé dregs. It gasped and drowned.

Dyer watched them, warming to them. It was clearly a routine they had developed over the years. "That's all very well, miss," he said, "but concerning the aforementioned Monica Gardiner . . . "

May stifled another laugh, then seeing Dyer's alarmingly stern face – a stern face she had been imagining for months, looking rather like Dyer's and sitting at the back of her class judging all her works and finding them wanting – she sobered up, coughed. "It's just that Monica expressly told me not to give out her address." May looked across at Gord. "She didn't want any riff-raff harassing her."

"That's as may be," Dyer said, "but I'm sure you'll appreciate . . . "

May took out a notebook, wrote Monica's address and handed it to Dyer. "You're really looking for Arthur, aren't you? You think he may be holed up with Monica?"

"I'm not at liberty . . . "

"Well, take it from one who knows. Arthur's no murderer." May gave her colleague a prod. "Is he, Gord?"

Gordon shook his head. "'Course not."

Dyer nodded, and looked at the address. "Seaview Road," he said. "Near the sea, is it?"

"Any nearer and it'd be in the sea. Poor Monica was flooded out her first winter there. She'd bought all new carpets with her lump sum, too."

A piercing bell made Dyer jump. He watched the life draining out of the faces of May and Gord as they gathered their textbooks, bags of exercise books, together. May sprayed her tonsils with Gold Spot. Dyer's heart went out to them.

"Fancy missing your next period, do you?" he asked.

Their eyes lit up, like children offered the exact same thing.

"How?" May asked.

"Yes, how?" Gord asked.

"Using the powers invested in me as a police officer, I would like to ask you some questions in furtherance of my investigation into the *Dying in Style* murders."

May stifled another giggle, then went off in search of

the deputy head to tell him the glad tidings. As she left the room, she heard Dyer ask Gord, "Does the name Hector Parris ring any bells, sir?"

❧ ❧ ❧

That morning a body was gathered up into a police launch. It had been spotted belly-up by a commuter walking to work across Blackfriars Bridge while repeating an apt stanza from *The Waste Land* – something he did every day of his working life . . .

The body of LP Lomax arrived at the mortuary at about the same time as Dr Edith Gonne. She had been forced to back her car to allow the ambulance out of the gates.

It took her most of the day to reach down her list to the body.

When her assistant came in, wheeling the sheet-covered stretcher, he said, "A drowning. From his wallet we have identified that the man's name is LP Lomax. A stereo headset was found trailing from a pocket. Inside a portable CD player. Rather a good one. The sort people kill for."

"Oh, yes?" Dr Gonne asked. "Was there a disc inside?"

"Yes, there was," the assistant replied. *"Dido and Aeneas."*

The pathologist took the sheet from the naked body of LP Lomax. She at once recognized the face. "What time was he found?" she asked her assistant.

"Seven this morning."

"He'd been in the water ten hours," Edith said.

"You're sure?"

"Certain."

"But you haven't . . . "

"No, I know I haven't. It's just that I was there when he jumped. Odd, isn't it? I tried to stop him, if reaching out with a hand and grasping his arm is 'trying'. Anyway, this gentleman's last human contact when living was with the person who will have most intimate contact with him after death. Get him ready, will you? I need a fag."

Lighting up in her office, Edith saw a hearse backing into the yard. The back was opened and a pine coffin placed inside. "Bye-bye, Miss Mullin!" Edith said. "Eternal rest to you."

❧ ❧ ❧

"You'll have to tell the police, Arthur," Monica said.

"No," Arthur Whitworth replied.

Cyril Parkinson and the literary editor had been murdered. The press had made the connection and people were buying *Dying in Style* in great quantities. Monica had come back from Smiths to report that there was a notice in the bookshop window saying that the book was available within but that, when she went in, she had seen only empty display stacks where once it had been.

"But you've *got to*, Arthur!"

"What would be the point of that, Monica? With your evidence, they'd eliminate me from the list of suspects straight away but they'd be no nearer to catching the real murderer, would they?"

"But at the moment they're probably not looking for anyone except you, are they?"

"They think I'm dead."

"But without a body they're probably assuming that you arranged it all."

"Why would I arrange it all, Monica? To get the book

selling? And how would I enjoy the fruits of the sales in a prison cell for life?"

"Well, who do you think is doing it?"

"I wouldn't put it past any of them."

"Who?"

"The publishers for a start. Cutting Edge was on the edge. Giles Gibbons told me that he was depending on *Dying in Style* to get them out of trouble. A lot rode on that book."

"And you think that they'd go to this sort of length to publicise it?"

"Yes," Arthur said.

"Really?"

"No." Then he thought about it. "Too obvious. They'd have known they'd never get away with it."

"So, if it's not you and it's not the publishers, who is it?"

"I don't know, do I?"

"You wrote it."

"No, I didn't; I wrote a story and someone's stolen it for his own purposes."

"You talk as if one of your stories had been adapted for a television series."

Arthur smiled for the first time that morning. "I wish!"

"You can go off people, you know," Monica said, meaning it. "You were a far nicer person when you were teaching. Do you know that?"

"Nice is for cake," Arthur said.

"No it isn't! Nice is for anything I choose. You *were* nice at St Mary's. Now you're . . . "

"Heartless, callous, cold, calculating, egomaniacal, bitter, twisted. Not Nice."

"A bit of that, yes."

"You'd like me to be nice again, would you?"

"I would."

"And I'd be nicer if I went to the police, would I?"

"You would. You know you would. It's so bloody obvious."

"But don't you want to see what happens, Monica? Don't you want to see the end of the story? If I go to the police we'll never know how it would have gone."

"I don't get you, Arthur."

"Well let me spell it out, then. I've been through every emotion in the book since coming to you. I've felt guilt about blowing people away in print – people I could see before my eyes as I wrote. I've been wondering what cold . . . what *evil* . . . part of me could have set this rolling. But now that it is rolling I know the answer. It's story that's at the bottom of it. Stories are what we want and what I always wanted to make. Now millions of people are reading one of my stories because it's becoming true. I can't – I won't – walk into the middle of it and say "That's it!" It's started, so it'll finish. I trust I make myself obscure?"

"I'd better get a copy of *Dying in Style*," Monica said.

"Why?"

"To see what's in it for me."

"You won't tell the police, will you?"

"I'll have to think about that, Arthur," she replied, moving towards the kitchen. "I won't do it behind your back. I'll tell you first if I'm going to."

"That's good of you, Mon."

Monica turned. "Good? No, I don't think it's good. Quite the contrary, I'd say."

❧ ❧ ❧

Giles Gibbons invited Jim Smart to dinner at the Garrick. It was, he felt, the very least he could do.

Jim had arrived on time, then excused himself straight away to visit the gents. Giles got him a drink and waited.

Jim returned. "It's very impressive, isn't it?" he said.

"I can't believe this is your first time at The Garrick?" Giles said, "Didn't I ever bring you?"

"No," Jim said, "I'd have remembered."

"But we have been out together, haven't we?"

"Several times. Joe Allan's usually."

Giles winced.

"I expect you're planning your retirement," Jim said.

"Not just yet, Jim. But I can't deny that *Dying in Style* is getting me set fair to living in style."

"It's a pity the author couldn't be around to see it, isn't it?"

"It is a pity. Royalties are building up."

"You think he may be behind the murders?"

"The thought had occurred to me."

"I see LP Lomax, the music critic, is the latest to go. We had a sudden surge in the shops when the news broke."

Giles nodded. "They reckon this one may have been just a suicide. Grief-stricken over Cyril Parkinson, people say. There's no accounting for taste. Everything going all right with supplies? I've been working damned hard to keep you in copies. Had to refuse a request from Australia for a hundred thousand of the English edition to keep you topped up."

"We're OK. At the moment."

"Have you read the book yet?" Giles asked.

"No. Keep meaning to but . . . you know . . ."

"How are things with young Mandy?"

Jim looked to left and right, "She's gone, Giles. Left a note saying as how she needed time to think. No address. No telephone number. Nothing."

"I'm sorry, Jim," Giles said.

"What do women want, Giles? What?"

"Search me," Giles replied. "Still, I'm sure she'll be back. It's not as if it's the first time."

Jim shook his head. "Not sure I want her back, Giles. A man can take only so much. I'm only flesh and blood when all's said and done."

Giles nodded understandingly. "You know that Cutting Edge is back to being a one-man operation again, do you?"

"Sorry?"

"Roberta, my publicity person, has resigned. She refused to see me. Flowers I sent to the hospital were returned."

"Still, she's had a shocking time," Jim said. "Makes me see my troubles in perspective when I see what others have to go through."

Giles nodded his agreement. "How true! How true!" he said. "You know, one of the last things Roberta did before she was hurt was write a glowing report on Arthur Whitworth's new novel. We're rushing it through the presses now, then straight into the shops. No review copies. I'm going to put a dedication to Patrice and Morag in it. Something like, 'To Morag Aitken and Patrice Luala: RIP'. What do you think? I think Arthur would have liked that." And Giles stared at his glass of champagne, eyes glazed by sorrow.

"I think that's fine. We'll take a few hundred thousand off your hands."

"Now that's what I like to hear, Jim," Giles said.

Jim looked worried again. "I hope you don't mind my saying this, Giles . . . " Jim said.

"Fire away."

"You look . . . I don't know . . . tired. Have you thought of taking a holiday?"

"I'd love to, Jim," Giles replied, "but at the moment it's out of the question. All I can manage is the odd weekend in the country. Still, when the pressure's off . . ."

"It's been a hard time for you, hasn't it?"

"It has, Jim. It has," said Giles Gibbons. He lifted the champagne to his lips and drank it down.

❧ ❧ ❧

When Morag Aitken was electrocuted in her shower, Monica said that enough was enough. If Arthur wouldn't inform the authorities then she would. He tried to persuade her, to convince her that turning him in would not change anything. When she told him that he'd changed his tune since last she brought up the matter, he said that, rather than face all the publicity, the press, the cameras, he'd walk back into the sea.

"Arthur," she said, "you didn't do these terrible things. Why are you so worried? What you'll have to face is nothing compared with what that poor girl . . ."

"Morag . . ."

" . . . With what Morag went through. Are you going to just let this go on? You said yourself that Morag had been a great friend to you."

"She has. But how will it change anything?"

"You're tying me up in knots, Arthur. You've got to think about me for a change. I don't want this to go on any longer. It's making me ill with the strain."

Arthur nodded. "OK," he said, "if that's what you want."

"Tomorrow, we phone the police. They'll come round and we'll tell them everything."

Again the nod.

"I'm going to bed now, Arthur."

He did not follow her into her room. He lay on the sofa looking out at the sea, thinking of everything that had happened.

The murderer had departed from the plot. If he or she had followed the book with care, it ought to have been Roberta who was killed. That might indicate that the murderer was a stranger to the workings of Cutting Edge. Or, perhaps, the murderer wanted to appear to be a stranger, to make an error accidentally on purpose.

Now that Morag was dead, who would help him work out the finer details of his books? Morag had been indispensable to him from the start. Perhaps the murderer wanted to remove all his supports one by one: his agent, his editor . . . all the people who had helped magnify his spidery writing into widely-distributed books. It just wasn't fair. It wasn't fair . . .

Arthur Whitworth caught himself. If Monica knew what he was thinking! It wasn't very *nice* was it? He was reducing all those lives to so many stepping-stones along his path to writing fame and fortune. What had happened to him?

But what would become of him without Morag, without Audrey? Mind you, with the book selling the way it was, perhaps their deaths were contributing to his future, his fame, his pension fund. Once he and Monica had explained everything to the police, he would be given a ticking-off and be able to retire back to write in well-heeled obscurity. There would be a queue of Audreys, of Morags, waiting to help the rich author climb to ever-greater heights But . . .

Arthur's brain spent the night – often against the commands of his consciousness and Janus conscience – working out plots, sub-plots – planning future novels in a cushioned solitude.

Only as dawn broke did he fall into dreamless sleep.

At eleven he woke to sunshine through the windows. He thought of Monica, wondered why she had not woken him. Panic at the thought that she might have left the house and gone to inform the police gripped him. He went to the front door, but the chain was on. Ditto the back. He approached Monica's room, knocked at the door. No reply. He opened it and saw Monica curled up on the bed. The duvet was on the floor.

Arthur went over to her and shook her. There was no response.

"Come on, Mon. Wake up, love!" Arthur said.

But Monica Gardiner, though always willing to do all she could for Arthur Whitworth – being dead, could not help him out this time.

ぐ ぐ ぐ

Jim Smart entered his empty house the following Friday night. The sound his key made in the lock, the way the door opened with a dead echo, reminded him of the emptiness of his home.

As he did most evenings, ever since Mandy's departure, he made straight for the drinks cupboard before he had even taken off his jacket. Pinned to the gin bottle, a typed note:

Jim:
If you want to get in touch
Ring this number and mention Mandy and Jafnna
334 5563

Jim looked at the note, wondering what it meant. Then he opened the gin. He turned on the television, flicked channels as he drank one gin after another. At ten he read the note again. He reached for the phone and rang the number.

A private sex club. He mentioned Mandy's name and the dour man on the other end said he'd been expecting a call. He'd be welcome any time. Jim phoned for a taxi and went to the club.

Jim Smart walked up three flights of steep stairs. He opened the door on the cinema and fumbled his way to a seat in the dark. He sat surrounded by upwards of twenty silent men, all watching the screen. His attention wandered. The gin had not made him drunk, merely blank. He looked around, away from the gyrating bodies, aware of the airless atmosphere of the place, the slight nausea brought on by the drink, compounded by the complicated congress on the screen, the unremitting cheap music.

The film ended with sprays of semen or wallpaper fixative, with spurious moans and cries and close-ups. The screen went blank. The silent men shuffled in their dark, unsatisfied, never satisfied, wanting more.

Then, Mandy was on the screen, walking along a deserted beach. Palm trees swayed. *All Kinds of Everything* was playing. She took off her top and the seats in the cinema creaked. Three fishermen, beaching their boats, saw her. They approached, wishing Mandy good-day. They coaxed her towards a beach-hut. Mandy seemed unsure of herself.

Inside, the men took Jim Smart's wife, then, when they were sated, a group of soldiers arrived, took the fishermen away, while Mandy cowered on the bed. The soldiers returned.

Jim sat engrossed, seeing in full colour what had been getting into Mandy all that time. He felt himself shrivelling up; his spare tyre bit into the metal of his belt-buckle. He knew as Mandy took, strained, accepted, gobbled and sucked, why he had never been able to come close to satisfying her. No one body could come near to giving Mandy what Mandy required. He started to weep. His nostrils filled up with snot and this, perhaps, stopped him from detecting the smell of smoke which, emanating from a fire started in the room below the cinema, began to fill the black room.

A man spoke in the dark, "Jesus Christ, we're on fire!"

A short silence, then a stampede for the door. But Jim Smart could not move. He was rooted to the spot at the sight of Mandy's face, ecstatic, surrounded by five erect soldiers' penises, like fire-hoses, fencing, then shooting, over her. And none able to calm her, bring her either satisfaction or peace.

Flame reached the projector. The image on the screen stopped. Black bubbles seared the image of Mandy and men. Then all crackled to black.

❧ ❧ ❧

Philomena Higgins MP punched the alarm-clock a second after it went off at six and rose from bed. She stretched, her arms in the air, then out to the window where the sun and her constituents were rising, or thinking about it. She embraced them all with some life-enhancing exercises, popped a number of anti-oxidant fortified vitamins and went downstairs for the milk, keeping her fingers crossed that the newspapers had arrived.

Opening the teak front door of the modernised Tudor farmhouse she and her still-sleeping husband occupied on the brighter fringes of her constituency, Philomena looked about. Milk, but no newspapers.

Carrying two pints of Gold Top back to the kitchen she

wondered about changing newsagents. To console herself for the lack of something to read, she flicked on the radio.

Another murder. A bookbuyer called Jim Smart, along with twelve other men, had been found dead amidst the rubble of a burnt-out sex shop. The newscaster said that arson was suspected.

Philomena tutted as she measured a concoction of oat-bran, muesli, wheat germ and honey into a bowl. Then she pressed open both bottles of Gold Top with her thumb and added the top of the two pints to her cereal.

"How many murders was that?" She'd almost lost count. There was the agent, the literary editor, the critic, the girl from the publishers, the African, and now this Jim Smart. Lucky that Arthur Whitworth was sticking to the plot of *Dying in Style* and not bumping off characters from other novels.

Philomena sat down at the breakfast-bar and started eating.

When Arthur Whitworth's third novel, *The Ends of the Earth*, was published, several friends of Philomena had pointed out that they thought she was definitely the woman MP in the book, who called ecologists eco-fascists, who wore loud suits and loved publicity of any sort, who poured scorn on the idea of a federal Europe.

Philomena had read the book and hadn't much minded the portrait painted of her. She was all the things the author accused her of . . .

Nevertheless, the doings since publication of *Dying in Style* had given Philomena the odd twinge. What if the murderer widened his net to cover other characters? What if, after the insult of stealing them for "fiction", he went a step farther and stole their lives?

Now that you couldn't move for seeing the population deep in *Dying in Style* perhaps the author would think it time to resuscitate his other moribund efforts with a few more murders.

Philomena Higgins prepared her husband's tea. While he was drinking it, all grunts while she talked – he didn't become even vaguely human until eleven – she would lay out her clothes for the day, run the bath and have a jolly good soak.

As she mounted the stairs she felt a twinge of pain in her stomach. She took no notice of it, thinking that the oat-bran might be the cause. But it did not go away. She was lying in her bath when agony struck and she wriggled in the tub, causing a tidal wave of watery foam, as she fought to get away from the pain.

Terry Higgins, alerted by the groans and sounds of sloshing water, went into the bathroom to see what the matter was. He found his wife, her head under the water, trying to stifle the agony. He manoeuvred her out of the bath and onto the bath-mat, where she rocked back and forth before writhing, climbing the walls of the bathroom with her feet. He rang the ambulance but by the time he got back to the bathroom Philomena Higgins was dead.

ꙮ ꙮ ꙮ

"The same poison that killed Cecil Parkinson. Injected through the aluminium milk-bottle tops," Edith told Dyer over the phone.

"It's enough to put you off the milkman, isn't it?" Dyer said.

"No, it isn't, Timmy," Dr Edith Gonne retorted. "Milkmen provide a valuable social service. They're the best neighbourhood watch we have – them and postmen. Buying milk from supermarkets is an anti-social act."

"Yes, Edith," Dyer said.

"Must go. I've a shocking day ahead of me. Sundry men burnt to a crisp in immoral circumstances. Shocking way to go. Why is it always men?"

Dyer turned to Constable Keeley and relayed what he had been told. "He's departed from the text of *Dying in Style* again. Do you see any connection with the books?"

"A character like Philomena Higgins – she was a noisy MP called Bridget O'Toole in *The Ends of the Earth* – gets killed. But not by poison injected through milk-bottle tops. The 'milk-bottle top murder' was in *Teacher*, if I remember rightly . . . "

"Hold on," Dyer said, "I'm in a mess. What you're saying is that the character murdered is from another of Whitworth's novels?"

"Yes, sir."

"Which one did you say?"

"*The Ends of the Earth*, sir, the one about polluters."

"But the manner of the murder was from another book?"

"*Teacher.* That's right," Keeley replied. "You see, there's this other bully in the school, apart from Haddock. He's called Maddox and he's been preying on this kid called Michael Mahon – known by all and sundry as 'Molly' Mahon because he's really effeminate – runs away from footballs, runs messages for bullies, has his bus-fare intimidated away from him on a daily basis. Anyway, Molly Mahon is sent to collect this other bully's milk at breaktime and he poisons it. As far as the plot of *Teacher* goes, it's a red herring. Teacher has only killed Haddock and three members of the Inspectorate." Keeley stopped, trying to remember. "Oh, yes, and the Minister of Education."

"So the murderer is doing a real pick-and-mix job on Whitworth's books. Any idea why?"

"Don't rightly know, but it's all publicity. Good for Whitworth's other books."

The phone rang. Dyer picked up. "Morning, Mr Gibbons."

"I've rung to ask if there's been any progress in the case," Giles Gibbons said.

"I was sorry to hear about the death of Mr Smart."

"A great loss, both to myself and the world of books generally, Chief Inspector."

"Quite so. The post-mortem's today. We've men combing the site of the sex club. It's a bit early to connect the death with the other murders, however."

"I think you'll find it fits."

"The late Mr Smart was married, wasn't he?"

"Sort of. To tell you the truth, Jim was rather unfortunate in his choice of women."

"His wife can't be traced."

"Mandy travels a lot."

"Where to?"

"All over the place. The last time it was the Jaffna Peninsula."

"Where's that?"

"Shame on you, Chief Inspector. It's on the news all the time. Sri Lanka."

"That's probably why I'm only a Detective Inspector and not a Chief Inspector. How do you spell 'Jaffna', sir?"

"J-A-F-N-N-A."

Dyer repeated the spelling. "Did they get on, you know, Jim and Mandy?"

"It was what you might call a stormy relationship," Giles Gibbons said.

"Right, sir," Dyer said. "I'll keep in touch. You're not planning any foreign travel yourself, are you?"

"Why do you ask?"

"If you do, keep us posted, won't you, sir?"

Giles Gibbons rang off without replying.

Dyer looked at the shard of paper on his desk.

Jim:
If you want to get in touch
Ring this number and mention Mandy and Jafnna.
334 5563

The number had been that of the burnt-out porno club. Odd, though.

"How would you spell 'Jafnna', constable?"

"Not quite sure, sir."

"It's been on the news a lot recently. Tamil Tigers and that."

Keeley wrote the word, then he crossed it out and wrote it again. "I think it's either J-A-F-F-N-A or J-A-F-N-N-A. Not sure which. I suppose it could be J-A-F-N-A."

"Find out, constable."

While Constable Keeley was out of the room, Dyer tried to think it through. Two more murders in as many days, one – maybe – following the plot-line of *Dying in Style*, the other apparently drawing inspiration from other Whitworth books. What was the sense in that? Apart from anything else, would it not deflect the public from the novel they were following, the novel that was selling worldwide, sending tabloid circulation through the roof, causing a migration of film crews to Britain? Still, on closer inspection, departing from the text was clever in a way. It postponed gratification, wound up the tension like a roll-over in the National Lottery. Also, it turned the spotlight onto other books in Whitworth's output. It helped shift merchandise.

For shifting merchandise had to be what every single

one of the murders was about, didn't it? If Whitworth were alive and carrying them out then the motive had to reach deeper towards hell than simply taking revenge on critics and publishers; it had to plumb the depths of filthy lucre.

But, this being the case, Whitworth would never get the benefit. Whether or not he was apprehended, his massive royalties would never reach him. No, all the way along the line, it was the publishers, printers, booksellers and the wider world of print and visual media who benefited. But then . . .

Dyer felt a headache coming on.

Keeley returned. "I looked in *The Readers' Digest Atlas*, *The World Book of Facts*, and I phoned the Sri Lankan Embassy." Keeley said proudly.

"So what's the verdict, Constable?"

"J-A-F-F-N-A."

Dyer nodded, looked down at his desk. "You'd think someone who visited Jafnna would be able to spell it, wouldn't you?"

"I suppose so. Why?"

"Just a thought," Dyer replied. He stood up, put his Golden Virginia tin in his pocket along with his cigarettes. "Right. Time to pack your jimjams and your bucket and spade."

"Why, sir?"

"We're off back to sunny Morecambe."

❧ ❧ ❧

Arthur lifted Monica and lay her down on her bed. He closed both her eyes, but they sprang open again. He broke down then, slumped by the side of the bed and moaned.

In the midst of it he wondered about his motives. Was he moaning for the death of his friend – perhaps his only friend – or for the fact that the plot had taken another twist which he, its instigator, would never have envisaged, for the simple reason that it was unexplainable? Or was it that, by weeping like the protagonist in some Victorian melodrama, he would show the heavens and Monica's wandering angry soul that he was not to blame?

But of course he was to blame. If he had obeyed her pleadings after his death was first announced none of this would have happened. But he had been so wrapped up in the unfolding of the nasty little plot that he could not bring himself to call a halt.

Writing was like that. Like alcohol or cigarettes, it took over, loading down one side of the personality, banishing balance. Everything had taken second place to the stories he spun. Like some awful Rumpelstiltskin weaving fool's gold from common flax, he had forgotten the world, allowed himself to become addicted to the magic of the word-processor, the whirling of the spinning-wheel, until he could no longer see what feelings were being hurt, lives undone, real-life characters shot through with his fictional arrows.

He was Janus. He was a twopenny-halfpenny Midas. Everything he touched in his living two-faced swoon turned to fool's gold.

Arthur Whitworth reached out to touch Monica's cold hand. As he made contact with it, he saw himself being seen touching it. He invented adjectives to describe the feeling of it.

What if he had done it? What if, after falling asleep, he had sleepwalked his way into Monica's bedroom and suffocated her? No, he couldn't have done that, could he? He wasn't a sleepwalker. He wasn't a murderer. Monica had always told him that he was a well-meaning man, a fine teacher, a decent colleague. Nice. How had things ended up like this?

Arthur stood up, took one last look at Monica's remains and walked from the bedroom. He picked up the telephone and listened to the dialling tone until a woman's voice told him to replace it. He wondered what the recorded voice was doing at this moment in real life. Was she at home? Recording other messages? Had illness stuck? Was she alive? Had recording her voice – a voice heard by millions – diminished her in some way? Or did she lift the receiver of her phone two or three times a day, wait and then get a thrill of pleasure from hearing her own voice? Did she tell her husband and children to pick up and listen. "Mummy's never far away. Just pick up the phone and listen!" And what did the children make of their mother's sweet-strict voice? Would they swank to their friends? Would they keep it dark, feel ashamed? The voice was set free upon the world. There was no knowing what effect it had upon the listeners. A neutral thing, one might think; but perhaps it set people lusting, longing, aching, to possess or destroy the disembodied voice.

He replaced the receiver – cutting dead the voice – walked to the window and swished open the curtains. A calm eggshell-blue sea mirrored the sky.

Not a bad place to write, he thought. He looked about in Monica's bureau, found paper and a pencil. Then he moved a side-table in front of the window, and started:

The coldest heart would have gone out to Peter Rushton when he woke up to find his wife dead beside him. And not only dead, murdered, if the dagger protruding through her nightdress was any indication.

Peter Rushton did not move a muscle. Later he was to

wonder why he had been so calm. He knew it looked bad. He could never have mentioned it to the police. It was so odd, to lie there minute after minute, feeling his wife's blood seeping through to him across the mattress, soaking his pyjamas like wee in a wet bed.

Guilt rose up. He was having trouble believing he had not done it. He had taken out a huge policy on her life just weeks before; he had at odd times wished her dead; he had . . .

Arthur stopped. No, that wasn't leading anywhere. He balled the paper between his fists and started again.

❧ ❧ ❧

A month later, two days after the death of Philomena Higgins, Dyer and Keeley knocked at Monica's door.

"Nobody in," Dyer said, after a decent interval. "Same as the last time."

"Nice spot, sir," Keeley said.

"A bit bleak in winter. Don't you think so, Desmond?"

Keeley looked out at the sandbanks and the sea beyond. "Magnificent, though. With good double-glazing it'd be heaven, I reckon."

"Ring again, constable," Dyer said. "All alone, would you be? You wouldn't fancy some company?"

"I'd like to try it alone and then I'd see. There's no one in."

"Try again. Desmond," Dyer said. He looked back at the view. "What sort of person would you live with in such a place, Desmond?"

"Not sure, sir."

"You haven't found a young lady, then?"

"No, sir. There's still no answer."

"Let's have a look round?"

They went round the cottage. Dyer tutted at the unkempt garden, the closed curtains.

Back at the front door again, Dyer said, "Looks like she's still away."

"Looks like it."

"What do you think, Desmond?"

"I think it's very close to the sea. And fairly close to the spot where Whitworth's boat was found."

"Get a warrant, constable," Dyer said.

⁂

When Dyer and Keeley, together with two uniformed officers, broke Monica's front door down and went into the house, they found Arthur Whitworth hunched over his writing-table. He had not even stirred when he heard the sledgehammer blows on the door. He merely continued frantically writing.

A stack of paper covered in Arthur's tiny handwriting lay in a neat pile on the floor next to his chair.

He did not turn, did not stop writing, when Dyer said, "Mr Arthur Whitworth?" . . . and he did not reply.

Dyer signalled Keeley and the others to search the cottage. Then he stood opposite the seated writer and took the pen out of his hand. Arthur Whitworth let it go, watched it slowly deserting him like, he thought, a space rocket deserting a planet, leaving the space wanderer – himself – marooned and hopeless. He stared as the pen disappeared into Dyer's breast pocket. Then he looked up at the face of the the policeman.

"I think that's enough writing for today, Mr Whitworth," Dyer said.

There was an exclamation of shock mixed with repugnance from one of the uniformed men, who had been struggling to open the door of the bedroom. This he had found hard to do as Arthur Whitworth had sealed the door shut with bath sealant when the smell of Monica's decay had proved a distraction to his work.

Dyer, telling the very pale policeman to keep an eye on the seated writer, went off to the bedroom.

In the weeks that passed between Monica's death and the police raid on her cottage, Arthur Whitworth wrote continually, only ceasing when he could not keep his eyes open. Two pints of milk were delivered each day and he had survived on this and on what he could forage from Monica's freezer. He did not watch television, nor listen to the radio. All appetite for the realisation of the plot of *Dying in Style* had left him once he took up his pen to write the new opus. And once the room in which Monica lay had been sealed and the olfactory reminders of her had lessened, then disappeared, he even lost awareness of where he was, how he had got there, who had been killed in such circumstances. The new story that flew effortlessly from the nib of his pen consumed him.

Dyer came back from viewing the remains. He whispered to the constable to get the forensic department over and returned, a mite reluctantly, to Arthur.

"You've got a bit of explaining to do, sir," Dyer said.

Arthur Whitworth said nothing. He looked at his right hand, at the little bump on the left side of his middle finger, stained with black ink. He formed his hand into a writing-grip and as he did so an idea came and he wanted his pen back. He did not see why he could not have it. He had done nothing wrong, had he?

Arthur Whitworth made a lunge for Dyer's pen-pocket. Dyer misinterpreted the move and slapped the hand away, then caught Arthur in an armlock.

Arthur groaned, then said, "My pen!"

"No more pens today," Dyer said. "You might do yourself a mischief." And he slowly released his grip on the writer's arm.

Arthur held the arm and looked at the page he was writing. Yes, with his pen he could fill it and fill it well. He had been in mid-flow when these people came in. They had interrupted what promised to be a fine scene.

"I think you'd better come with us, Mr Whitworth," Dyer said. He signalled to Keeley and the remaining policeman.

Arthur Whitworth was led – just as he was – from Monica's cottage.

The daylight surprised him. The lighthouse, the view of the sea, the gunmetal sky. It was all too much and he shielded his eyes. In the back of the police car he sat fisting his eyes, biffing the cornea, retina and lens into generating spectacular colours. A dark pen, like his own Platignum, wandered across the colours, dropping again and again out of vision until he massaged it back. Then, it disappeared to be replaced by a red-glowing rowing-boat lapping on a purple and green sea.

He opened his eyes then, remembering. The car was travelling along a straight dual carriageway. He closed his eyes. The red boat was back. Then himself sitting howling in the shallow sea. Monica opened the door to him and, in the midst of showing him around the neat cottage, was flung back and throttled. He opened his eyes and looked to left and right at Keeley and the uniformed constable. "You think I'm a murderer, don't you?" he said.

"The thought had occurred to us, Mr Whitworth," Dyer replied, from his position in the driver's seat. He eyed Arthur Whitworth for a moment in the driving-mirror. Arthur looked back but the policeman's gaze was too much for him and he closed his eyes.

The red boat, half submerged, wandered across his vision. Lines from a Chinese poem he had taught his classes came to his mind. *"I think of my little boat, and long to be on my way,"* Arthur Whitworth thought.

It was only when Dyer responded that he realised he had spoken out loud. "There'll be no little boats for a while, Mr Whitworth. Not until we've sorted a few things out."

❧ ❧ ❧

Reactions to the apprehending of Arthur Whitworth were immediate. TV crews from all parts of the world were sent up to Morecambe, and the town, settling back into its sleepy rhythm after a busy summer, awoke to find itself the centre of attention. Landladies of B and Bs on the verge of closing for the winter, saw what was in the wind and postponed the arrival of decorators, cancelled their cruises and Indian summer tours to sunspots to cater to the inundation.

Dyer and Keeley were very soon the centre of attention. Dyer told a press conference that it was patient, step-by-step legwork that had led to the arrest. He declined to give further information but felt sure that many people might be able to sleep more easily in their beds that night.

Keeley, deemed to be more telegenic, was left to give the details of the arrest and the finding of Monica's body.

"Are you looking for anyone else in connection with the *Dying in Style* murders?" a voice from the sea of faces asked.

"I don't think so," said Constable Keeley.

Dyer intervened, "We're keeping our options open. Early days and all that," he said.

ꝺꝺꝺ

Arthur Whitworth quite liked the look of his cell. It was warm, with a small table and chair that would do for writing. A basin and flush-toilet in the corner. A high, undistracting window through the mesh of which he could see the sky. As the door clanged shut on him standing in the middle of the cell with his hands bunched on his pants to keep the beltless pants up, his shoes laceless, relieved of watch and St Christopher medal and chain, he felt like an anchorite. All he lacked was pen and paper.

This was denied.

He tried the bed, then lay down on it. Not a bad bed. He dreamed of the story he had been conjuring up before being so rudely forced away from his idyll. He dropped off, still dreaming.

ꝺꝺꝺ

"The bugger's asleep!" Dyer informed the station sergeant as he looked through the spy-hole into Arthur's cell.

"That's not so unusual. A lot sleep," the station sergeant, a bluff, overweight man of about forty-five, called Hetherington, replied. "It helps them forget the fix they're in. It's the ones who pace you've got to watch."

"We'll leave him today, sergeant," Dyer said. "Tomorrow morning we'll start on him. I have the feeling he'll be cooperative. I might even get him to write his own statement."

"It must be a relief for you, sir," Hetherington said. "Still a lot of people are going to be a bit disappointed. To tell you the truth, I'm a bit disappointed. According to *Dying in Style* the detective in charge of the case was going to get it next."

Dyer twinkled. "I think the nightmare's over. Or the fun. A lot of people have been really enjoying it. Have you noticed? Whitworth had a good run for his money, though, you have to admit."

"Me and the wife have all his books," said Hetherington. "After that Philomena Higgins copped it we thought we'd better have a go at the others so as not to be caught napping."

"I think that one was an aberration; a red herring as they say in the books."

"Do you think he'd sign them?"

"Who?"

"Arthur Whitworth."

"Sign what?"

"His books. That'd make them worth something, wouldn't it?"

"Ask him," said Dyer. "But do me a favour, wait until he's been charged, will you?"

"I will," said Hetherington. "I wonder what he'd like for his tea?"

❧ ❧ ❧

"It's 'The World Tonight' on the line," Giles's secretary said. "Can you do an interview over the phone?"

Giles nodded and picked up the telephone.

"We're very happy and relieved that the prime suspect has been apprehended," lied Giles. "It's been a terrible time. Nobody felt safe. I've lost some very good friends and colleagues. I feel bereft. Yes, of course all this has added considerably to sales, but that doesn't make up for the loss of friends, does it? Neither does it make up for a great mind – and Arthur Whitworth *had* a great mind – going over the edge into madness. No, I don't know any more than you. I don't think I am catering to degraded tastes by distributing Whitworth's books. We published him faithfully for many years *before* all this started, remember. We're also about to publish another novel by the author. It was planned way ahead of all the dreadful happenings. Yes. It's called, *Mantra for a Fading Messiah* . . . Cutting Edge . . . who else? Price £16.99 and worth every penny. Thank you."

Giles put the telephone down. It had been a busy day. From his desk he had fielded a succession of phone calls asking for reactions to the arrest of Arthur Whitworth. He had done his best to milk what might be his last chance of publicizing *Dying in Style* and the rest of Arthur Whitworth's books.

The trial would, doubtless, keep the public's interest on the boil but with the end of the murders the best part, the prime publicity, was over.

In one way, Giles felt a bit let down. It was a pity, after all, that Arthur Whitworth had been arrested before all the murders were replicated. Still, he mused, he wasn't privileged to live in a perfect world; things quite often did not turn out the way they did in novels. Stories in real life were left hanging. But it was a pity. Giles, like Hetherington, the station sergeant in Morecambe, and tens of thousands of others had been waiting for the policeman to get it.

Not that he – or anyone else – actually wanted the policeman dead. No, they didn't. They just wanted the excitement of the policeman getting it. It was, Giles thought, rather similar to switching on the news and hearing that some really spectacular event had occurred: a plane crash, a terrorist outrage, an assassination. It perked the evening up wonderfully, this feeling of shared story, of being comfy in the lounge while four hundred souls had departed this life in claustrophobic panic, in a rush of nail-full wind . . . People's tutting and shaking of heads were awash with mixed motives, bordering on the hypocritical. A part of people really enjoyed other people's violent deaths.

Still, it looked as if the policeman was out of danger now that Arthur Whitworth had been caught. Groucho's would start to swing again as publishers, critics and media folk came out of their shelters at the all-clear of an arrest, saw that they'd lived through the threat that Arthur Whitworth had posed.

"I think I'll go there," Giles said, "I've earned a bit of a celebration."

Before leaving his office, Giles telephoned his solicitor – a close friend – asking him to represent Arthur Whitworth.

❧ ❧ ❧

Sergeant Hetherington knocked on Arthur Whitworth's cell door and went in, carrying a tray.

"I've brought you your tea, Mr Whitworth," he said.

Arthur sat up, then swung his legs over the side of the bed and scratched his head. "Thank you," he said.

"You've had a good long sleep. You looked so peaceful there I didn't like to disturb you before, but I'm going off duty shortly and I wanted you to have something to eat."

"I'm not hungry."

"I've done bacon butties for you. You can manage a couple of those, can't you? In *Teacher*, that chap you called 'Teacher' always took bacon butties with him to school."

"You've read *Teacher*, have you?" Arthur asked.

"Me and the wife have read all your books, Mr Whitworth."

"Did you like *Teacher*?"

"It was a really great read," said Sergeant Hetherington. "And I'm not just saying that; it really was."

"I put a lot of myself into it."

"Did you, sir?"

"I used to be a teacher. Head of English at St Mary's."

"Well I never! Still, I suppose it's always a good idea to write about what you know. I sometimes think I should write a book about being a station sergeant. You wouldn't believe some of the . . . "

"I'll take a bacon butty, Sergeant."

Sergeant Hetherington put the tray down on the table. He moved the chair slightly to intimate to Arthur that he should sit there. "We mustn't let our standards slip just because we're in unfortunate circumstances, must we?"

"I expect not," said Arthur, "but you know I really quite like this cell. It's very peaceful. The only trouble is they won't give me pen and paper."

"Won't they? Well I'll have a word with them. I expect after you've been interviewed they'll change their mind about that."

"Do you have anything I could read?"

"I think that can be arranged. You eat your butties and drink your tea and I'll go and search something out."

❧ ❧ ❧

Detective Inspector Dyer Interviewing Arthur Whitworth. 29 September. 10:05 a.m.

D: Your name is Arthur Whitworth of Who'll Do It Up Cottage, Blubberhouses?

W: Yes.

D: And are you a writer of thrillers?

W: I wouldn't call them that. I write morality tales using the "thriller" genre as the form.

D: And are you the author of one such "morality tale", *Dying in Style*?

W: Yes.

D: In that novel, an author who has been pilloried by critics determines to get his revenge.

W: Yes.

D: By killing off critics, agents, publishers?

W: Yes.

D: Did the book sell well, Mr Whitworth?

W: Initially? Before the fuss?

D: Before the fuss.

W: No. It was remaindered.

D: "Remaindered" . . . what does that mean, Mr Whitworth?

W: It means the hardback edition didn't sell and was offered to bargain bookshops. I believe upwards of a thousand were pulped.

D: And how did that make you feel?

W: Suicidal.

D: In *Dying in Style* the author is also suicidal for a while, but he decides to channel his angst into getting even. Isn't that what you decided to do, Mr Whitworth?

W: No.

D: Do you know why you're here today?

W: Yes.

D: And do you think you deserve to be here?

W: Yes.

D: Aren't you here because you tried to get your own back, to bring your fiction back to life, by actually carrying out the murders you described in the novel?

W: I can't deny that that has happened. What I deny is that I carried out any of the murders.

D: So you are not responsible for what happened?

W: I didn't say I was not responsible.

D: Audrey Saunders, Cyril Parkinson, Fidelma O'Mahoney-Gunton, Morag Aitken, Patrice Luala, Jim Smart, Monica Gardiner . . . you're responsible, but you didn't do it?

W: That's right.

D: Did you get someone to do your dirty work for you? A contract killer?

W: Nothing like that. I am responsible because I told the story. Telling the story got it off my chest, allowed me to dismount from my hobby-horse. It also, however, released it from my head. Do you know the story of Pandora's Box? It's not a completely apt metaphor, but letting all the demons out gave me some hope. I had thought that to confront the critics with their own lack of ethics might silence them. I was wrong, of course. They killed the book. But every year they kill thousands of books, thousands of people's best efforts.

D: And you consider this to be immoral, do you?

W: I consider that they get between the author and his audience. Like barbed-wire or bars on a window.

D: I'm no expert, but don't critics have expertise? Aren't they qualified to judge what's good and what isn't?

W: They would certainly think so.

D: But you don't?

W: I think it's part and parcel of the same thing.

D: What same thing?

W: The writing of a book is very hard work. Taking a book to bits is the easiest thing in the world. Writers open themselves up in the hope that their work will strike a chord: show readers what they had not thought of, give words to what they think all the time. Criticism on the whole is a closed shop. The reader as often as not does not know where the critic is coming from. Is he a follower of this or that "movement" in literature or style? A believer in this or that philosophy of life? Who is he? What gives him the authority to stand in judgment? Does he believe in something? In nothing? What is his subtext? All I can usually say about a work of art that I do not like is that I don't like it. But to commit myself, to stand as judge, jury and executioner, demands a certain type – and in my view a not particularly wholesome – type of person.

D: I must say I enjoyed your books more than the critics said I would. It made me think they knew something I didn't.

W: Thank you.

D: But to get back to responsibility. You feel that you are "guilty" of these murders because you "imagined" them? Am I right?

W: Yes.

D: And that's the extent of it?

W: Yes.

Dyer went on to question Arthur Whitworth about his movements from the publication of *Dying in Style* until his arrest.

D: And what about Monica Gardiner?

W: I can't explain her death.

D: Did you kill her?

W: I don't think so. I can't remember doing it.

D: Can't remember?

W: I've told you what happened. I woke up and found her dead.

D: Mr Whitworth, that's a horse that won't run. Even if we accept that somebody else is responsible for the other murders, Monica Gardiner's death comes right to your door. You and her all alone in an isolated cottage.

W: I know.

D: But you're telling me that you didn't do it?

W: I'm telling you that I don't think I did. I've thought about it a lot since – when I could bear to. It's possible that I sleepwalked and killed Monica. I can't explain the death. I can't explain any of the deaths.

D: What did you do between Monica Gardiner's death and your arrest?

W: I wrote mostly. My new novel.

D: Wasn't that rather callous in the circumstances?

W: Extremely callous. Monica and I were good friends. I knew the police would come eventually. You took much longer than I'd expected.

D: Would not an innocent man have informed us?

W: I didn't know what to say. Monica, I suppose, was my alibi. I'd been with her since trying to commit suicide, while all the murders were occurring. With her death my last hope went.

D: So you see your situation as hopeless?

W: I do.

D: And you may well be correct, Mr Whitworth. You will be held, pending our investigation of Monica Gardiner's death. Do you have any questions?

W: Might I have writing materials?

D: No.

❧ ❧ ❧

Dyer rang a bell and Station Sergeant Hetherington appeared at the door of the interview room to conduct Arthur Whitworth back to his cell.

Arthur walked ahead of Hetherington, who carried a Marks and Spencers bag. When they arrived at his cell, he unlocked the door and ushered Arthur inside. Then he went in with the prisoner.

"I've brought you your books to sign."

"That's nice," said Arthur.

"You don't mind?"

"Mind! I'm delighted."

"Here you are, sir."

Hetherington lay the stack of books down on the table and gave Arthur a Bic.

"Who shall I make the dedication out to?"

"'To Sheila and Jim Hetherington' will do."

Arthur sat down and wrote in all the books.

"Thank you, sir," said Jim Hetherington. "Sheila and I completely agreed with what the critic said about *Teacher*." Jim quoted from memory: "'*An excellent novel from a master.*' We think that about all your books."

"I wouldn't say that," Arthur said modestly. "Actually, the critic didn't write that. He wrote '*An excellent first novel from an ex-schoolmaster.*' Some creative editing took place."

"But still," said Sergeant Hetherington. "Thank you again, Arthur. You don't mind me calling you Arthur, do you?"

"You're more than welcome," Arthur replied. "Might I keep the pen?"

"I'm sorry, sir," Sergeant Hetherington said, all stern. He reached for the pen. "Strict instructions. More than my job would be worth."

"I only want to write."

"I know you do, sir. Let's just hope everything will turn out OK and then you'll be able to get back to it again."

"Everyone thinks I committed the murders."

Hetherington thought so too. He did not, however, say what he thought. "How about a spot of lunch, Arthur?" he asked.

The tone of the man's voice, his refusal to answer his query, added to by his kindness, nudged Arthur Whitworth over the edge, though it was a tiny drop down. Like falling off the kerb. Nevertheless, he began to weep. He tasted a tear with a tongue. Salty, yes. A weak solution, as when a river feels the first ripple of tidal flow from the ocean. It looked as if there was going to be a whole lot more of that from now on . . . and time to come up with an apt metaphor.

❧ ❧ ❧

People who had felt they were going to be "next" or like several of the murders, a deviation from the plot, relaxed once Arthur Whitworth was safely in custody.

The following Sunday's *Independent* dared to print a long article by a critic in which he excoriated Arthur Whitworth's use of "self-conscious post-modernism" while roundly attacking all the writer's novels as "cheap". The critic used a false name – Paul Golding – to disguise himself, but it plainly sent signals to people that the heat was off. It was safe to return for a bask in the soupy waters of literary London.

When news reached Anne and Win Whitworth that Arthur was alive and had been arrested, they were thrown into confusion. A side of Anne and Win was very pleased that their nephew had not died, but it was inconsiderate – and typical – of the silly boy not to have told them.

In the time since his death Anne and Win had watched the real-life killings of characters similar to those done away with in *Dying in Style* with a heady mixture of pleasure and trepidation. In some ways it seemed like an answer to prayer. Somebody was simply doing the decent thing; somebody who felt as strongly as they did about the wicked treatment their Arthur had been subjected to.

But as time went on and death was piled upon death even Anne and Win, whose appetite for vengeance they had thought insatiable, began to feel that it was going too far. The murders of Audrey Saunders and Cyril Parkinson would have been enough to teach the beastly media a lesson. But it just went on and on.

Then, when they heard that Arthur was not in fact dead but very much alive and under police custody, Anne and Win added two and two and joined the rest of the country in believing that the answer had to be that Arthur was the culprit.

"I think we're to blame, Win," Anne said. "It just goes to prove what I've always said,"

"What do you always say?"

"Example is the root of all evil . . . and all good," Anne said.

"How do you mean?"

"Well, if we hadn't killed off that Bill Baker for interfering with Arthur in the park when he was a nipper, maybe Arthur wouldn't have gone the same way."

Win thought about that. "I wish we hadn't told him," she said at last. "I wish we'd kept it dark."

"It was my fault," Anne said, "He was always wandering off and he just wouldn't be told. I thought telling him would make him think twice."

"It got him back to bed-wetting, just after I thought the buzzer contraption had done the trick."

"And it got him going on thinking about murders. Remember those stories for the school magazine?"

"What are we going to do? We can't just let him rot in gaol, can we?"

"I don't know what we can do." Anne said. "Still I think we should visit him, don't you?"

"It's going to take more than a visit."

Solomon, Anne and Win's aged black cat, jumped up

on Win's lap. She stroked the cat. "I don't know . . . " she said.

"You're wondering if Arthur's worth all this fuss, aren't you?"

"To tell you the truth," Anne said, "I really do feel let down. He could have dropped us a line while he was playing dead."

"It's typical of Arthur," Win said. "Typical. Remember the time he wandered off on Saltburn beach? He let us in for a whole day's search and when we found him he just didn't understand what we were worried about."

"And that was *after* the Bill Baker episode. He just wouldn't learn," Anne said. "He looked so lovely in those little shorts, though. You couldn't be angry with him for long."

"So what do we do?"

"Well, we can't leave him to face this. I think we'd better go and tell the police that we did it."

"But we didn't do it!" Win said.

"You know what I've been thinking?" Anne said. "I've been thinking that just one more murder might get Arthur off the hook."

"I suppose we might as well hang for a sheep as a lamb. I keep seeing that Bill Baker. Even after all the years that have passed, I still keep thinking we're going to have to pay for what we did to him," Win said.

Anne did not reply. She was thinking. The prospect of spending the rest of her natural life being the plaything of the types you saw on "Prisoner Cell Block H" did not appeal to her in the slightest. She thought and thought until Win sighed pointedly beside her. At last she said, "What we do is finish off the story. That'll convince the police that it can't have been Arthur, won't it?"

"You might be right," Win said.

"And you know what Arthur always said, don't you?"

"He said such a lot."

"He used to say that the first chapter and the last chapter were the hardest."

"We're up to it, though, aren't we, Anne?" Win said.

"It might be the end for us," Anne said.

"We've discussed it, though, haven't we? I'm ready for the off myself. It's you that keep wanting to see another spring. To my way of thinking, once you've seen that special offer of bulbs from *Radio Times* coming up the once, you've done it."

"Fetch down our copy of *Dying in Style*," Anne said. "I want to see who's left to kill."

❧ ❧ ❧

"The coroner's report on Monica Gardiner's in, sir," Keeley told Dyer.

"What does it say, Desmond?"

Keeley scanned the documents.

"A massive stroke. Natural causes. That's the gist of it."

"Bloody hell!"

Sergeant Hetherington knocked on the door of Dyer's office. He waited for the "Come in!" but when it didn't come he knocked again and opened the door.

Through the haze of smoke Hetherington made out Dyer sitting behind his desk, his elbows on it, his hands – one holding a smouldering cigarette – under his chin. Constable Keeley sat on a radiator, his back to the open window.

"What is it, sergeant?" Dyer asked.

"There's something I need to talk to you about, sir."

"Go on."

"Well, you know you've forbidden the remand prisoner, Arthur Whitworth, from having writing materials?"

"Yes?"

"Well, I thought I ought to mention that it isn't on. We're breaking the law. Prisoners have a right to writing materials."

"I know that, sergeant," Dyer replied, "but seeing as they mean so much to him that's the reason I'm keeping them away from him. It's a ploy to help me break him. I know I'm bending the rules, but . . ."

"I know that," Sergeant Hetherington said, "but it's Mr Whitworth's solicitor that pointed it out. I think it's probably the right time to give him what he wants."

Dyer didn't seem impressed.

"You never know," continued Hetherington. "Not giving him them hasn't worked. Being generous might soften him up. Also, you never know what he might write." Sergeant Hetherington twinkled. "Might be something incriminating."

Dyer turned to Keeley. "What do you think, constable?"

"I think Sergeant Hetherington might have a point. And, of course, not giving him pen and paper is illegal."

Dyer sighed, "Give him paper and pencil, sergeant."

Sergeant Hetherington brightened straight away. "Right away!" he said, and left the room.

Dyer turned around to face Keeley. "We haven't got a thing on him. There's nothing to link Whitworth to the other murders . . . "

"Apart from the books. I'd say you couldn't get better circumstantial evidence than that."

Dyer shook his head. "I think he's off the hook, Desmond," he said. "Failing any hard evidence – and there's none that I can see – we wouldn't get a conviction."

"It doesn't seem fair," Keeley said.

"What do you think?"

"I think he's guilty. I mean, he's got the motive; he had the opportunity. Monica Gardiner's no alibi. I hate the idea of him walking away free."

Dyer laughed. "You'll get used to that if you continue in this line of work, Desmond. It happens all the time. Still, in Whitworth's case, I doubt he'll ever be free. He's got an albatross round his neck from here on in. And that albatross is called *Dying in Style*."

ණ ණ ණ

Keeley left the room. Dyer picked up the telephone.

"Edith, it's me."

"You're in a right mess, aren't you, Timmy?"

"Help me, Edith."

"The Lord helps those . . . ."

"We've got to release Whitworth. There's nothing to connect him to the murders except the obvious – and that won't hold up."

"Where's he been all this time?"

"He says he was with his friend, the late Monica Gardiner, and she died of natural causes."

"Well, if Whitworth didn't do it, who might have?"

"The publisher, I suppose. Giles Gibbons. But he's got alibis for the times of the murders. We've been tailing him, tapping his phone. There's not a whiff of suspicion."

"It's easy enough to get a contract killer, I hear."

"I know. If it's that then we're really stuck."

"Over to you, Timmy!"

"Come back to me, Edith!"

"What's your status with that young bobby with the assets?"

"We're just good friends."

"I will come back to you, Timmy, on condition that you stop smoking the minute I enter the flat."

Dyer took out a cigarette and lit it. "Right you are, Edith."

"And no messing about."

"No messing about."

"One other thing. I want you and young Constable Keeley to do a spot of lifting. Thursday at eleven. My office." And Edith told Dyer about Patrice's funeral. "Can you help?"

Dyer said they would.

"Where's Whitworth now?"

"Down in the cells."

"And he's going to be released, is he?"

"After I've talked with him once more."

❧ ❧ ❧

Arthur Whitworth did not look up when the keys turned in the heavy lock and a frowning Dyer stood in the doorway next to a beaming Sergeant Hetherington. For a couple of seconds all that could be heard was the scratching of HB pencil on writing-pad.

Dyer coughed. "Mr Whitworth?"

"Yes," Arthur said, still not looking up from his table.

"I'd like to have a few words with you." He turned to Sergeant Hetherington, "That'll be all, sergeant."

"Right you are, sir."

Dyer sat down on the bed under the cell window. Arthur continued writing. Then he stopped, reread a sentence or two, moving his lips as he did so, and crossed out a couple of words.

"What are you writing, Mr Whitworth?"

"I can't tell you that, I'm afraid. Not until it's finished."

"I could take it from you, you know," Dyer said, "I'd be perfectly within my rights."

Arthur leaned back on his chair, yawned and stretched. "I'm writing an historical romance."

"That doesn't sound like your sort of thing."

"I know. But I've spent so much time trying to come up with the real culprit for these murders that it's been tying my brain in knots. I'm trying to do something that will distract me. The trouble is I still believe it was me. Everything points to me."

Dyer felt he knew what was coming. He didn't fancy hearing all that pained angst again. While in a way it made some sense, Whitworth's argument held about as much water as the ethical coffee or powdered milk debate. He was like the types who agonised in supermarkets believing their shopping decisions weighed heavy with ethics. According to those arguments, everyone was guilty of everything. Edith, for instance, had once pointed out that, by smoking tipped cigarettes, Dyer was spreading fag-ends of insoluble pollution that people a hundred – or was it a thousand – years hence would have to pick up. The nervy notions of neurotics. He sighed. "Why?" he asked.

"For the reasons I gave you before. You see, I *am* the killer in that I wrote the scenario. I gave the nudge. Do you ever consider 'The Nudge', Detective Inspector?"

"You'll have to explain that."

"It's easy. You bump into someone in the street and you nudge that person's life a fraction. His life's route will never be quite the same again. You get a builder in and have changed that builder's life just by the phone call. Then, when he drives out to the house, he's nudged again and again. It happens all the time, happens so much that we don't give it a thought. But think of the world of story, of ideas. 'Books That Changed My Life' is a sort of cliché. But they do change lives; they nudge people in all sorts of directions. I'm called a 'thriller' writer. Some people read upwards of two or three thrillers a week. All those methods of murder! All those motives! Lots of nudges. Lots of ideas planted into the heads of people who, without the book, would never have given a thought to methods of dispatch, to the how and the why of murder. Imaginations running riot cause mayhem."

"You make writing sound a bit on the immoral side."

"I know."

"But you're still doing it?"

Arthur looked down at his writing-pad. He nodded. "Looks like it, doesn't it?" His face seemed to crumple as if he was on the verge of tears. "I can't help myself."

Dyer thought of his smoking, of his promise to Edith that he would give up when she came back to him. In the starry-eyed blue-sky world of the future all things were possible.

"I've come to tell you that you're free to go."

"What?"

"Free to go. We'll need to know your whereabouts, but apart from that . . . "

"You mean you're not charging me?"

"No."

Arthur Whitworth looked around his cell. "I'm being released?"

"That's about the size of it."

"But I don't want to be released!" Arthur exclaimed. "It isn't right to release me!"

"Your solicitor's been banging at our door."

"Well, he had no business to."

"Solicitors, when they're engaged, tend to think the

person who's paying them wants to be released. Yours is a real pain in the neck, by the way. Where did you find him?"

Arthur Whitworth did not reply. He gazed at the writing-paper in front of him. "Where would I go?" he asked at last.

"That's not . . . ."

"I mean, I can work here. Sergeant Hetherington's been wonderful to me. All the staff have been wonderful. And I'm managing to write."

Dyer thought for a moment that this kind of reaction might be sufficient to have Arthur Whitworth sectioned. "I'm sorry, Mr Whitworth," he said, "there's no way we can keep you. Unless you confess to the murders."

"I've already 'confessed'."

"A proper confession. With chapter and verse. All the details. Where you obtained the poisons, how you managed to gain access. That sort of thing."

"Details were never my strong point, Detective Inspector. I was always concerned with other things."

Dyer was exasperated. "Mr Whitworth," he said, "we're dealing with real life here. This is not a piece of tale-spinning. If you committed the murders you'll know all the details. It stands to reason."

"I committed them *in my mind*!" Arthur shouted. "Doesn't that make me guilty?"

"From a moral angle, it well might; but we're dealing with the law here and, as far as the law is concerned, you're not guilty."

Arthur looked desperate to Dyer. "Look," he said, "I know from Sergeant Hetherington that the media are everywhere. They've broken into my house to take photographs of the murderer's study and bedroom. If you release me they'll be after me. I couldn't take that. I really couldn't. I'd kill myself."

The two men looked at one another. Dyer was thinking cruel thoughts. If Arthur Whitworth killed himself the case would be closed. Lots of loose ends, of course. But there was no denying that the heat would be off. He would be put onto a fresh case, some tabula rasa without all the conundrums of this one, perhaps. But then the realisation came upon him that he was beginning to agree with Whitworth about his protestations of innocence. Perhaps he was only guilty to the extent that he had set the ball rolling with his damned book.

"I'll see what I can do, Mr Whitworth," Dyer said. "Can't make any promises, mind, but we might be able to charge you with obstruction of justice if you like. I think that will stick, don't you? As a favour. Between you and me . . . Meanwhile I'll talk to your solicitor and tell him how you feel."

"He already knows. I think he fancies himself, though. All the publicity and that . . ."

"Ah, yes. Publicity," said Dyer. "Publicity makes monsters, doesn't it?"

Arthur Whitworth turned back to his work. "I don't mind how you do it," he said, "but please don't set me free."

Then, as Dyer wondered, Arthur Whitworth continued writing.

❧ ❧ ❧

Two days later, at 10.45 in the morning, Roberta Coleman arrived outside the building in which Dr Edith Gonne worked. She was wearing a dark raincoat over jeans and T-shirt, carried a portable tape-recorder, a single red rose and the papers that Edith had given to her in hospital.

A man passed Roberta at the entrance, looked at her.

Roberta wanted to lift her hand to cover the scars on the left side of her face, the pink eye-patch that covered her sightless eye. The man, she knew, had been looking at her scars. They would always from now on look at her scars. Those scars were her advance publicity.

Roberta walked into the building and asked at Reception for Dr Edith Gonne. She followed the directions along the corridor, and knocked at the third door on the left, marked "Duty Pathologist".

Edith answered the door. She was dressed in her best black suit. Her hair had been recently cut and styled.

Edith greeted Roberta, noting the livid scars on the side of her face. Still, given time, they would calm down. Already they gave to Roberta's youthful face a sage, mysterious tinge. Even the patch was somehow attractive . . . Peter Pan doing an impression of Captain Hook.

"We're all set," Edith said. "Timmy and Constable Keeley should be arriving shortly."

"I'm scared," Roberta said.

"Don't be. Have a coffee."

"Thank you. Would you mind if I smoked?"

Edith did rather. She saw the packet and knew that she was going to give way. Already she saw herself five minutes in the future, a stub and a little ash in front of her on the desk, feeling defeated, feeling a little unwell. "Not at all," she said.

"You?" Roberta said, offering her packet.

"I don't mind if I do."

Dyer and Keeley came in as the two women were in the middle of their cigarettes.

They did not speak much. Eleven struck on nearby Big Ben. Edith looked at Roberta. Nodded.

They went outside by a side entrance. The coffin lay in the back of Edith's Volvo. They had collected it earlier from an understanding undertaker on the Essex Road. Edith unlocked the car and Dyer and Keeley carried it back into the building.

Roberta followed them down a long corridor and through a metal door into a room lined with doors like those of ovens. There was a name on each door.

"Are you sure, Roberta?" Edith asked, her hand on one of the doors. "We can manage, you know."

"I'm sure," Roberta said.

Edith turned the handle while Dyer removed the lid from the coffin. A sound of metal runners and Patrice's body, swathed in a plastic body-bag, slid out. Edith looked at Roberta but her face gave nothing away.

"Right," Edith said, "we each take a corner and lift him into the coffin." They positioned themselves. "At the count of three," said Edith. "One . . . two . . . three . . . " and they transferred Patrice from the tray to the coffin.

Keeley placed the lid on top, and started screwing it down.

Dyer and Keeley followed Edith's Volvo through the clogged streets towards Highgate Cemetery, where Roberta had bought a plot close to Karl Marx's grave.

"Miss Coleman's a lovely girl," Keeley remarked.

"You've noticed, have you? I told you she was, Desmond. I'm not wrong about everything, am I now?"

"I really admire what she's doing. It takes guts."

"She's doing what she can. Patrice is the father of Roberta's child, you know."

"I didn't know that, sir."

"Neither did she. They told her she was pregnant in hospital. You can see as how she might want to do all she can for the father. It's all too late, though. Mind you, if what Edith believes is to be believed, maybe it isn't too late."

"We'll solve this thing, sir. We've got to."

"Ah, the strong black and white emotions of the young," Dyer said, "I remember them well. I envy them indecently. Be patient, Desmond. Something will turn up, as a wise man – in the days when men were allowed to be wise – once said."

"But I don't see how we're going to do it, sir. I mean, if Whitworth's innocent . . . "

Dyer lit a cigarette. He did not reply.

ᴥ ᴥ ᴥ

In the cemetery two workers helped them carry the coffin from the Volvo to the grave. They prayed as best they could as the coffin was lowered, then Roberta took a spade. She dug shovelful after shovelful of earth on top of the coffin until Keeley went over, gently took the spade from her and got on with the task. Roberta played a tape of *Missa Luba* and stood alone while the task was completed. Then she placed the single red rose on top of the mound.

The four mourners stood in silence around the grave until the flash from a camera brought them to themselves. They looked up to see a man running away.

"Who told the press, I wonder," Dyer asked.

"Someone from my former life, I expect," said Roberta Coleman. She let herself be led away by Constable Keeley, while Edith and Dyer followed.

ᴥ ᴥ ᴥ

"So what are you going to do now, miss?" Keeley asked.

"Call me Roberta."

"Roberta," Keeley said. "Another coffee, Roberta?"

Roberta nodded, gave Keeley a smile and looked around the Hampstead cafe. In the corner sat Alicia Thomason-Thompson, the publicity manager for Scimitar Books, chatting with Diana Simms of On The Shelf. All these women with three syllable names ending in "a". She had been one of them, of course. Once.

Alicia Thomason-Thompson looked Roberta's way, but seemed not to recognise her. Was it the scarring, the eye-patch? Was it the scent of death coming off her, fresh from the soil of Patrice's grave, soil that still clung to her shoes?

Constable Keeley was off at the counter fetching her another cup of cappuccino, being ticked off by the waitress for not waiting for her to deign to serve them. She saw his embarrassment as he turned back to her. She smiled at him and patted his chair, warming it for his return.

"I'm going to get myself a proper job," Roberta said.

Constable Keeley, sitting himself down, looked confused.

"You asked me what I was going to do now," Roberta said. "Then you got distracted."

"You're not staying with Cutting Edge?"

"No. I've already resigned."

"Will you go to another publisher?"

"I doubt it. I want out of publicity. I've had enough." She fingered her scars, not to make a point, but that was what Keeley picked up.

"I see," he said.

"Yes," she said, taking her hand away from her face. "I thought I might train as a nurse. If they'll take me."

"Why?"

"It'd be a complete change," Roberta said. "I need a complete change." The waitress arrived, took the order and left. "Still all that's on hold until after the baby."

"Will you be able to manage?"

"I'll manage."

"I've had a career change," Keeley said. "I used to be a plumber."

"Are you glad you left plumbing?"

"I'll tell you when we've solved the *Dying in Style* murders."

Roberta nodded. "Are you married, Desmond?"

"No."

"No." She felt tears threatening. "It was a good funeral, wasn't it? We managed everything very well between us, didn't we? Without strangers."

"We did."

Keeley looked at his watch. "I'll have to be going soon," he said.

Roberta nodded. Alicia Thomason-Thompson seemed to be looking straight at her, but could still not see past the scars. How many times had they talked? At how many literary gatherings? All gone. All dead.

"I'd like to see you again, Desmond," she said, still looking at Alicia Thomason-Thompson. Then she turned to Desmond Keeley, saw him wriggle, straightening his tie. She thought of Patrice holding a bottle of white wine in the crypt of St Martin's. Neither Patrice nor Desmond fitted. Both, despite the difference in backgrounds, were maladroit, uncomfortable. More than anything Roberta wanted to join their world, a real, uncomfortable world where people laid the cutlery all wrong, opened tins, had a stab at living honestly.

"I'd like that," Desmond said. He took out his Metropolitan Police diary, ripped a page out and wrote down his name and address for Roberta Coleman.

"Good," she said, folding the paper and putting it away in her purse. "I'll phone you when . . . when . . ."

"Take your time. I'll be there, Roberta," Constable Keeley replied.

ꕥ ꕥ ꕥ

"Penny for your thoughts?" Edith asked.

She was sprawled on the bald sofa. It was newly toupeed with a rug bought by Timmy Dyer. He had bought several rugs in a sale at a branch of Edinburgh Mills. These he had used to cover a multitude of sins in the dingy flat. Warring tartans fought for ascendancy in the freshly painted room.

Dyer, washing dishes, turned from the sink. "I've two really. I was wondering where the *Dying in Style* investigation goes from here. And I want a fag."

"Me, too," Edith said. "Take deep breaths, Timmy. Isn't it wonderful to smell the freshness in the flat?"

"No," Dyer said.

"The craving will go. Your mind will clear. Who knows, you might even get some inspiration about the case."

"It isn't inspiration we need, Edith: it's proof. Evidence."

"Surely the circumstantial evidence would be enough, Timmy?"

"No, it isn't. The milkman at Monica Gardiner's cottage says that the milk was taken in every day – money left in payment every Friday – right up to the time when we arrested Whitworth. Also, if you saw him, spoke to him, you'd sense that he just couldn't have done it. Those murders took a different sort of personality, a 'doer', a planner," Dyer said, trying to convince himself.

"But he thought up the murders in the first place, didn't he?"

"That's exactly it, Edith. He *thought* them up. but having the energy to actually carry them through, well, Arthur Whitworth just doesn't have it. Give him a warm room and a bit of grub, a notebook and pencil, and he's as happy as Larry."

"But if not Whitworth, then who?"

"Search me, Edith. Sometimes we think it has to be Giles Gibbons, because he's making such a lot out of it. The bookbuyer's wife is also under suspicion, but she's disappeared off the face of the earth. But, failing anything that links Gibbons to any of the murders, all we can do is monitor him. And I have to say that he hasn't put a foot wrong."

"Where's Keeley now?"

"Trying to pin something on Giles Gibbons."

"You like Constable Keeley, don't you?"

"Very much," Dyer said. He looked over at Edith. "Don't worry, Edith. He's too good for me."

"Meaning I'm not, I suppose."

"You know exactly what I mean, Edith. You don't mix yesterday's milk with today's. Would you like a coffee?"

"No," Edith replied, "it makes me want one."

"I know," Dyer started to pace. He picked up his dog-eared copy of *Dying in Style*. "Would you like me to read to you, Edith?"

"If you must," Edith said.

Dyer read the account of the last murder in the novel, that of Chief Inspector Harrington a week after the arrest of the author.

Edith listened, a slightly pained expression on her face.

When Dyer had finished, Edith remarked, "That's a bit far-fetched, isn't it?"

"Yes and no," Dyer replied. "It is, I believe, what's known as surreal. Have you read the book, Edith?"

"No."

"Well, it fits in rather well. You see, all the way through we keep hearing about Chief Inspector Harrington's obsession with rare birds' eggs. It's his Achilles heel. He's a law-abiding man in every way, but he just can't resist robbing birds' nests for his collection. It goes right the way back to childhood. Searching for birds' eggs was what got him interested in becoming a detective. So, at the end, when he gets a tip off on the network that there's a red kite's nest in Clissold Park, he can't help himself. He has to go and see if he can find it."

"So what triggered the knife in the cuckoo clock to come out and stab him through the eye?"

Dyer slammed the book shut to illustrate his exasperation. "I've just read it, for Christ's sake! It's a booby-trap!"

"Don't blaspheme," Edith said.

Dyer spelled it out. "He climbs the tree that's marked with a chalk arrow and reaches into the nest. He trips the wire that sets the cuckoo clock chiming. Instead of a cuckoo there's a knife and it . . . honestly, Edith!"

"But how did it manage to get him right in the eye?"

"I don't know!" Dyer said, pacing the room, smoking his fingernails, wondering if he could think up a convincing excuse to go out for a walk. "Maybe it was a really accurate cuckoo clock, handmade for the job."

"But," said Edith doggedly, "if the murderer's in gaol, who done it?"

"I don't know, do I?" Dyer said. "It's the last murder in the book and it was supposed to get the reader wondering."

"So does the reader find out?"

"No."

Edith was silent for a while. She watched Dyer pacing,

knowing exactly what was going on in his head. "I don't call that a very satisfactory read, Timmy," she said. "Maybe the critics were right to give the book the thumbs down. I mean, a writer lets down his readers' expectations at his peril."

"Well, I thought it was rather neat myself," Dyer said.

"It sounds like an old story to me," Edith said, giving Dyer one of her loaded looks. "Shall we watch the news?"

Edith made room on the tartan sofa. Dyer slumped down. He searched about. Edith could feel his bad temper vibrating across the tartan rug. "Where's the clicker?"

Edith felt Dyer's hand pushing down the fluff and halfpenny-holding cracks in the sofa. "Forget it, Timmy!" she said. "Let's make tonight like real old times."

"Better not, Edith," Dyer said.

"Don't be so tight, Timmy."

"There may be something interesting on the news . . . "

"There's nothing interesting on the news. It's a soap opera dressed up. Nothing adds up. A bit like *Dying in Style*. Make Edith feel good, Timmy. Be generous. This is real life. We only get the one stab at it I hear."

"Edith . . . ."

"Come on, Timmy. I've been feeling as dead as my cadavers, Timmy. Can't you help me?"

Timmy Dyer, already despairing at the thought that there would be no post-coital cigarette, did his best to welcome Edith home.

~ ~ ~

Desmond Keeley sat in front of the news, rolling a bottle of Bishop's Finger between his palms. He was not quite sure what he felt. It was the first time in several weeks that he had not spent most of the evening with Dyer.

It was nice to have a bit of peace, to be back in his little flat, away from the tension that came when Dyer looked at his young constable a little too long, and sighed. But that was a double-edged sword for, exiled from the flat because of Edith's return, he felt an odd sense of loss – like a beauty queen whose time is up. He was no longer in the limelight of admiring eyes, no longer keeping constant company with someone who thought him the bee's knees.

Keeley had, much to his credit he thought, managed to fend off Dyer's oblique advances. But he knew he had given good value, knew that the older man got a peculiar frisson from having him around. There was another factor in the equation, too; Keeley had been brought on by Dyer, been allowed to achieve things beyond his station as constable. He had been flattered by the attention, by Dyer's appreciation of his skills in both the plumbing and the policing department. Dyer had, in short, woken Keeley up to his potential and to the power and promise that lay like a pearl within the soft callow shell.

He allowed himself to think of the future as the portentous music introducing "The News" started. He saw himself, married to Roberta, living in this space. A baby-bouncer in the corner. He a bobby, she a nurse. That would be good.

"Early days," he said to himself. "Mustn't let my imagination run away with me."

The news had thus far been of little interest. Single currency, the teacher shortage . . . then the news that Arthur Whitworth had been remanded in gaol for "Obstruction of Justice". A reporter outside the police-cells where Whitworth was detailed the story, questioned by the newscaster who seemed greatly put out that murder charges had not been made.

But Keeley was far more interested in scanning the

people behind the reporter. A couple of young boys jumping into camera-shot and sticking out their tongues at the viewing public, a knot of newspaper reporters and, close to the steps of the police-station – almost out of shot – two elderly ladies holding placards. He got up, went close to the screen trying to read what the placards said, but the item was over and the news passed on to Ulster.

Still, Keeley thought as he watched, odd those two old ladies with placards. Who could they be?

He finished his bottle of Bishop's Finger and went to the fridge for another. He came back, turned off the television and tried to think about ways of trapping Giles Gibbons. But the picture of the old women with the placards kept coming back. Was this inspiration or was it just curiosity?

He picked up his phone and rang Morecambe.

"Station Sergeant Hetherington."

"It's Keeley here, sergeant."

"Nice to hear your voice, young man. I thought you might have forgotten us. Did you see us on the telly?"

"That's why I'm ringing. Could you do something for me, sergeant? Outside I noticed two old ladies holding placards. Could you go outside and see what's written on them for me."

"I know what's on them. One says 'Arthur Whitworth is innocent!' and the other 'Free Arthur Whitworth'."

"Thank you, sergeant. Two crackpots, I suppose."

"No, at least they seemed very sane to me. They went on at me about habeas corpus until upon my word I was completely tied up in knots."

"Who are they, do you know?"

"Yes, constable, I do. They're Arthur Whitworth's aunties, Anne and Win. Lovely ladies I will say; real gems if you get me. Refined. We will not see their like again. I've sent tea out to them a couple of times."

"Have they seen Whitworth?"

"No, of course not. I'm under strict instructions from Arthur. No visitors. He wants to be alone."

"Do the ladies know that?"

"I've told them no visitors are allowed. Wouldn't want to hurt their feelings, now, would I?"

"No, of course not," Keeley said.

"How are things back in London? Any progress?"

"Not much," Keeley said, then, thinking he had said too much, he added, "Still, I'm not at the centre of the investigation. Just a humble bobby, me."

"Well, best of luck, constable."

"Thank you, sergeant."

And Keeley heard Sergeant Hetherington put the phone down.

He stood up and paced the length of his living-room. How could he have been so stupid! It might not add up to anything, but not to have thought of Arthur Whitworth's relations! A grave omission. He tried to think. Those aunties had been mentioned. Had he heard Dyer talk about them? Why had they not at least been interviewed?

Anyway, it was Dyer's fault. He was just the new boy learning at the feet of a more experienced man. While there was much that was impressive in Dyer, it was clear that he was a hopeless detective in many ways. Laziness was his problem. He'd been at it too long. By rights his job ought to have been handed on to younger, leaner, keener, more active minds.

And, if they had failed to make the connection with Arthur's relations, what else had been omitted?

❧ ❧ ❧

Giles Gibbons was feeling restless and dissatisfied.

Though Arthur Whitworth's new novel, *Requiem for a Fading Messiah* had reached second place in the hardback charts, it had failed to knock *Dying in Style* from Number 1.

He tried to console himself by looking at the paperback top ten. There Arthur Whitworth's novels occupied eight out of the ten spots. So why was he feeling dissatisfied? Cutting Edge had never been in better shape. He was in the middle of negotiating a buy-out of the much larger Knock Out book company, truly a minnow swallowing a salmon. He was seldom off television and radio. The Sunday papers profiled him. He had written "A Life In The Day Of . . . ", he had reviewed the TV offerings for Boxing Day, he had eaten more dinners in more five-star restaurants than Will Self or a wise man ought. So why did he feel so miserable?

Giles Gibbons understood his condition to the extent that he knew his achievement was the cause of his unhappiness. For years he had struggled, pushed, wheeled and dealed for the profile, the influence, the fame, the attention, the aura, that now, since *Dying in Style*, he had obtained. And that was partly the trouble. He had reached the peak and lacking another hill to climb, he was getting bored with the new perspective.

He also missed Roberta's presence. Not to mention Morag, even Jim Smart, his stepping-stones. What were the last two, the remaindered two, thinking, if they were thinking, of course? Were they cursing his every breath, his every blink of eye . . . marvelling at his dissatisfaction with life, with consciousness?

He found himself wishing that he could close the book called *Dying in Style* and concentrate on his new project, a series of novels that would stretch the boundaries of taste and decency to the limit. The written word married with virtual reality five-senses software for those with the funds. The whole package was to be entitled, *Absolutely Disgusting*, or AD, for short. It would generate its own publicity, as the morality police descended upon it, big guns firing.

All around the country Giles had novelists working. In his place in the country he had Mandy producing the typescripts which would answer the question "What do you do for encores?"

Placing his palm down on his musical mat to coax *The Blue Danube* to flow, Giles Gibbons waited, dreaming of bad publicity.

ꕥ ꕥ ꕥ

Keeley came into Dyer's smoke-filled office the following morning. "I thought you'd given up," he said, making for the window.

"Don't tell Edith, Desmond," Dyer said. He produced a large toilet-bag from the drawer in his desk. "With these little babies, Edith will never know." And he tumbled the bag's contents onto his desk: a pump of breath-freshener, strong mints, a drum of whole cloves, gum, both nicotine and regular, mouthwash. "How's that? I made Boots' day."

"It's not what I'd call honest, sir. A bargain's a bargain. And if you're not giving up smoking, what else aren't you giving up?"

"The rest is gone," Dyer said, glancing at Keeley's crotch. Keeley closed his legs. "But I'm not ready to stop the fags; not until the *Dying in Style* murders are solved."

"Talking of which . . . " Keeley said.

"Go on, constable," Dyer said, tumbling cloud-cover back into the toilet bag.

"You know that Whitworth's got two aunties?"

"Yes," Dyer replied, "they live in Leeds. Arthur Whitworth was brought up by them after his parents died."

Keeley hadn't known that. He stopped. "Well . . ." And Keeley described watching the television news the previous night.

"So?"

"So they should come under suspicion."

"Why? Because they happen to be related to Whitworth?"

"Partly. I was just theorising. I mean, if they're related, they might have been angry about the reaction to Whitworth's books. Who knows, they might have taken it into their heads to avenge their nephew."

"Don't think so." Dyer said. "All the planning. A fair bit of technical know-how. I did get the boys in Leeds to interview them, you know. As good as gold. They make the best seedcake in Yorkshire, according to Detective Inspector Timmins. Also, Detective Inspector Timmins visited them on the very day that Patrice Luala was killed. He found them vacuuming a Morris Minor. Anyway, how old would you say they were?"

"In their seventies, I'd guess," Keeley said.

"Wouldn't have the energy."

"Now who's underestimating the old?" Keeley said. He was feeling a trifle put out at having the theory that had kept him awake for much of the night drenched in cold water by Dyer. "*Some* older people have quite a bit of energy, will power and tenacity," Keeley added pointedly. "Arthur Whitworth's aunties had enough energy to go up to Morecambe and wave banners."

Dyer raised an eyebrow. "Meaning I don't, I suppose?"

That was precisely what Keeley meant. "No, of course not, sir," he said.

Dyer caught Keeley in a steady gaze, then dropped his eyes. "I understand what you're saying. Leave it to me. I'll look into it. But I want you back to checking on Giles Gibbons."

"Sir . . ."

"I know it looks hopeless. He's as good as gold counting his money and becoming a media star in the process. But I still have this hunch. There is one murder to go, you know . . ."

"The policeman."

"Yes," Dyer said. "Off you go, Constable Keeley."

"Yes, sir," Keeley replied, wishing he could get back to the beat. He arrived at the door, opened it, then turned when he thought he heard Dyer speaking to him. "What did you say, sir?" he asked.

"Mind your back, constable," Dyer said, enunciating meticulously, as though addressing an infant or a dimwit.

"You too, sir," Keeley replied, almost tenderly.

❧ ❧ ❧

Sergeant Hetherington knocked at Arthur Whitworth's cell door. He was holding a tray on which was a covered plate. Next to this was a small box given by Anne and Win who, unable to gain admittance, had decided to send in a bakewell tart.

Arthur was lying on his bed.

"Sleeping, Arthur?" Sergeant Hetherington asked.

"Dreaming, sergeant."

"What sort of dreams, Arthur?"

Arthur, smelling bacon butties, sat up and swung his legs onto the floor where they met a pair of slippers kindly sent in by Sergeant Hetherington's wife, Sheila. "I'm dreaming of big busts, Jim."

"That's disgusting, Arthur."

Arthur noticed the little parcel next to the plate. "What's that?"

"A present for you. From two ladies."

Arthur opened the box and found a small, perfect bakewell tart. "How kind!" he said, "I haven't had a bakewell tart since I last visited my aunties in Leeds. And I couldn't touch it because of the shocking time I'd had at a reading. It all seems years ago."

"The tart is from your aunties. They've been outside demonstrating for your release."

Arthur smiled. "They've never been able to do enough for me, sergeant. I've been the most ungrateful of nephews. Out of sight out of mind. All that. I'd visit, you know, but it was only out of duty. What a shit I am!"

"It's lucky for all of us we get treated better than we deserve," Sergeant Hetherington said.

"There wasn't anything they wouldn't do for me. Always taking my part. Always . . . "

"Eat it before it gets cold," Sergeant Hetherington said.

"What was that you said?"

"The bacon butty. Eat it."

"Ah . . . yes." Arthur said.

"My Sheila," said Sergeant Hetherington, "is worried like mad about me."

"Whatever for?"

"Because, according to the last murder you wrote about in *Dying in Style*, the policeman in charge of the investigation gets murdered."

"But you're not in charge of the investigation, are you?"

"Try telling Sheila that. When I tell her I'm only a glorified skivvy she won't believe me. Then she says that several of the murders didn't follow the book in every detail. She says it might just be a policeman."

"Maybe you should mind your back," Arthur said. "Fancy a piece of tart? There's too much for one."

"I wouldn't say no," said Sergeant Hetherington.

Arthur cut the tart in two halves with a plastic knife. He looked at the two halves, reached out to give Sergeant Hetherington the one he judged the smaller. Then he saw Anne looking at him disapprovingly through the hatch of the past. He handed Sergeant Hetherington the larger piece.

They tucked in.

"Not bad, is it?" Arthur said.

Sergeant Hethington could not speak. His mouth was full of a delightful combination of pastry and sweet-spicy filling. Then, finally, "A glimpse of heaven, Arthur!" he said.

"I think I'd better see my aunties," Arthur said.

"But I thought you didn't want . . . "

"I think I'd better make an exception. It's not every chap has relations as solicitous as mine, in spite of everything. I think I'd better see them . . . you know, to put their minds at rest."

"Next time I see them," said Sergeant Hetherington, "I'll tell them."

Then, licking his finger, Sergeant Hetherington started picking up every single crumb remaining from Anne and Win's bakewell tart.

❧ ❧ ❧

Early that evening Dyer called Constable Keeley.

"Listen to this, Desmond," he said, adding, "have you a pen and paper handy?"

"Never without one," Desmond replied.

"This is a note that was waiting for me when I got

home. I quote: 'Dear Chief Inspector Dyer: If you want to find out who the *Dying in Style* murderer is, come to Hampstead Heath at Midnight. An ancient oak has fallen across the path leading from West Heath Road to Jack Straw's Castle (you probably know it). I'll meet you there at 12.' It's signed: 'A Friend'. Yes, and there's a PS: 'Come alone!'"

"Don't go, sir!" Keeley said.

"I'm going, constable."

"But you know as well as I do who is the last to be murdered. It's a set-up, sir."

"It may be a set-up. constable," Dyer replied, "but I've got a dependable sidekick. I want you to get on the trail of Giles Gibbons. Get over to his house straight away. If he leaves home – assuming he *is* home – ring me on the mobile and tell me. I won't move from here until I hear from you."

"How do you know it's Giles Gibbons?"

"I don't *know*, constable. I suspect. Now get a move on."

* * *

Dyer paced the flat. He ached to smoke. He ached to be off, to be doing something. Half an hour passed . . . three-quarters. Finally, Dyer, desperate for nicotine, went into the lavatory, stood on the pedestal, opened the small top window and lit the cigarette, exhaling each greedy puff out of it. Some of the smoke seemed to curl around, back into the toilet, preparatory to telling tales on him. Still, he'd solve that with half a can of Haze.

The telephone rang. Dyer exhaled a lungful of smoke through the window, dropped the fag-end into the toilet water and made off for the phone.

"Giles Gibbons has just left his house," Constable Keeley said.

"Where's he headed?"

"Hard to say. We're just approaching the Holloway Road. He's indicating right, sir."

"OK, constable. Now's your chance to be all you can be, as they say in the underwear adverts. Don't lose him. I trust I'll meet you behind a tree at midnight."

"But . . . "

"All the best, constable," said Dyer. He rang off, went back to the toilet and hazed the air there; searched under his bed for his leather jacket; drank a glass of water; at once wanted a pee; held his breath in the haze-stinking toilet; flushed – noting with dismay that the guilty cigarette-stub had failed to flush; picked it out, swaddled it in a foot of Andrex, flushed again – successfully this time; and left the flat.

Only when he was halfway down the stairs did Dyer remember that he had forgotten to leave Edith a note.

Still, he thought, *I won't think about that tonight. I'll think about it tomorrow. If tomorrow comes, that is.*

❧ ❧ ❧

Edith Gonne approached the Highbury flat and found that someone had stolen her parking-place. She had to go two hundred yards down Highbury Hill to find one.

It was nine o'clock on Friday night and Edith was looking forward to an evening with Timmy. Dinner, a dinner bought module by module from Marks, a couple of bottles of wine, then an hour or two in front of the telly with "Eurotrash" or whatever else Channel Four had dreamed up to cater for the Thank-God-It's-Friday, perhaps already-dreading-Monday, pissed population.

Edith backed the car into a gap between a Rover and a Volkswagen caravan. She turned off the lights, fiddled with the key and reached across to clamp on the steering-wheel immobilizer. She was surprised, upon looking out of the front window, to see Timmy Dyer, done up in his leather jacket, smoking a cigarette, pass right by the car.

Had Dyer been looking in Edith's direction he would have been sure to have seen her. But he was looking elsewhere, trying to read by the light of the street lamp what looked like a letter.

Edith let Dyer pass, wondering what to do. Of course, she could have got out, made after him, had a scene. But she was tired; a feeling of defeat was edging through her. Obviously Timmy was up to his old tricks again. He was definitely back on the fags, though she had suspected that for three or four days. There had been a definite aroma about him, haloed by peppermint, that hinted a falling away. Judging on past performances it was only a matter of time before all his resolutions collapsed. Still, the day before yesterday – nauseated by a decaying cadaver – she had fallen away too.

Dyer never wore that leather jacket except when he went cruising. He had told Edith that he had given it away to a chap begging in a doorway as a token of his new leaf, his new self. Another lie. The bugger had probably just hidden it in the garage – the garage filled with odds-and-ends – then taken it out when his lust rose up.

Resolving to lock Dyer out of both her life and their flat, Edith walked towards the front door. She postponed crossing the road until a gang of rough-looking, intimidating kids had passed by. Then she darted into the block. She locked herself into the flat, giving an angry double turn to the latch. She started unpacking her groceries. As she was placing some packaging into the swing-bin, Edith noticed an envelope. She picked it out and read, "Chief Inspector T Dyer" followed by the address. Funny, she thought, promoting Timmy like that. "Detective Inspector" was Timmy's station, about as far along as Timmy would ever go.

The envelope was empty. Perhaps that was the piece of paper Timmy had been reading. She thought. Her heart melted. Maybe, after all, Timmy was out and about on police business. After some minutes of thought, some more reading the complicated instructions for her solitary meal, Dr Edith Gonne put everything into the microwave and then unclipped the security-chain, clicked the lock of the Yale to allow a friendly key to turn. Then, though it was not cold in the hall of the flat, she shivered.

She said a prayer for the soul of Miss Mullin.

❧ ❧ ❧

Constable Keeley started to shake as soon as he put his mobile away. Two cars behind the black Jaguar of Giles Gibbons, surrounded by Friday-night traffic, pavements full of people leaving an Odeon, Keeley did not think he had ever felt more alone. The red lights on the Jaguar seemed to look into his soul, like devils' eyes, sussing out exactly who he was and what he was doing.

It was barely nine o'clock. If Giles Gibbons was planning something at midnight, then he had some time to kill.

Some time to kill. The phrase set off Keeley's shiver again. His hips in the seat of the plain red Metro shuddered; his hands, when they released their tight grip of the steering-wheel, shook as if palsied. He kept asking himself what the matter was, what had got into a fellow – himself – whom he was normally able to count on.

Maybe, after all, he was not cut out to be a policeman. Maybe plumbing was more his style. A start and a finish to a job, and no threat to life and limb apart from the odd stroppy householder.

Traffic slowed down towards Archway. Then everything stopped. The car between himself and Giles Gibbons made a shrieking U-turn to avoid the jam. A gap of twelve feet was all that remained between himself and the man he had been told to tail. Constable Keeley, trying to keep calm, inched forward, stopping a foot behind the rear of the Jaguar. He smelled the fumes of it coming through the Metro's ventilation system. His imagination acted up and he saw himself fanning in mustard gas, expiring there with traffic hooting and farting his requiem.

Suddenly, before he knew it, the jam had cleared. Giles Gibbons's car shot away, up the hill towards Highgate. It went through an amber Pelican crossing adjacent to the Whittington Hospital. Keeley was thinking of jumping the red light but a group of people were crossing. He stopped, waited for the line to cross and, just before the crossing went onto flashing-amber mode, took off up the hill.

There was no sign of the Jaguar. Keeley drove through Highgate Village trying to think whether Giles Gibbons would have gone on north towards Finchley, or would direct the car towards what – if he was indeed the murderer or the informer – was to be his midnight destination. Opting at the very last moment for Hampstead, Keeley turned sharp left and at once found himself a few yards from the red tail-lights of the Jaguar.

Keeley braked, but the Jaguar had picked up speed and was putting distance between them. Had Giles Gibbons been waiting for him? Only at The Spaniards did Keeley come close behind the Jaguar, caught in a single-line-queue. He thought he saw Giles Gibbons looking at him through his wing mirror. Did he suspect he was being followed? If so, did he recognise Keeley? That was doubtful; they'd only met on one occasion. And then he had merely held a door open.

The Jaguar joined a queue of three cars trying to enter the car park at Jack Straw's Castle. Lights gleamed from inside the pub. Keeley could see a tall young woman draining a pint, gesturing. What was she saying? He did not follow the car, but took a complete revolution on the mini-roundabout adjacent to the pub, then drove around the large pond to the south-west. He parked, half the width of the Metro on the kerb, and walked towards Jack Straw's Castle.

❧ ❧ ❧

"Your aunties are outside," said Sergeant Hetherington.

Arthur's heart jumped and sank. "Show them in," he said.

Sergeant Hetherington, left the door ajar and disappeared. Arthur got up off the narrow bed and smoothed himself down. His belt and shoe-laces had been returned, but the shirt and pants were police-station issue. Looking down at himself, at his crumpled clothes concealing a soft, tiring body, he felt ashamed and vulnerable. He was ten again. A little kid with a wet bed and two formidable aunties about to descend.

When Arthur's father had left his mother, Anne and Win moved heaven and earth to locate him. They found him at last living with a woman in Whitby and pushed him into contributing to the maintenance of Arthur and his mother. Then, when Arthur's mother had died with the same suddenness as Monica, Anne and Win moved him in with them, accepted all the slings and arrows a grieving, mixed-up ten-year-old could throw, pestered school on his behalf, sorted out the bullies who assailed him, kept him at his books.

All through his life Anne and Win had batted on Arthur's team while he took all credit for his achievements. Duty calls had dwindled into the occasional postcard. He had all but forgotten the stepping-stones he crushed while crossing life's river.

But they had held his torch aloft. "Blood is thicker than mortar!" as Win had said. "Nobody does down the Whitworths and gets away with it!"

Arthur heard Win say, "Funny smell. This way, is it?" He smoothed down his clothes and waited on tenterhooks for the cell door to open. He wished he was dead.

"You've lost weight," Anne said.

"Not that you didn't need to," Win said.

"No. Not that you didn't need to."

Arthur kissed his aunts, smelled Yardley and rouge from a little blue compact on their cheeks. Was it really there or *had it been* there? Did seeing them spark old sensations? He sat Anne down on the chair, Win on the bed.

Sergeant Hetherington was hovering. "How about a nice cup of tea, ladies?" he asked.

"Two sugars in both," Anne said, testing the chair, hearing a creak, inspecting the legs.

"Milk?"

Anne looked at the sergeant. "Of course," she said.

"I think it was you two ladies who were responsible for the bakewell tart."

"It was for Arthur," Win said severely.

"It was too big for me," Arthur said. "Sergeant Hetherington and I shared it."

"Only shop-bought," Anne said, to devalue the gift, to devalue the recipient.

"Lovely, it was," said Sergeant Hetherington.

He left the cell, closing the door.

Anne looked to left and right. "It's got damp," she said.

"It's not so bad," Arthur said.

"Why won't they let you go, Arthur? They must know you had nothing to do with those murders," Win said.

Arthur looked at Win. Always far smaller than Anne, she seemed to have shrunk considerably since they had last met in Leeds. "They've charged me with obstructing the course of justice," he said. "That way they can hold me until . . . until . . ."

"But you've done nothing!" Win said.

Arthur said nothing.

"I mean," Anne said, "you were with that Monica all the time, weren't you?"

Arthur nodded. "Maybe they think I paid someone else to do the murders," he said. "I don't know what's going on in their heads, to tell you the truth."

"Well, don't worry about all that for the moment. Things will work out. We've got good news for you, Arthur." Win said, "Every bookshop we pass is chock-a-block full of your books. You can't turn on the television without hearing some gink talking about them. The Yanks and the Japs are obsessed. Me and Anne don't bother to go into bookshops to place them where everyone can spot them any more. There'd be no point. When all this is over you're going to be really well-off, Arthur."

Arthur stood up. His chair fell back. He paced. "But it isn't going to be over! I'm finished!" Arthur paced the linoleum, pointing to it and out to the limited horizons of the grubby walls. "This is my world from now on! This is all I will ever see!"

Anne righted the chair. Win placed herself in Arthur's

path. “Don’t take on, son. Everything will work out.” She guilded him back to his chair.

Obedient, he let himself be seated, listened as they cooed consoling phrases into his ear.

Sergeant Hetherington came in with the tea. On a plate were piled several bars of Kit Kat. He poured the tea, offered the Kit Kats. Arthur heard Anne and Win complaining about Rowntrees being bought up by Nestlé’s and Sergeant Hetherington expressing surprise. He heard Win telling Sergeant Hetherington that Kit Kats were definitely shorter than they had been. Of course, you couldn’t prove it, all the longer ones having disappeared down gullible gullets . . . even dear old Branston Pickle was owned by Nestlé’s. Everything was owned by Nestlé’s, she continued. And what wasn’t owned by Nestlé’s was owned by some Yank. It was disgusting, she said; nothing was as it appeared. There was no honesty left in the world. And what with the Internet and those ugly big dishes on everyone’s houses there was nowhere for the world to go but downhill. Sergeant Hetherington agreed that it was disgusting and Anne and Win – bonding in shared pessimism – nodded at the truth of that. Anne added that, at a time when the world’s moral antennae needed to be at their most acute they were, in fact, at their most blunted. “They’d go through the floor if they weren’t so blunt!” Win said.

Arthur did not contribute to the conversation. He thought how much he had taken from the conversation of these two women; how much he owed them. They had made him what he was. *Aunties, that Bill Baker . . . he . . . he . . . made me . . .* He, the author, the tell-tale, tale-teller, creator of easily-told cheap thrillers, the solitary vomiter-forth of diseased ideas . . . he was the one responsible. Every word written, every song sung, every image caught on film was a nudge with implications. All on whom the muse descended were sundered by a brain-splitting blade of mixed motives. Vanity riding a hobby-horse of the Apocalypse. A wet kid whispering into a shocked ear.

"Who are you nudging?"

Arthur was back. He saw Sergeant Hetherington draw back as if hit.

"I'll just leave you alone for awhile. I'll come back for the tray in a few minutes," he said, plainly discomfited. He scurried from the cell.

"What's the matter?" Arthur asked.

"That policeman told me a smutty joke," Anne said. "Then he had the gall to give me a nudge. I ask you!"

"He's harmless. He's been very good to me, in fact."

"And so he should be!" Win said. "You're an innocent man and an author!"

Arthur nodded, looked uncomfortable, bit his nails. "How's Solomon? He must be five . . . six?"

"He's ten and a half," Win said.

"Never!"

"He is." Anne said. "And don't bite your nails."

Arthur stopped.

"And take your elbows off the table," Win said.

Arthur did so. "Who's looking after him?"

"Mrs Flynn. You remember Mrs Flynn?"

"Of course I do," Arthur said. "Is she still as religious as ever?"

"I don't call what Mrs Flynn does 'religious'. It's nothing short of idolatry," said Anne. "Remember all those plaster statues?"

Arthur nodded.

"Well, she's built what she calls 'A Grotto'," said Anne.

"In the *front* garden," added Win.

"With the Virgin Mary and some kneeling French peasant.."

"It attracts some shocking types."

"Still, she's good with Solomon, isn't she?"

Both aunts agreed – with some reluctance – that Mrs Flynn was good with Solomon.

Arthur was sweating. All the questions he was going to ask had evaporated. "Well," he said, "I hope all the murders have finished now. It's been a nightmare."

"They oughtn't to keep you here," Anne said.

"No, they oughtn't to keep you here," Win said.

Arthur didn't say anything. He couldn't think of a single thing to say. They sat like that.

"Mrs Flynn's been going to see some mad woman in the West of Ireland," Anne said.

"On a coach," Win said. "She comes back in a state."

"This woman lives on an island and she bleeds all the time. Says as how she can see into priests' souls."

Arthur smiled. He had not heard what Anne was saying. "They're not going to let me go," he said. "They're going to keep me here until they've found the evidence to pin the murders on me."

They looked at him. Then they looked at one another.

"That isn't going to happen, is it, Win?" Anne said.

"No, Anne, that isn't going to happen."

"It *is* going to happen," Arthur said, almost shouting. "It is! I know it is! There's nothing you can do to stop it. Not this time. I'm on my own."

Anne came up to Arthur, put her arm around him. "Have we ever let you down before, son? Have we?" she asked.

Arthur was weeping, tasting the tears. *Like weak sea, like a lick of the bark of the Judas Tree, like . . .* "No," he said.

"Well, we're not going to start now, are we, Win?"
"No, we're not going to start now."
"But . . . " said Arthur.
"But me no buts, Arthur Whitworth," Anne said.
"Here's a nice hanky. Blow your nose," Win said.

❧ ❧ ❧

Sergeant Hetherington came in to take the tray away. He looked shamefaced.

"We'd better be off," Anne said.

"Are you going home to Leeds?"

"No. Not just yet. We'll be in tomorrow," Anne looked at Sergeant Hetherington frostily, "if that's all right?"

Sergeant Hetherington said of course it was.

Anne and Win kissed Arthur, Anne dryly, Win sloppily, The difference of touch tolled bells of cerebral braille, peeling back across the dark decades. They left him alone. When the door had closed, Arthur lay tummy-down on the bed and swore at himself into the suffocating pillow. Then, after a few scant minutes, he fell asleep with his thumb in his mouth.

❧ ❧ ❧

Constable Keeley waited in the carpark while Giles Gibbons was drinking in the pub. Two or three times in the course of his two-hour wait he looked through the window to see if Gibbons was still there.

The fourth time Keeley looked – at about 11.25 – the bar-stool on which Giles Gibbons had been sitting was empty.

Keeley had time enough to wonder whether Giles Gibbons had gone to the lavatory when he felt something stick into his back. He drew a sharp intake of breath and was once more shaking uncontrollably. He felt a trickle of urine pass, sufficient to soak through his Y-fronts and dribble down his thigh.

"You know who it is, don't you, constable?" said Giles Gibbons. "No sudden moves, as they say. God, I feel like such a cliché. Still, it has to be done. Walk straight ahead, towards the Jaguar, Constable Keeley."

Keeley did as instructed, still perversely aware of the damp in his pants. A group of women were leaving. They eyed him. Did they see? He was amazed at himself for worrying about how he looked at a time like this.

As he meekly approached the Jaguar, Giles Gibbons told Keeley to veer to the left. Pushing him with the prodding object . . . was it a gun? A knife? Keeley went down the steep bank that led onto the Heath. Once on level ground, they walked almost side by side.

"Why are you doing this?" Keeley asked.

"You'll find out."

"I don't understand."

Giles Gibbons prodded Keeley forward.

They walked on and on, round and round. At least that was Keeley's impression. Then Keeley was being pushed off the track and across a dark meadow. A hunter's moon was rising to the south and its glow, aided by the city's aura, profiled a fallen tree.

"Stop here," said Giles Gibbons. "No, don't turn around. Sit down. There. On the ground."

Keeley did as he was told. He was shaking violently, knowing that any second he would half-hear a report, half-feel a searing pain, half-smell cordite and, before the report had echoed, the pain registered, the cordite stench spread from victim to killer, he would be dead. He would be dead. He would be dead and he didn't know what "dead" meant. He didn't know! He didn't.

Midnight struck. Shaking, Keeley listened to the bell, convinced that at the last stroke his life would end. What to think about? Sorry, God! Forgive. Wish I'd stuck to plumbing. Ten . . . eleven . . . *so this is how it feels* . . ." More warm liquid trickling down his leg.

Then, quite suddenly, the whole glade was bathed in light. Floodlights positioned far away angled in, turning the shadows of Keeley and Giles Gibbons huge. Then tiny white fairy lights came on, weaving through every branch and twig of the fallen oak. Ten yards away a long table had been laid under a branch of the tree. The fringes of a white tablecloth, blown by the wind, shifted like shining, ghostly mist. Around the table sat naked manikins, their faces moulded and painted into the features of all the murder victims. Audrey Saunders, Cyril Parkinson, Morag Aitken, Fidelma O'Mahoney-Gunton, Patrice Luala – all sat helpless and frozen at the dinner table. Waiters appeared and popped corks, hors d'oeuvres were served.

Dazed, Keeley approached the table. "Thought you might enjoy a little celebration!" Giles Gibbons called out. "Sit down,"

Keeley sat down. Men appeared and took photographs. "A few publicity shots," Giles said. "Hope you don't feel we're being intrusive. Part of the launch for Cutting Edge's 'Absolutely Disgusting' series. Two birds with one stone. Couldn't let the opportunity pass by." Then Giles Gibbons strode to the head of the table. Behind him, a red curtain. A large red tassle hanging down. "One more surprise awaits!" he said, and pulled the tassle. Keeley's mouth dropped open when he saw Dyer tied to a tree. He was naked, apart from his leather jacket.

A silence, interrupted by the hooting of an owl. The photographer took more pictures. Keeley stood up and ran over to Dyer. He released him. More photographs.

Dyer, like a ragged doll, crumpled onto the ground.

"You all right, sir?"

"No, I'm not fucking all right, Desmond," Dyer said. "I'm fucking ruined, that's what I am! Fucking ruined!"

"I'll arrest the lot of them, sir!"

"Leave it, Desmond. I got myself into this."

"How, sir?"

"Never mind that; just get me out of here, Desmond."

"Where are your clothes, sir?"

Giles Gibbons, who had been watching the scene from the table, came over. "Give the Chief Inspector his clothes, would you?"

A man stepped out of the shadows. Tall, muscled, tanned. White T-shirt. He handed Keeley a mess of clothes.

Dyer looked at the man. "I thought my luck had turned when you came along," he said. "I should have known."

The man smirked. "Poof!" he said.

"I don't see why we can't arrest them all," Keeley said.

"Are all ex-plumbers this innocent?" Dyer asked, as he stumbled into his pants.

"So what do we do, sir?"

"Just take me home. It's finished. And what's more to the point, I'm finished," Dyer replied.

❧ ❧ ❧

"I could take you back to my place," Keeley told Dyer as they made their way back to central London in Keeley's car.

"No, I'd better face Edith, constable," Dyer said, "I'd better warn her."

"Warn her?"

"About my picture in the papers."

"Your picture, sir?"

"Haven't you worked out what that little happening was all about, Desmond? It was about publicity, and I'm to be on the receiving end."

"But how did they get you into that position, sir?"

Dyer sighed. "I got myself into that position. I arrived in plenty of time. Nothing seemed to be happening. I decided to have a look around – I have been up on the Heath before, Desmond – and that handsome chap happened along. And the rest . . . well, we'll draw a veil."

"But how do you know the press will get the pictures?" Keeley asked.

"I know because Giles Gibbons told me."

"Isn't there a way to stop him?"

"Don't think so. Invasion of privacy won't hold water, seeing as it's a public place. Not all the papers will take it, but I can think of one or two that will. Then there's the foreign press. I tell you, Desmond, I'm going to find out how bad it can be. That's me finished as far as the police-force is concerned. Still, better look on the bright side: I'll be going out with a bang. Well, almost."

"I don't know what to say, sir."

"Say nothing, Desmond. Still, tonight has been a learning experience. We know what Gibbons is capable of. He has, as they say, come out."

"He certainly has, sir."

"You and I, Desmond, we've seen the Promised Land. I may not get there with you but I think that, with application, you'll get there."

"Straight home, sir?"

"Yes, please." Dyer said. "And Desmond?"

"Yes, sir."

"Will you come up with me while I face Edith? It could be I'll be evicted."

"Of course, sir," said Keeley.

"And one more thing, Desmond?"

"Yes, sir?"

"Stop calling me 'sir'."

❧ ❧ ❧

Constable Keeley stayed just long enough to make sure that his boss would be let into the flat. After a long grilling from Edith, Dyer had been sent to bed. Edith stayed up, wondering about it all.

She had surprised herself by not feeling as angry with Timmy as she might have been. After all, he had gone up to the Heath with an honourable mission in view. He had, in a way, been taking his life in his hands. Trouble was, his feet of very crumbly clay, when confronted with the atmosphere of the place after dark, had taken over. A cuckoo in the eye. Still, Timmy was right about one thing: he was finished as a Detective Inspector. His shambling, serendipitous approach to investigation had been forgiven for years – after all, he usually got his man in the end; but being found in flagrante delicto – or as good as – would surely do for him.

Still, she thought, out of humiliation might come humility. Out of all this might emerge a chastened man.

Edith slept fitfully on the settee. When she brooded awake she could hear Timmy's snores, raucous and content, coming from the bedroom.

She lay on until six. Then she got up to take a walk, to search for the Sunday papers.

❧ ❧ ❧

ABSOLUTELY DISGUSTING
On page 2 of this paper there is
a photograph that will shock you.
The man in charge of the *Dying in Stlye*
murder investigation, Detective Inspector Timothy Dyer,
caught by the cameras at the "launch"
party of Hampstead Heath
for Cutting Edge's new venture. *Absolutely Disgusting!*
Also pictured, manikins made up as the
Dying in Style victims.
Is this sick or is this sick?
Turn to page 2 – and pages 4 to 8 –
to decide for yourself.
One things for sure, you'll find it absolutely disgusting . . .
And you'll be absolutely right!

Edith turned to the inside pages and looked at the pictures. Then she closed the paper.

A second tabloid showed Dyer on the front page. Under a headline, THE LONG **** OF THE LAW? they had printed the same photograph of a trussed-up Timmy Dyer. A self-righteous story guzzled up a further two pages. Edith placed the paper back on the shelf and bought a packet of cigarettes and some gum.

She walked along the Holloway Road, smoking and thinking. Then, turning along Drayton Park, she climbed back up to Highbury and went into her church to catch early-morning mass.

During the mass, standing, kneeling, sitting, with the rest, Edith was thinking of other things. Only when the priest elevated the host did her mind come back to eternal truths.

Forgive us our trespasses; as we forgive those who

trespass against us . . . A hard saying in the circumstances, she thought. *And lead us not into temptation.*

The thoughts, unprompted, came back; dark thoughts of vengeance. Edith prayed for the restoration of equilibrium, for peace of mind, for Patrice – cold under Highgate soil – for Roberta . . .

Roberta. She would have a chat with Roberta. One injured party might be able to balm another. The thoughts continued, miserable and vengeful, as members of the congregation shook her hand as a sign of peace. Shortly after, while all the good people queued to take Communion, Edith Gonne knelt on in her pew and did not approach the altar. She wanted to, but did not dare. Not in the circumstances; not with these thoughts, these murders she was committing in her heart. They had, she believed, already put her soul to death.

ↀ ↀ ↀ

"Where's Sergeant Hetherington?" Arthur Whitworth asked the young station sergeant whom he had not seen before.

"A few days off duty, Mr Whitworth. He's just gone, as a matter of fact."

Arthur nodded.

"Your aunties are here to see you again, sir."

"Couldn't you say I'm ill?"

"They're all packed up, ready to return to Leeds."

"Show them in."

"Right you are, Mr Whitworth."

A minute later Anne and Win came in. They were all dressed up, both wearing hats which Arthur remembered from decades ago.

"We hate to leave you like this," Anne said.

"Yes, we'd rather stay. But Solomon . . ."

"Mrs Flynn wants to go to Lourdes tomorrow. She got a cheap package."

"I quite understand," Arthur said. "I . . . I . . ." He started to cry.

"Don't cry, Arthur. Everything will be all right. Don't cry, love," Win said.

Arthur took Win's offered handkerchief. He smelt its scent as it dried his tears. "Sergeant Hetherington will be sorry to have missed you," Arthur said, for something to say, as a reminder.

Anne smiled. "We saw him on the way in."

"I gave him a bakewell tart," Win said, "seeing as he'd liked it so much and everything. Also," she added, "I was feeling that I'd been a bit hard on him. He can't help it if he's not well brought-up, can he?"

"It was nice of you," Arthur said.

They talked for half an hour about nothing in particular. Then Anne said that they'd have to go.

"I don't know when I'll see you both again but, believe me, I love you." said Arthur.

They kissed him one by one . . . Anne dry; Win sloppy. "We understand," Win said.

"We know what writers are!" Anne said.

They left him there.

ఌ ఌ ఌ

The same sergeant brought Arthur his lunch. He didn't say anything. Arthur slept all afternoon, dreaming of Giles Gibbons.

Teatime arrived and the sergeant brought it in. "Terrible thing has happened, Mr Whitworth . . ." the station sergeant said.

"What? What terrible thing?"

"Sergeant Hetherington is dead. Keeled over in the middle of his Sunday lunch. They think it was a heart attack."

❧ ❧ ❧

Anne and Win Whitworth returned to Leeds. Neither spoke much for the first forty miles of the trip. The roads through the Dales were meandering, the weather wet and windy. Each was alone with her thoughts.

Only as the road widened and straightened towards York did they say what was on their minds. Anne spoke first.

"I think it's time, Win," she said.

"I knew you were going to say that. What do we do?" Win asked.

"I think we do what we discussed. Are you able for it?"

Win nodded. "It's the only way to get them to release Arthur, isn't it, Anne?"

Anne gazed through the windscreen at the wipers pushing the rain away. Tears threatened, but she willed them back into the reservoir behind her eyes. Now was not the time for them. Maybe in a few hours' time, with Solomon on her lap, with Win beside her in this car, her breathing becoming shallower as Anne clasped her hand and whispered endearments . . . then might be the time to let tears come.

"Are you sorry it's turned out like this, Win?" Anne asked.

"Are you sorry?"

Anne thought. "I'm sorry we had to kill," she said.

"Are you?" Win asked.

"No, not really. I'm sorry it was necessary."

"Was it necessary?"

"Oh, yes. I think so. Family honour. If we hadn't done something to help Arthur, I couldn't have lived with myself."

"But do you think Arthur appreciates all our efforts?"

"Not at the moment," Anne said, "but in the fullness of time I'm sure he will."

"Yes, I'm sure he will," Win said. She turned to look at Anne, frowning behind the wheel, staring at the road ahead. "Are you frightened?"

Anne was rather, but told Win that she wasn't.

⁂

Anne and Win Whitworth, together with Solomon, were dead by the time the police – alerted by Arthur when he heard of the death of Sergeant Hetherington – knocked at their front door.

Having collected Solomon from Mrs Flynn, they had driven north to a favourite piece of moor close to Hutton-le-Hole. There in a lay-by, they manoeuvred the car to face east and the sunrise before offering Solomon a morsel of poisoned salmon.

Solomon sniffed the offering on Win's palm. Anne and Win held their breath. If Solomon refused to eat his death there was no possibility that they could do so. The old cat sniffed, looked at both Anne and Win in turn – a long, deep look that seared their souls – and finally, with delicate tickling licks, ate the fish.

They watched the cat piano Anne's lap, prior to settling down on it, curling into its last sleep. Then Anne, moving slowly, carefully, reached for the thermos and poured Win her coffee.

Win smiled, took the cup and drank it. Then she gave Anne a kiss on the cheek and closed her eyes.

Anne refilled the cup and drank it down. Sweet, milky coffee with a bitter aftertaste. She stared ahead of her as a grey light rose on the misty moor. Now was the time for the held-back tears to flow. But nothing happened. She looked out steadily feeling her eyes, as though weighted with lead shot, trying to shut. She fought her heavy lids – the curtain that was fighting to close on her life. *If only he'd stuck with teaching*, she thought.

A gash of red cut the sky. The sight was too much for her and her eyes closed. She was dimly aware of Win's breathing, the warmth of Solomon in her lap. Then something that, at first, seemed like nothing. It was sad in a way. All this nothing. But then, with a sudden sense of wonder she realised that it was not nothing. Dots of light rose like stars before her eyes, approached, turned into living shapes, into recognisable people.

"You're dead!" Anne told Bill Baker.

Bill Baker nodded. He was joined by Sergeant Hetherington. They started to accuse her, to criticise her, with an eloquence born of resentment, in the limbo of their sleep.

"I'm sorry!" Anne told them. She felt Solomon scratch her. Then silence as, across the endless sky, a light appeared and approached, turning into what looked for all the world like one of Mrs Flynn's plaster statues. Anne quaked.

ॐ ॐ ॐ

<u>To Whom It May Concern</u>

Anne and Win Whitworth being of sound mind
wish to state that we and we alone
are the murderers.
Many years ago, we killed Bill Baker of Accrington Street
for fiddling about with our nephew.

When we saw how wicked the people
were being to Arthur's book,
we decided to continue our zero tolerance policy.
We are sorry for any inconvenience caused.
We also wish to state that we committed
these murders without
any accomplice being involved.
Yours truly,
Anne and Win Whitworth.

ꟹ ꟹ ꟹ

Arthur Whitworth was released from custody, though *denied further sanctuary* was the expression that he communicated to Dyer and Keeley as the phalanx of press and TV cameras faced him at the police station entrance. Blinking at the arc-lights he stood behind a row of microphones and made a general confession to the world.

Arthur reiterated everything he had told Dyer about his partial culpability. He added that he was guilty of an inability to realise the implications of his actions. He was shallow, had neglected his nearest and dearest and had to accept responsibility for the love decaying into madness that had taken over Anne and Win.

He realised that he was the "beneficiary" of the murders. The royalties on his book sales had made him a millionaire many times over. He would see to git that the money was used to make restitution – though restitution, he knew, could never be adequate – to those hurt by what had happened.

No, he was not planning another book. He did not have any plans.

Arthur Whitworth left the podium and struggled towards a waiting taxi.

"Where to, sir?" the taxi-driver asked.

Arthur was sitting in the back seat of the Jaguar. He tried to reply, but his mouth would not work. It felt as if he had been chewing powdered bone. Instead, he thought, *A cold uninhabited island far to the west.*

Through the thin insulation of the car window, he watched the cameras aimed at him, the men shouting question that clouded the glass. Publicity was courting him, though it felt more like gang rape.

The driver coughed. "Where to?" he repeated.

The padded grey roof of the car reminded Arthur of a leaden sky. The lamp of clouded glass in the centre brought back his aunts' ceiling light in the Leeds lounge. The bodies of wasps and flies had upset him when as a child he looked up at the lamp, letting its light drill into his retina, and took the image away with him, locked in the fast-shut bags of closed eyes. The black smudges had followed him into sleep and brought on nightmares.

Arthur's gummed tongue warred with hard palate and teeth. "Out of here," he told the driver at last.

The Jaguar sped away with several cars and motorcycles in hot pursuit. Arthur, knees tight together, pushed himself further down in the seat until his bottom was half off. He heard Win say, "Sit up straight!" He let himself fall some more.

Soon the car was negotiating the centre of Morecambe. Arthur was seeing everything from the angle of a child. Shop signs, lamp standards looming, high windows, a patch of grey sky. The sky panicked him. Through that window to and from the unknown the dead were watching him, wishing him harm, aching for vengeance. He farted then and, shocked at himself, pulled himself up in the seat, smelling its leather melding with his own stink. The window next to him descended as if by magic and the eyes of the driver met his.

The car shot a light then turned left with a squeal of brakes. Another left and it lurched to a halt, causing Arthur to slip down the seat again.

"We'll wait here until the hounds lose the scent. Then we'll head for home," the driver said, reaching into the glove-compartment for a handkerchief.

"Home?" Arthur asked, "I have no home."

The driver removed his cap and wiped his brow with the handkerchief.

Arthur sat up straight. "It's you, Giles."

"The very man," Giles replied. "You took your time recognising me."

You took your time recognising me . . . Arthur meditated on the tossed out phrase. It could serve as his epitaph, as the flash on his once-remaindered, now phenomenally successful, novels. It might be written on his gravestone in the lonely churchyard in Blubberhouses, or across his forehead – carved with a penknife. *Penknife . . . pen. Knife.*

"You seem a bit depressed for a man who's got away with murder." Giles said.

"You did it, didn't you Giles?"

"I wouldn't have done anything if it hadn't been for you, Arthur. I'm weak willed and easily led. Your story made me do it."

"But I didn't do anything!"

"I suppose you're right. In a way. But writing a story isn't worth a bean unless it's published and read. And I did that for you, didn't I? I made the world sit up and take notice of Arthur Whitworth!"

Arthur saw Giles's cool eyes in the driving mirror. He stared back at his publisher frankly. "Look at me, Giles!

Do you think I like what you see? Do you think all this publicity has made me happy?"

Giles returned Arthur's gaze for a moment. Then he pulled himself away, looking to right and left. "You'll feel better when we get home. I have a home, Arthur. In the country. I've got your greatest fan in residence. Remember Mandy Smart? Another hopeless addict of your tales. She'll make you feel human again."

"You did it, didn't you?"

Giles turned onto the main road. "I'd prefer to think your dear aunts did it. They admitted it after all."

"You know they didn't."

Giles smiled. "OK," he said, "let's just say that *we* did it. Publisher and author in a frantic dance of death. But, dear Arthur, you lead. I, devoted reader that I am, merely followed. Let's leave it at that, shall we? After all, you've got your royalties to count. What are you going to do with the money, Arthur?"

And Arthur Whitworth, seeing the shadows of dead insects in the hanging lamp of the lounge in Leeds, wanting to weep but fearing Anne and Win's reaction, said what he had been thinking since getting into the car. "A cold, uninhabited island far to the west . . . with a jetty and a rowing-boat."

"You could buy an archipelago, Arthur!" Giles said.

ꟹ ꟹ ꟹ

Desmond Keeley was driving while Dyer watched the blinking diode on the electronic map set up on the dashboard. They heard, over the purr of the Jaguar, the conversation between Arthur Whitworth and Giles Gibbons, a conversation that the machine was recording on digital tape.

"What do you think, Desmond?"

“A stroke of luck, Timmy,” Keeley said.

Keeley, with the aid of Sergeant Durry, had planted the equipment in Giles Gibbons’s car the day Dyer’s picture appeared in the papers.

“I reckon we deserve it. I told you we’d get Gibbons one way or another, didn’t I?”

“You did, Timmy. You did.”

“The icing on the fallen cake of my career,” Dyer said. “It just goes to show, there’s nothing that beats basic plodding police-work. Can’t wait to tell Edith. Not too fast, Desmond. We don’t want to give him the least idea he’s been sussed.”

“No, of course not,” Keeley slowed down. “What I don’t understand is how Whitworth got his aunties to try and kill Sergeant Hetherington.”

“We don’t know that he did.”

“You don’t think the aunts might have had hopes for the royalties?”

Dyer moaned. “Don’t, Desmond! Let’s not think that. The poor things are dead. They were adoring aunts and Whitworth’s greatest fans. A powerful combination, Desmond. Quiet affection without a hope of reward. The aunts were the only ones in this whole sorry business with a pure motive. It’s a rare commodity in this world.”

“We may never know for sure,” Keeley said, signalling to overtake a lorry.

“Don’t overtake, son,” Dyer said. “Not on these roads. We’ll get there eventually. Anyway, you’ve got a good woman to court.”

Keeley obeyed his boss. Thinking of Roberta Coleman, he drove at a steady 40 mph towards the arrests, admiring the dusk-shadowed scenery; feeling rather good, grateful to be alive, young and in love at such a time and in such a place.

❧ ❧ ❧

Partly shielded by the luxuriant ivy growing around the kitchen window of Giles Gibbons's country house, Roberta watched Mandy Smart preparing dinner. Mandy uncorked bottles of red wine, placed them on top of the Aga, inspected a simmering soup on the hot plate, opened the oven to poke a roast.

A stylish dinner table for three had been laid in the centre of the room. Mandy placed flowers on it.

A car approached up the drive. Mandy heard it, came to the window.

Roberta had to pull back into the dark of the ivy.

When she looked around the foliage, Mandy had brought out of the fridge a magnum of champagne. This she carried out of the room.

Sounds of greeting, squeals from Mandy, the pop of a cork.

A long moment passed. Then Giles Gibbons, Arthur Whitworth and Mandy Smart came into the kitchen holding champagne flutes. The three toasted one another with the champagne. Arthur fondled Mandy's right breast. Giles fondled her left. Mandy laughed, throwing her head back, tossing back her blonde hair. It described an arc, like a halo, over her head.

Seeing that they were standing together in the centre of the kitchen – as close together as they would ever get and remain in the vertical – she raised the shotgun, aimed with her good eye and watched the happy trio enjoying their last moments. She squeezed the trigger, but then relaxed it. Vengeance was within her grasp. *In a second she could be watching as Mandy dropped the champagne, swooning to death; as Giles crashed back against the table; as Arthur Whitworth – blood gushing from his face – tottered forward towards the broken window and the smoking shotgun. Perhaps he would stand in front of her for a moment, swaying, looking through the window. Then, rocking from side to side like a red rowing-boat on a swollen sea, he would see her and speak. What would he say? "I didn't do it, you know. Not really. Not really. Not my fault." Tottering. Clumsy. "Is this the end?" Then falling like a stone against the window. The broken pane knifing his neck. A pen-shaped shard hitting the jugular . . .*

But what about the future? What about the baby and Desmond Keeley? She might get away with it but would she be able to live with it?

Roberta lowered the gun and watched the three seated at the table. She pushed the shotgun into a leather bag and then heard the approach of a car. The three inside heard it, too. She watched their faces. The looks from one to another. Mandy swivelled her champagne glass. Arthur felt his throat. Giles put a finger into his mouth and bit down. She heard a loud banging on the door, saw the three bow their heads as if in prayer over the table. That sight was more pleasing to Roberta than the carnage she had thought to cause. She smiled and tip-toed away to the secluded lane where Edith, Roberta's repenting accomplice, waited in the driving seat of the Volvo, reciting the fourth Sorrowful Mystery of the Rosary.

❧ ❧ ❧

Back in her flat, Roberta turned to face the front door. Little white spots of filler showed where the pellets had hit the door and surrounds. Tears came. She soaked them up with slaps from her sleeve.

Then Roberta Coleman walked over to her book shelves, scooped up all her signed copies of Arthur Whitworth's books and dropped them into the swing-bin next to the sink.

She regarded the books there amidst the detritus of kitchen waste. For a moment, a knee-jerk morality made her want to pick them out, wipe them down and replace them. After all, a writer was not what he wrote, was he? Beautiful blooms grew on septic tanks. She considered this, but then her mind and heart retraced the last year and hardened her resolve. It was an obscenity even to have those books in the flat at all.

Roberta pulled the plastic sack out of the swing-bin, knotted the top and carried it down the tiled stairs of the building. Outside the front door, down the side passage, stood the large, communal bin. She heaved the sack over the top and heard it land softly on the rest of the rubbish.

She was about to re-enter the building when a shadowy figure appeared at the front gate. Roberta let out a little cry.

"Did I give you a fright?" It was Desmond Keeley. "I didn't mean to. It's just I was passing and I thought I might drop in. I mean, if it's convenient. I have news."

"Yes, of course," Roberta said. Keeley followed Roberta upstairs. "You'll have to forgive the state of the place. I've turned into a real slob since I gave up work."

They went inside. Keeley appraised the flat. "It's all right," he said.

Roberta looked around, seeing the place new-minted. "Yes, it is, isn't it?" she replied.

The End